**Praise fo...
Award–win...
EVELYN VAUGHN**

"Magic and mayhem blend seamlessly in *Something Wicked*, making for an absorbing tale that's not to be missed."
—Jennifer Bishop for *Romance Reviews Today* (www.romrevtoday.com)

"I just read *AKA Goddess* by Evelyn Vaughn. What a fabulous book! I fell in love with the sexy hero, Lex Stuart. Every time he came into a scene, my heart constricted wonderfully."
—Gena Showalter, author of *The Pleasure Slave*

"Evelyn Vaughn's excellent love triangle, complex characters and believable heroine leave readers wanting more."
—*Romantic Times BOOKclub* on *AKA Goddess*

"It's funny. It's romantic. It's unexpected. It's everything I would want in a great read. Finally, the Bombshell line lives up to its promise. This book rocks."
—*www.allaboutromance.com* on *AKA Goddess*

"The author's characters continue to be particularly well written, making *Her Kind of Trouble* an emotional roller coaster as well as a fast-paced romp."
—*Romantic Times BOOKclub*

Available in September 2007 from Mills & Boon® Intrigue

Lost Calling

EVELYN VAUGHN

⊙™MILLS & BOON®
Pure reading pleasure

*First published in Great Britain 2007
by Harlequin Mills & Boon Limited,
Eton House, 18-24 Paradise Road, Richmond, Surrey TW9 1SR*

*THE MADONNA KEY series was co-created
by Yvonne Jocks, Vicki Hinze and Lorna Tedder.*

ISBN: 978 0 263 85750 4

46-0907

*Harlequin Mills & Boon policy is to use papers that are
natural, renewable and recyclable products and made from
wood grown in sustainable forests. The logging and
manufacturing processes conform to the legal environmental
regulations of the country of origin.*

*Printed and bound in Spain
by Litografia Rosés S.A., Barcelona*

EVELYN VAUGHN

has written stories since she learned to make letters. But during the two years that she lived on a Navajo reservation in Arizona – while in second and third grade – she dreamed of becoming a barrel racer. Before she got her own horse, her family moved to Louisiana. There, to avoid the humidity, she channelled more of her adventures into stories.

Since then, Evelyn has canoed in the East-Texas swamps, rafted a white-water river in the Austrian Alps, rappelled barefoot down a three-storey building, talked her way onto a ship to Greece without her passport, sailed in the Mediterranean and spent several weeks in Europe with little more than a backpack and a train pass. While she still enjoys channelling "travel Vaughn" on a regular basis, she also loves the fact that she can write about adventures with far less physical discomfort. She now lives in Texas, where she teaches English at a local community college.

In 2005, Evelyn won the prestigious RITA® Award from the Romance Writers of America for her first Bombshell novel, *AKA Goddess*. Feel free to contact Evelyn through her website, www.evelynvaughn. com, or by writing to: PO Box 6, Euless, TX 76039, USA.

This book would not be possible without the other brilliant authors who helped create and who put in the hard work of writing the series. Of these authors in particular, I must acknowledge:

- Jenna Mills – *Veiled Legacy* – for so many of the details and plotlines, and for Scarlet,

- Cindy Dees – *Haunted Echoes* – for her constant good humour, fast writing and for reading everything I wrote,

- Sharron McClellan – *Hidden Sanctuary* – for her technical help, archaeological know-how... and for the grins,

- Carol Stephenson – *Shadow Lines* – for stepping in like she belonged here (because she did),

- Lorna Tedder – *Dark Revelations* – for her mystical expertise and

- Vicki Hinze, for Myrrdin.

I also owe thanks to our incredible agents, including Paige Wheeler, Roberta Brown, Pattie Steele-Perkins and Richard Curtis, for some high-level wrangling.

Then there are my readers: Thanks to Kelly, for really getting Catrina; to Juliet Burns, for insisting that I write more; to Toni, for sitting over my shoulderwhen I needed her; and to Sadhbh, for helping with the French details. (And a special thanks to MP/Karmela, for her suggestions about redeeming Catrina.)

And much gratitude to my editor, Natashya, for her super support.

But as for dedications?

This book is dedicated to all the women who have suspected they might be extraspecial, and just weren't quite sure why.

Chapter 1

Once, during the terror of the French Revolution, a handful of women fought for starving citizens, rescued innocents marked for death—and watched their dreams drown in a sea of blood. They risked their lives for a collection of ancient Madonna artifacts, in the hopes that someday one of their descendants might use them to save the world.

That first earthquake was not my fault.

Even if God did smite sinners, would He not use the standard thunderbolts? I am no saint. But even I haven't the conceit to claim an entire natural disaster!

My grandmother could. One of her favorite sayings was, "This is your fault, Catrina." Although if anyone could will earthquakes into existence, *she*… But I digress.

A rush of feathers and coos startled me from self-pity as I strolled from the hospital. Grateful for the distraction, I looked up. Doves burst from the sycamore trees that lined the avenue and scattered into the blue Parisian sky. Hmm.

I glanced over my shoulder to see that, *certainement,* the slight, gray-haired figure who'd been following me on and off for more than a week had returned as well.

I ignored him to look back to the birds.

"What is wrong now?" I whispered—I am French, by the way, but I will translate for you.

I snorted at my understatement. A great deal was wrong. I had gone months without a lover. My job as curator at the prestigious Musée Cluny dissatisfied me of late. That damned old man really was following me, though I had yet to manage a confrontation—I feared he had something to do with a past mistake of which I am not proud. And the grandmother who had raised me, no matter how poorly, lay dying in the nearby Hôpital Saint-Vincent de Paul.

But did I mention, months without a lover?

Fine. If you must know, my grandmother was of even greater concern than my sex life *or* the mysterious old man, at the moment. *Grand-mère* disliked me even more than I disliked her, but in a rare attempt at decency, I had just visited her.

Who would have thought so old and sick a woman could shout so loudly or throw flowers with such vehemence? But today, our mutual disdain had held a terrible undercurrent of finality.

Far easier to worry about birds.

At first, I thought I heard the rumble of a truck's approach. But I saw only automobiles and scooters darting along the Avenue Denfert-Rochereau. A young couple, strolling and cuddling ahead of me, looked about in concern. Springtime in Paris meant music and sunshine and love and flowers and birds—

Fleeing, frightened birds.

My legs trembled, as if the visit with *Grand-mère* had upset me more than I cared to admit. Unlikely. Finally, I recognized the sensation from my two years in the USA.

In California, to be exact.

Earthquake!

Logic denied my unsteady legs. Surely not. *In Paris?*

Then the sidewalk rolled, buckled. I fell hard against an iron fence circling a sycamore and caught at it, clung to it. Other pedestrians ran or stumbled, their shouts lost beneath the earth's alien growl.

So much for logic. An earthquake. *In Paris*.

Losing my balance on the pitching pavement, I managed to secure one elbow around an iron bar, trying to take everything in. The old man had caught himself against a lamppost. Even in chaos, his stare unnerved me. The young couple stumbled together. Her hand wrenched from his as she fell to the asphalt.

The bastard ran on without her. Over the woman's screams for him—his name, it seems, was Eduard—the very earth began to shriek in protest, like something huge and maddened.

Clinging beside the sycamore, on my knees to lower my center of balance, I watched a crack open and dart into the road—quick, like the run in a nylon, but not as straight. This was worse than I'd seen in California.

It ran right under Eduard's lover's hips.

Her screams choked into horrified whimpers.

The crack widened beneath her. Jagged chunks of concrete crumbled into the fissure spreading, gaping across the avenue. Dust plumed upward. A smell of tearing cement burned the air. Once-solid ground shifted, sagged. The din crushed my ears.

And that foolish, abandoned girl had to look over at me, wide eyes brimming with terror.

I am no saint, but…*merde*.

I tried reaching toward her with one hand, hoping the little fence would hold. "Quick! Come here!"

Since she may have been a tourist, I repeated the command in English. Then exasperated German.

Surely the little fool understood *something!*

All she had to do was crawl toward me. Instead, as one of her knees dropped into the widening crevice beneath her, she began to weep.

Better her than me. Lest it escaped you, I am not a very nice person. And yet…she looked so very helpless.

With a groan of disgust, I loosened my elbow-hold on the fence and attempted to hang on with one hand, tight and sweaty on the iron. I stretched closer toward the girl. *"Now!"*

She stared at me and trembled. My fingers began to slip on the age-pitted iron. I wanted my elbow hold back.

"Fine," I screamed at her. "Die, then!"

The motivational ploy, were it one, had no effect. Suddenly the ground heaved harder, surging up, then dropping. The crack stretched wider, now gushing dust. Steel reinforcing bars ripped from the buckling concrete they had once supported. The girl's legs dropped into the opening, as if the earth were swallowing her. Her nails tore on the pavement as she tried to hold on.

Gravity sucked her downward.

And unexpectedly—under some sisterhood impulse?—I let go of the fencing and dove for her. Spread flat across the walkway, I reached for her wrists with both hands and actually succeeded in catching one. That gave me purchase to grab the other and hold on.

As she dropped deeper into the fissure and my chin slammed into the asphalt, I recognized my mistake. I swore. Loudly.

I was not saving her. She was dragging me down.

This is why I avoid being nice! Now I could not let go even if I tried, not without beating her off. The idiot dug into my wrists with what nails she had left, sweat stinging the wounds she inflicted. Straining—to escape as much as hold her—I tried to bury my face into my own shoulder, to catch even one breath that wasn't thick with debris. I choked instead. I couldn't get my knees beneath me. I couldn't find purchase. My body slid inexorably toward the widening hole.

With a final shriek, the girl vanished into the road's gaping maw. I lurched forward with her, then caught on the edge. Jagged asphalt cut me under my arms as I momentarily held her. She kicked and writhed upward— *now* she struggled to live?

My arms felt pulled from my shoulder sockets as I inched forward. Downward. The lip of torn rock dragged past my breasts. Past my ribs. I was hanging headfirst, into depths I could only imagine. For the record? I dislike heights. And then—

Then I dropped into the void.

This is your fault, Catrina, I thought, as dusty darkness swallowed me. Worse, I knew of nobody who would even care.

Except perhaps the mysterious old man. Depending on why he was following me in the first place.

Regaining consciousness was a pleasant surprise, relatively speaking. I ached from scrapes, bruises, and pulled muscles. My wrists bled from the helpless girl's nails. I'd landed on something hard and uneven, so my back half felt little better.

On the plus side, I was alive. I am quite the fan of survival. Especially my own.

The earth no longer pitched. It loomed in total stillness, as earth should. Compared to the chaos of before, the muffled cries from the street above and the distant car horns and wailing sirens, seemed almost peaceful.

Dust-thick sunlight and sycamore leaves filtered down past broken pavement perhaps four or five meters above me. Nothing more damaging seemed in immediate danger of crashing down. On the ground just in front of me…

Amidst some dirty white fragments, a small key gleamed.

Perhaps I could not think clearly. Oddly drawn, still gathering my senses, I reached, touched it….

A sea of red—red hats, that is. A drumroll. Uncertain steps to the scaffold. She clenches her teeth, tries to breathe past the stench of blood-soaked wood. She mustn't vomit the swallowed key, or the soldiers will find it, might find everything. If she must die, her secret must go with her.

Better it lie dormant than be destroyed.

They strap her, standing, to the bascule. It, and she, drop into place. Her neck fits easily into the lunette, sticky with the fresh blood of her sisters, her friends, blood that stains the basket into which she must stare.

It is either that, or close her eyes. And her eyes will close soon enough.

The crowd shouts encouragement to the executioner and insults at her. They call her a traitor—she, whose idealism helped launch the utopia that has now maddened into slaughter. Here lies proof that her ideals were born too soon. Such savagery is no way to change the world.

Certainly not to change it into any place she would wish to live.

As ever, she tries to distract herself with story. This is when the hero should arrive, sword flashing and musket barking, to save her. It does not work. Her hero is long gone.

The drumroll reverberates louder, louder, or is that her racing heart? Then, worse—it stops. Does the executioner move? Is that the sudden slide of the blade?

Somehow—impossibly, wonderfully—she pushes herself backward. She wrenches free of the ties binding her to the bascule—were they not properly fastened?— and rolls to her feet, blind to the deadly thud behind her.

There remains a chance. Still a chance!

I blinked, swallowed hard and quickly pushed myself into a sitting position. Something bit into my hand. I looked down to realize that I had cut my palm on a broken rib bone. Not mine.

That was somewhat less disturbing than the vision of blood and guillotines that had shaken me, even when I shifted my gaze.

An unattached skull leered back at me as if delighted for the company. Near it, arm missing and chest half-shattered…

Apparently, I had landed on a skeleton. Perhaps a victim of the Revolution? To consider that would involve remembering the vision, which I was not ready to do. Instead, I drew my knees beneath me. Now I noticed a second skeleton, and a third. They lay in a hewn cave the size of a freight elevator, cluttered with rubble and debris.

I stopped counting when I noticed the girl who'd dragged me down. Unlike my other companions here, she moaned, alive.

Absently pocketing the key, I crawled past another skeleton to reach her and touched her shoulder.

She opened her eyes with a start, looked past me…

And began screaming. Loudly. With echoes.

"Stop that!" I've often wondered if slapping hysterics will really silence them, or if that is merely dramatic convention. I was quite ready to try it, but she slumped to the floor, unconscious. So instead, I looked over my shoulder.

A white avalanche of skulls and femurs and hip bones sloped downward from the remaining rock overhang to the floor. We'd fallen into the catacombs.

We weren't wholly safe. There might still be aftershocks. The earthquake itself…

My cat, I thought fleetingly. *The museum. My flat.*

Those had to wait.

The catacombs are not as popular a tourist site as the Tour Eiffel or the Moulin Rouge. But I'm no tourist. As a teenager, I'd played at being a "cataphile," dating a budding anarchist who'd delighted in urban exploration beyond the city's "do not enter" signs. We'd found hidden routes into the labyrinth from Métro tunnels and sewer systems, him for the sheer thrill of it. Me, I'd gone for the history, too, and the defiance.

And for the unabashed sex.

Thus I was familiar with the catacombs' *raison d'être.* By the late eighteenth century, the cemeteries of Paris had overflowed with remains. The solution? Quietly disinter several graveyards and move the skeletons into deserted limestone quarries. Over the next few decades, approximately six million bodies were relocated and stacked for maximum efficiency into an estimated 300 kilometers— that means 185 miles—of tunnels.

"Hello?" called a female voice from above. "Are you okay?"

I squinted upward, but—against crumbling bits of rock and the mote-thick sunshine—I could only tell that our would-be rescuer could not be much older than me—thirty—as she leaned well over the edge of the rift with no apparent fear of falling.

"Define 'okay,'" I challenged. The girl beside me moaned.

The woman up top laughed an infectiously bright, musical laugh, as if I had intended to amuse her. I had not. "I saw you help that girl. That was so noble!" Perhaps she thought that excused her informal *tu*. She spoke fluently, but was not French.

Since I do not laugh so easily, I said, "Is it bad?" The only sirens I could hear remained distant. I imagined collapsed buildings, broken gas mains, fallen trees. Emergency services were likely too busy to get to us just yet.

"The landlines aren't working, and nobody's mobile phones will turn on. But some men are bringing a fire hose," the woman said. "I'm Scarlet, by the way. Scarlet Rubashka. I was on my way to the observatory to watch the solar flares when the earthquake hit. Can you believe it? An earthquake in Paris. I never would have imagined I'd get pictures of something like that. I'm a photographer. What's your name?"

A nearby gasp distracted me from this seemingly endless exposition. The girl beside me had come to again. Her eyes widened—

I put my hand over her mouth, before she could start. "I am Catrina Dauvergne," I told them both. "And my head hurts."

Only when the younger woman recovered herself enough to blink a few times did I carefully remove my hand.

"My ankle hurts," she said forlornly. Then she gasped and recoiled. A huge fire-hose nozzle landed beside me, its heavy canvas hose flopping across my head, and I understood what had frightened her this time.

"Oops," called Scarlet Rubashka, from above. "Sorry!"

They'd tied knots into the hose—more like loose loops, fire hoses not being particularly flexible—as hand- and footholds for us to climb. Because of the girl's twisted ankle, I wrapped the hose around her so that the men up top could lift her.

More crumbs of pavement rained down as they did. I backed into a shadowy corner, out of the worst of the stony deluge, and tried to convince myself I wouldn't be buried alive. *Alone.*

Then again, with five or six skeletal friends lying about me, not counting the thousands of partials that made up the debris of the back wall, I would not be alone, would I?

"Eduard!" exclaimed the girl happily from above me, as she reached safety. "You're safe!"

I rolled my eyes—and Scarlet, again leaning over the edge to keep watch on me, laughed. I could make out her fiery red halo of short, dyed hair.

"Now you, Catrina!" she called, as soon as they'd freed the hose and again dropped it. This time it did not hit me. "Hurry, before this place caves in!"

As I stepped forward, I kicked something. Under centuries of dust and dirt, in the filtered light, it looked like a large jar, cracked but held together with wire wrapped around it. Near it lay the rotting remains of a wooden form with the sloped top of a letterbox, like a portable writing desk. How very odd.

The catacombs only held bodies, not belongings. Who would be buried with her writing desk?

"Please, Catrina," called Scarlet, as if she truly cared.

Considering her easy smiles and laughter, she probably was one of those women who truly *did* care. About almost everything. Especially puppies and bunny rabbits.

I sighed, shook my head, and reached to catch one of the loops in the fire hose. My cut hand hurt as I tested my weight. Then I found a foothold in the lowest loop and pulled my aching body upward.

Once my feet left the ground I began to spin in slow circles. More debris broke loose from where the hose rubbed the edge of the broken pavement, and I ducked my head. This would be more difficult than I'd anticipated. Groping above me, I found another loop of canvas, steadied myself as much as I could while spinning and rose upward for a better foothold.

"Is the damage extensive?" I called, thinking again of my cat.

"Only right here, that I can see," Scarlet assured me. "It's odd that this one spot was hit so hard. Only three windows were broken, across the street. You're halfway there."

Dangling two meters from the ground, ducking my face away from the hail of dust and rock, I got my first full view of the underground vault into which I'd dropped.

Five skeletal bodies lay there, all beheaded. But unlike most residents of the catacombs, their heads had been kept with their bodies. So had a jumble of belongings—not only the letter box and the jar, but a whole scattering of moldy books, dishes, cutlery, even piles of rotting clothing. *Clothing!* From an era when it was unpatriotic to waste goods that other citizens could use, and when unpatriotic activities got one killed.

Well…perhaps from that era. Nothing of the debris denied my guess at the late eighteenth century.

This was not part of the standard catacombs. With no way in or out, it had remained hidden for over two hundred years. A story waited here, a mystery. A history in danger of being obliterated by either a cave in or road crews.

"Can't you make it?" called Scarlet, sounding worried. "Shall we try to pull you up, too?"

Once I left, how would I keep their story from vanishing?

The history of it called to me—and history is one thing I can never resist. I adore everything old, except my grandmother. So if neither my cat nor my employer immediately needed me…

I secured my handhold on the fire hose, hung for a long, spinning, thoughtful moment, swallowed hard—and let go.

This time, at least, I landed feet first.

"Catrina!" cried Scarlet.

"This is an archeological find," I called upward. "Someone should document and clear it before the city fills it in."

"Or before it collapses on your head?" Ah, so the redhead wasn't merely sweetness and light. That was somehow a relief.

"I will take that chance. I'll need lumber to shore up the walls. Lights of course. Photography equipment…"

Merde. What I needed most was someone with true archeological training. Someone whom I could trust not to contaminate the site…or to steal from it. And I trust so few.

To complicate matters, the professionals might be more concerned with damage suffered by the older Notre Dame or Sacré Coeur than this little time capsule.

One face flashed through my memory, as forcefully as my earlier vision of blood and beheadings. My immediate enthusiasm for the idea worried me, as he would not want to come—but come he would. The echoes of the past, from every corner of this little lost cave, worried me more. This was their chance to be understood, to be heard.

I will do anything to protect the past. *Anything*.

"Scarlet," I called, as if this new stranger and I were indeed friends. "I need to send for somebody at the Sorbonne. His name is Rhys Pritchard. Can you do that for me?"

"Yes, but Catrina, your grandfather..." Scarlet paused, looking around. "That's strange. He's gone."

I have no living grandfather—but I suspected I knew whom she meant. That damned old man. "What about him?"

"He said for me to tell you that he's now convinced the Black Madonna lives. Does that make sense to you?"

It did not. But neither did his very presence.

Or an earthquake. In Paris.

On the avenue outside, Pierre Grimaud watched the rescue efforts slow to a halt. Even more than the earthquake, the woman's refusal to leave the catacombs unnerved him. Could it be...?

But of course. *It was true*.

He slipped back into his ancestral locksmith shop and

shut the door, shot the bolts home. After pulling the window shades, he descended worn stone stairs to the ancient basement—and quickly cut the wire that had rung the warning bell, alerting him to this danger. Nobody must trace the mass grave to him, or through him, to his family's long-ago patron. For his entire life, the unassuming brass bell high on the wall had only ever rung when his father tested it each year and, once his father died, when Grimaud continued that traditional chore. He'd half believed the tales of family duty were mere myth, no matter how fervently he wished them to be true. When the bell had rung today, he'd first thought it because of the earthquake.

But the earth stopped moving. *And the bell still rang.*

Women had opened Pandora's box, pulled the trip wire and alerted him that a centuries-old danger was upon the world.

Grimaud's pulse sped with excitement. Of all the generations to keep watch, this had happened for him. *He* could be the one to fulfill his family's purpose. *He* could protect France, perhaps all of Europe.

This was so much better than his computer games.

Praying that the wire could no longer be traced to his shop, he returned upstairs and found the family Bible. The address he needed was written, in faded ink, inside the back cover.

Grimaud's hand shook as he retrieved a sheet of stationary. This felt enormous, like…like learning there truly were monsters in the closet—and only he and God could banish them.

The myths were real!

As his father's father's fathers had once promised
they would, Grimaud carefully wrote: *They are found.*
We must contain their evil. Send instructions.

Chapter 2

Dust and debris showered down from what was left of the overhanging rock as Rhys Pritchard descended the fire hose hand-over-hand, dropping the last meter as I had. "Cat, are you all right?" he asked, in Welsh-accented French. If one *must* corrupt the language with an accent, it might as well be Celtic.

I had stopped taking mental notes to watch his descent. I find the bodies of even average men quite sexy. This black-haired man, lanky and fit, qualified as above average, even in faded jeans and a worn T-shirt. The intensity of his concern distracted me. I suddenly wished I could have combed my hair or, worse, reapplied my lipstick since the earthquake.

He is this kind to everyone, I reminded myself. But I'd not seen him for months, and never with a five-day beard, as today. Rhys had adopted a scruffy, bad-boy image so at odds with his reality and the religious medals that hung together from a leather thong around his neck, that I doubted I could wrench my foolish gaze away from the dichotomy.

I hate appearing foolish, so asked, "How is the city?"

"Much of the power's out. The Métro stopped running. The radio has conflicting reports, some injuries, no confirmed deaths. But *this*—" He gestured at our sinkhole, his gaze still holding me. *"Are you hurt?"*

"I am fine," I reassured him, drawing composure around myself like armor. "This place is what needs your help."

Rhys stared at me, then looked at our cramped, unstable surroundings. When he turned back, his eyes flashed with what, on another man, might have been anger. "You're fine, are you?"

"But in need of archeological assistance," I explained. "If the roadwork above does not fall in first, the repair will likely destroy all this. I—"

"Archeological assistance?" He scrubbed an impatient hand through his overlong black hair. "I was on my way to give blood when I got your message! Catrina, I thought you were hurt!"

In fact, that *was* anger! Since I had no good arguments against giving blood, I simply lifted my hand, widened my eyes and pouted. "I cut myself."

Rhys took a deep breath, then let his head fall forward. Was he praying? If so, it was quick. When he looked back up, he'd regained his composure. Wrath is, after all, a deadly sin.

Sarcasm, however? Venial at most. "You must be in terrible pain," he conceded wryly. But as he did, because he was good and trustworthy, he dug a first-aid kit out of the satchel he wore slung over his shoulder. "How on earth do you bear it?"

I wrinkled my nose at him. But with him taking my hand in his—bigger, stronger, currently cleaner—I didn't risk speaking, lest he learn my secret. Not that I keep it very well. When he gently swabbed the blood-encrusted cut with an alcohol wipe, I caught my breath from far, far more than the sting.

"I am sorry," he murmured. Watching my face, he blew gently on the wound to cool it. I felt increasingly warm, instead, and had to swallow back a whimper of longing.

Shall I confess? *This* was why I'd avoided Rhys Pritchard these many months, like a dieter avoiding cake. *Because I wanted him.* I wanted him in ways that transcended mere chemistry…chemistry, yes, but by no means mere. I wanted him in ways even I did not understand. Frankly, I have no trouble getting men. But for months, I had not wanted *men. I wanted him.*

And kind or not, Rhys Pritchard did not want me.

He'd said as much the previous summer, the last time I'd thrown myself at him. You think I misinterpreted? I'd said, *You want me,* n'est-ce pas? And he'd said, *I do not.*

The exchange loses nothing in translation.

So…why did I hold so still while he smeared antibiotic ointment across the cut, then taped a bandage over his handiwork? Too easily, I fantasized every ministration into a caress, every fleeting glance into a mean-

ingful stare. With our heads inclined over his progress,
I smelled wine on his breath and drew the scent between
my own lips as I longed to draw....

"There you go," he said with harsh efficiency, releasing my hand and stepping back. "Are we done?"

"You're leaving? Without helping this place?"

"They're catacombs." Rhys shrugged, dismissive.
"They…"

But then he seemed to notice—how these five skeletons were not part of the orderly stacks, how
remnants of their daily life had been buried with them.
He sank into an easy crouch, to get a better look at
the closest remains. Then he whistled through his
teeth and looked back up at me with a soft, "What's
this, then?"

Somehow, I'd known that he of all people would see
what I saw.

"*Exactly.* These are not the usual catacombs. But if
we've any hope of understanding them, we must salvage
all this before road repairs destroy it. We will need volunteers to document items before they are moved, someone to speak to the Sorbonne about accepting them, and
of course someone to stay with the find, to guard it from
thieves."

"To guard it from thieves." Rhys's gaze cut back to me.

"Of course! Antiquities such as these may not look immediately valuable, but theft could prove a major…" *Ah.*

He knew the threat of antiquities theft. When we'd
met a year earlier, I…well…I'd *relieved* one of his
friends of a medieval chalice. She had herself stolen it
from its original resting place, destroying any hope of

establishing provenance and leaving a burnt abbey behind her. I'd been in the right.

Unfortunately, the best way to see that this chalice would be treated with respect, *sans* provenance, had been to find it a home with a private collector. So I had sold it. *Finis.*

Except…since then, I've had cause to believe I may have been mistaken about the woman's motives. Perhaps.

Well, who likes to be mistaken? Especially with that strange old man following me, and me with no better explanation than to think that Rhys's friend—who was quite wealthy—meant to have me fired or arrested? Better to avoid the subject. I had worked with Rhys Pritchard again, on a dive in Alexandria last summer. His good-natured manners had led me to hope that he understood why I'd gone behind his back to save the chalice. As it turned out, he did not.

He was simply good natured. And very well-mannered.

"Theft could compromise the site's integrity," I continued coolly, lifting my chin. "We cannot leave these artifacts *in situ*, but we can at least protect and document them before taking the salvage to a legitimate institution. If you do not wish to help, then do hurry on your way."

I even made a shooing motion with my hand, adding, "I am sure you have other good works to do."

Rhys scanned the cavern once more, seemingly torn. Again, he knelt by one of the bodies. With a pen from his pocket, he lifted something from the comb of a rib cage. He studied his find for a long moment. Then looked back up at me.

"I'll send for other students," he conceded. "I'll see

the department chair to arrange the necessary permissions from the Sorbonne, as well. You and I can take turns keeping watch, starting with me, tonight."

"With you?" My stomach lurched at a rumble above us. It resolved itself into the sound of a helicopter.

"You're moving like an old woman," he insisted. "*Go home*."

Instead of agreeing right away, I bent nearer the skeleton to see what he'd found to change his mind. Then I understood.

It looked to be some kind of Virgin Mary medal. Apparently, the people interred in this cave had been Catholic. Rhys was interested, I realized, in their martyrdom.

Just what I needed—another reminder that the man I wanted so foolishly had once been a priest. *Oui*. A priest.

Do you suppose that could also have something to do with his consistent rejection of my bad-girl charms?

"He's a *priest?*" exclaimed Scarlet Rubashka, as the two of us walked northward. It turned out that we both lived on the Left Bank, a mere seven blocks from each other—not so surprising, considering the area's popularity among students and artists. With the Métro not working, we chose to keep company for the walk. "Him?"

"He *was* a priest," I corrected her. Perhaps I'd shared that tidbit to justify his clear immunity to me. Scarlet had the kind of fine-boned looks that make other women defensive. Even her vibrant red bob could not disguise her natural beauty. "Now he is an archeology student. I do not know more than that."

"Perhaps he left the priesthood for you." She smiled at the thought. "And you just don't know it yet!"

"He hadn't met me then." Even I draw the line at trying to seduce men I *know* to be priests.

"Perhaps not in this reality, but in the reality of the heart?" Scarlet sped her step so that she could turn and walk backward, watching me. She spread her hands over her chest. "Perhaps your souls sensed each other across space and time."

I was not generally drawn to a man's *soul*, and cannot imagine any man foolish enough to be drawn to what's left of mine, so I said nothing. Perhaps her space-and-time comment also helped silence me. She had entertainment value, this Scarlet.

"He has a weakness for blondes," Scarlet decided. I am a dark blonde. "He came quickly enough when you sent for him."

"That," I noted, "is because he is painfully responsible. There is a difference, *n'est-ce pas?*"

"Not necessarily. I sensed a connection between you."

"Rhys does not like me. That is the only connection."

"No, he does not *want* to like you." She scowled and made her voice extra husky. "There is a difference, *n'est-ce pas?*"

Her mockery amused me. But I changed the topic to an almost certain distraction—*her* likely lovers. "And have you a soul mate? Someone who calls to you from across space and time?"

Scarlet sighed so deeply, her shoulders sank. "I like to think so, but he's running late. You know those fortune-telling kits you can get at bookstores? Rune kits, box-set tarot cards, tumbled crystals? I *adore* those. Perhaps it's because I'm adopted—I like to imagine myself having been left by gypsies, you know? Anyway, the runes and cards all indicate my soul mate is tall, wealthy and handsome."

"Really," I murmured, keeping an unusually close watch on the subdued streets around us. *Quel surprise.*

For several blocks, we'd passed quite a few abandoned cars. Even now that cars moved again, slowly in deference to the many darkened traffic lights, Paris seemed to hold her breath. The rumble of larger cars kept unnerving me deep down, as if they heralded another quake. Would an aftershock be so surprising?

"*Really,*" Scarlet exclaimed. "I wouldn't have gone looking for a rich, handsome man, but if that's what fate has in store for me…" She shrugged, bravely accepting the inevitable.

I almost smiled. "Fate is a cruel master."

"My soul mate may be adventurous, too. A man of mystery."

"Why do tarot cards never predict a short, poor, ugly homebody with no hidden depths?" I challenged.

Scarlet laughed. "What fun would that be? Any cards that would predict that have no place in my deck!"

Sirens continued to advertise the work of emergency services across the city. Rhys had told us there would be a curfew at dusk. And…*was someone following us?*

I hadn't seen or heard the gray-haired man since he'd delivered his strange message through Scarlet. *The Black Madonna lives?* A particular kind of medieval art is called the *Vierge Noir*, or Black Virgin—statues of the

Holy Mother, her complexion painted black. Could he mean those?

Likely he was a religious oddball, and I was unsettled by the day's drama.

"I feel it, too," Scarlet whispered, when I looked over my shoulder. "Eyes on us. I felt them even before you sent for Rhys. It feels like…like somebody is angry with us."

"What else is new?" Between my visit to *Grand-mère*, Rhys Pritchard's mistrust of me and the still-possible wrath of God implicit in the earthquake, I'd had enough censure for one day.

"Maybe we could trap whoever it is," Scarlet suggested, with what I already recognized as her usual enthusiasm. "Duck down an alley, hide behind some crates. When our stalker comes in after us, we can ambush him and hold him for questioning!"

Another glance over my shoulder revealed only an unusually quiet street, lined with quaint shops beneath several floors of apartments like mine. I would not be surprised if my imagination was getting away from me. Even after so short an acquaintance, I would be surprised if Scarlet's imagination was not. Hide behind crates and *ambush someone?*

Brandishing what, exactly? Our good looks and quick wit?

"Or," I suggested, "perhaps we could stay together for extra safety, take shelter in our nearest flat and lock the door behind us once we reach it?"

Scarlet made the invitation easier with her good-natured shrug. "That could work, too. Whose apartment is closer?"

As it turned out, hers was. But since I wished to
check on my cat and she had only plants to worry about,
we went to mine. Beyond the sensation of being
watched by *angry eyes*, no danger showed itself by the
time we reached my top-floor flat.

A few pictures and a mirror had fallen, and knick-
knacks lay on the floor, as did a toppled stool. Otherwise, the place seemed untouched by the quake. My
calico cat, Tache, looked up from the settee with a lazy
mew of welcome, her posture as unconcerned as if
Mother Nature had not gone on the attack.

As Scarlet crossed to Tache with an exclamation of
delight, I turned the lock on my door, then eyed my un-
intended guest. She knelt by the settee to sweet-talk my
cat, laughing when Tache pawed her cheek. I do not
make friends easily. But something about Scarlet
Rubashka struck me as familiar. Trustworthy, even.

"Have we met before today?" I asked, drawing the
tall, diamond-paned windows open. Being on the third
floor—what Americans would call the fourth—I felt
safe, and this way I could survey my entire neighbor-
hood from this little sanctuary of mine. It looked unusually quiet and, with the encroaching dusk, dark. In such
an ancient city, the power outage felt like traveling back
in time. "Perhaps at the Cluny, or…"

The memory, just beyond my grasp, taunted me.

"I would have remembered you." Scarlet plopped
onto the settee. "Although…I told you I was adopted,
right? Maybe you met someone from my birth family!
Can you remember a name? Brown hair? My natural
color is brown, and this is my real eye color."

She blinked her chocolate-brown eyes dramatically.

I shook my head, unable to follow her move from do-I-even-know-you to the level of specifics she wanted. Instead I quirked an eyebrow and suggested, "Perhaps our souls sensed each other across space and time?"

Scarlet Rubashka, it turned out, was almost impossible to insult. She grinned. "Mock me if you will, Catrina Dauvergne. But this is the dawning of the Age of Aquarius. There are forces at work in this universe that we can only begin to imagine."

Which made me think of the key I had found, and the awful vision I'd had upon touching it, and—

With a sinking feeling, I touched my pocket and swore.

Her chocolate-brown eyes now widened. "Excuse me?"

"I—" I hated admitting mistakes. Admissions just escalate into more trouble. So why did I keep talking? "I took something from the site. A key. I should have left it *in situ,* but I was distracted by a…a daydream, I suppose…."

Merde. I slapped my hands on the open windowsill. Rhys already thought me an antiquities thief, and now this.

Tache leaped easily onto the sill and began to wash her face, one paw at a time, pretending disinterest and, occasionally, glancing upward at the ceiling.

"May I see it?" asked Scarlet. "I love keys. I always wear this one—see?" From around her neck she drew a chain on which hung a silver filigreed key, far more ornate than the one I'd taken. "I've had it since I was a baby."

Fine. Sinking onto the settee beside her, I showed her

the little key from the cave-in. In doing so, I got my first good look at it myself. It was no larger than a woman's thumb, which made sense. I'd found it under the ribs of the skeleton, not around its severed bit of neck; its owner had swallowed it. On one side, faded by age, someone had scratched initials: *SdM*.

"A daydream, huh?" she urged, with surprising insight.

"Or a delusion."

"Or a vision. Keys have great symbolism…why can't they unlock doors into someplace or even sometime else?"

There really was something about this woman, wasn't there? Grudgingly, surprised at myself for admitting it, I recounted what I'd seen. Scarlet did not doubt the truth of it.

"So those women were killed in the Revolution!"

"We've no proof of that. In my…vision…the woman survived. But I found the key under a beheaded skeleton." I studied it. "I suppose I'll lock it up until I've more time to study it."

Since the site *was* already compromised.

"Proof schmoof. This key has something to tell you. You should sleep with it. Maybe you'll dream more information."

"Or perhaps this is absolute foolishness."

"No, it's not! I have a friend, Eve, and she's so psychic that she had to learn to shield herself. She—"

But Scarlet was interrupted by Tache letting out an angry screech. She leaped off her windowsill to streak beneath us.

And then—

A small, dark-whiskered man suddenly swung through my open window, right into my flat, apparently off the roof. He knocked a figurine off the shelf beside him with his hard, ungainly landing. Then he straightened, his expression menacing…and, I thought, quite insane.

"Give me the key," he demanded. "Now!"

If I'd needed proof we were being watched—here it was.

Chapter 3

Scarlet's hand flew to her neck and her own key.

"No." I sounded more composed than I felt. This was my flat, *my home* the man had violated with his oily, metallic smell and his wild eyes and his waving, scar-etched hands. He'd come off my roof? For a key!

"The evil mustn't wake," he insisted. "Give it to me!"

He did not say *please*. Still seated on the settee, where he'd caught us off guard, I lifted my feet to the edge of my coffee table—and pushed. Hard and sudden.

The table slammed into the intruder's kneecaps, knocking him to the wall. He let out a howl of pain. Then, with a roar, he lifted the table—and threw it at us!

I dove out of the way in one direction, Scarlet the other. The settee tumbled backward under the table's impact. Tache ran for the bedroom in a calico streak, seeming to limp.

Now I was angry.

"The key!" the man insisted, wheeling on me. So he wanted the "SdM" key, and not Scarlet's? Pocketing it as I regained my feet, I noted with some disgust that Scarlet raced for the apartment door and fumbled with the lock.

Coward, I thought, and, *serves me right, to trust her.*

I picked up an ashtray from the floor and pitched it at him, like a Frisbee. The man recoiled, lifted a protective arm, grunted at the impact. "Is it too late? Has the evil taken you—"

"Fire!" screamed Scarlet into the corridor. She was not fleeing after all. "Help, there's a fire! We were frying eggs, and a…a dishtowel caught on fire, and…um…*gas leak!"*

I leaped for the open kitchen and began to throw coffee cups. He clapped a hand to his face where I'd struck him, hesitated a moment longer, then bolted for the window.

"The whole place could go up in flames!" called Scarlet from the doorway. *"Help!"*

As neighbors called questions, I put down a dish and watched the stranger clamber out. Should I try to stop him, fight him further? I am a historian, not a warrior princess. He might yet fall to his death…even if I chose not to push him.

I did not push him, and he did not fall to his death.

After he scrabbled awkwardly back to the roof, I hurried to close and lock my window, and then the inside shutters. Then I went to the tiny, slope-roofed bedroom, to lock those shutters and to check on Tache in the near darkness. She sat on my raised bed, licking her white paw. When I tried to take a closer look, she protested and stalked away, no harm done.

I returned to the front room, where Scarlet was trying to explain the disturbance to my neighbors. "Since I've heard that it's better to cry 'fire' than 'rape,' I thought it might also apply to strange men who leap in off the roof, so—"

"She's drunk," I said firmly, by way of dismissal. "I will keep closer watch on her. *Bon soir*."

"Thank you for coming!" called Scarlet as I shut the door and locked its three required locks. As if the neighbors had brought us muffins, instead of simply checking to determine if their own flats were in danger. The room seemed suddenly quiet.

I lit several candles and began to clean up.

"Wait!" Scarlet stopped me with a hand on my arm. Still sore from my earlier fall, I barely held back a wince. "We need to leave this for the police, don't we?"

"I don't intend to ring the police," I told her.

"What? Why not?"

I lifted the settee back onto its feet and scowled at the scar on one curved wooden leg, instead of looking at her. *Because I did not like to ask anybody for help. Because the police were busy with other, more serious fallout from the earthquake.* "Because we have no telephone service, remember?"

And because I disliked the police. I had not liked them as a teenager, when my grandmother's response to me running away had been to have me arrested and leave me in jail over the weekend before coming for me, to "teach me a lesson." I did not like them now that I was someone who had, arguably, committed a crime. Just that once. But once was enough.

One misstep—and it would haunt me throughout my life. I hid my distress by straightening the coffee table. One of its legs wobbled.

"Rhys was right," Scarlet suggested, dropping the subject of the police. "You should rest. Shall I make you some tea?"

Still kneeling beside the abused furniture, I frowned up at her. Was she truly that unobservant? Or was she humoring me?

Something about the gleam in her brown gaze made me suspect the latter. An intelligent optimist? Intriguing.

I felt an unexpected rush of gratitude.

"Do you think you can manage tea without setting anymore dishtowels alight?" I teased, to hide it. I, too, knew of the advice about crying "fire" to get proper attention from bystanders. It was her level of detail that had amused me.

"Well, I *am* drunk," she admitted with a mischievous smile.

To my surprise, I found myself smiling briefly back.

And, silly or not, I slept with the key that night.

The drumroll reverberates. Or is that her racing heart? Worse—it stops. Does the executioner move? Is that the sudden slide of the blade?

Somehow—impossibly, wonderfully she pushes herself backward. She wrenches free of the ties binding her to the bascule and rolls to her feet, blind to the thud behind her.

She still has a chance! The crowd, usually so blood-thirsty, cheers for her escape. Alive with joy, she spins, ready to fight off further guards—

Only to see her decapitated body, even now strapped to the bloody bascule.

The joy stills in her. It does not make sense…rather, she does not want it to. But she needs to know. Ignoring the men who unbuckle her body and tip it like a broken doll into the gory coffin beside the bascule, she creeps forward, forces herself to look into the bloody basket on the other side of the blade….

Her own face, familiar despite the shorn hair and the bright blood spatter, stares up at her. Despite having no body, its eyes focus on her—and blink. It smiles—

With a gasp, I reared upward in my bed. Every muscle in my aching body screamed. Tache mewed a protest and shifted to a safer place on the covers. I panted, the drumbeat still in my ears, the smell of fresh blood in my nostrils, and the sight…

Mon Dieu. That had been no dream.

I didn't make it to the toilet before I threw up.

It was with mixed feelings that I approached the site mid-morning the next day. Historians must accept death, at least in general terms. But to have perhaps witnessed the execution of at least one of those victims, against all logic…

This very much unnerved me.

But I needed to uncover this woman's story. I wanted to see Rhys Pritchard again—perhaps with less foolish-ness? And this was *my site.* Not mine by means of ownership—the Sorbonne and the city had that—but mine by discovery. *And* visions.

I walked from the closest bus stop to what turned out to be the worst damage in the city—good news for Paris, if not for Avenue Denfert-Rochereau. The area had been cordoned off, and the only vehicles were EDF—*Électricité de France*—vans. Bright security tape circled the gap in the asphalt, and the top of a ladder extended a full meter from its top.

As I approached, having ducked under the tape, I could hear Rhys Pritchard offering an orientation to the morning shift.

"—done what we can to shore up the overhang, but don't underestimate the danger of collapse. Hence the waivers."

"There won't be another earthquake, will there?" asked a girl's voice. "Or aftershocks?"

"Our immediate concern is rain. But until someone clarifies what caused yesterday's—" Rhys fell silent as, with a steadying inhale, I stepped onto the ladder. Since I was looking down to watch my feet, I could focus not on the height, but on him squinting up at me through the trickle of sand, despite precautions that bumpered the ladder from the edge of the rock. "Ah, Catrina. Good morning. Watch your step."

At least, should I fall, he might catch me. Or not....

Need I point out that he looked delicious this morning? Rhys wore dust and exhaustion well, his thick black hair and careless whiskers gray with it, his eyes extra bright behind its mask. He'd triple-looped a bandana around his left wrist, likely for wiping his face, its color now indistinguishable from the dirt around him. As I reached the last two rungs of the ladder, in the close quarters, he became taller than me again.

He made introductions. The two volunteers were students, Josette and Charles—with better-trained archeologists flocking to the larger sites and the airports slammed, we could have done worse. I prompted him to keep speaking. "Do we expect rain?"

"Tonight, perhaps tomorrow, which is why time is of the essence. What's at stake here is not merely artifacts, but knowledge. Who were these women? Why were they not tossed into a mass grave like so many other— yes, Josette?"

I supposed that, as a teaching assistant, he must be in charge of classes. But his easy presentation surprised me, as did his immediate response to the young woman's raised hand. She asked, "But Monsieur Pritchard, how do you know they were women?"

"We cannot be certain without forensic analysis—another reason to exhume them. But considering how small the skeletons are, and their wide pelvic openings…"

"Not to mention," I added, spreading a hand toward one of the rotting piles of cloth just beyond Josette, "all the gowns."

Rhys's quick grin, white against the dust of his stubble, almost made me forget the rest of my evidence: *the visions*.

"But isn't that guesswork?" challenged Charles. Sitting on a portable table crammed against the sloping wall of skulls in back, he wore an expression of bored disdain as easily as he did his greasy ponytail. "None of it's a certainty."

"If you are looking for certainties in history," I warned, "you may wish to pursue a different course of study. Math, perhaps. There are absolutes in math."

"But *aren't* there absolutes in history?" Josette, who wore a crewcut, asked this of Rhys. If he taught classes, no doubt more than one student had a crush on him… perhaps as powerful as my own?

"History is subjective," he said. "Heroes from one era are vilified by the next. Many writings, like the Mayan codices, are destroyed after the fact for political or religious reasons."

Did he avoid my gaze as he said this last part? They did not know he'd been a priest.

"And people from preliterate cultures, or who were not allowed their own literature, are ignored or forgotten," I added. "As is often the case with women."

"There is that," Rhys agreed. Did we hold each other's gaze for a moment longer than necessary? I thought of Scarlet's insistence—*he does not* want *to like you…there is a difference*—and my mood lifted considerably.

Josette narrowed her heavily lined eyes at me—but I could not help it that I wore even work clothing well, or that the straps of my leather minibackpack, more practical than a purse for such work, emphasized my breasts.

"You mean we can't trust history?" protested Charles.

"We cannot blindly trust its objectivity," Rhys clarified. "But if we look closely, truth can linger beneath the surface."

Which was an excellent transition to setting them their tasks. As the students tried to document items without stepping on anybody—living or dead—Rhys filled me in on his progress. He gave me his notes and the signed waivers the Sorbonne had requested and informed me that city workers might come by to study why the earthquake had somehow peaked near this spot.

Forced to stand so close, I had difficulty paying full attention. Perhaps I was attracted to a good man like a visitor at the zoo, there to see a previously undiscovered animal.

"—three days at most, even if the weather stays fair," Rhys continued, as I drank him in, "which… Is something wrong?"

I should let him go. He'd been here all night, after all. "Just something Scarlet Rubashka told me."

"Did she make it home all right?"

Perhaps I was not the only one lingering? "She stayed at my flat. Since everything seemed so…unsettled, last night."

"You two got along?" Did he think me incapable of making friends?

I thought of how she'd hugged me before heading home that morning. She'd done it quickly, before I could stop her. And she'd helped me clean up the sick, after my nightmare….

I said, "At least she didn't steal anything."

Rhys folded his arms and squinted down at me. Something about his blue gaze saw far more than I show most people, especially men. The sensation frightened and intrigued me.

"Catrina Dauvergne," he challenged, "why must you pretend—"

But a voice from above interrupted us. "Rhys Pritchard!"

A look upward revealed one of the people I least wanted to meet again. The elderly Brigitte Taillefer was Rhys's boss at the Sorbonne. She had once been my favorite professor, when I'd attended the same college some years earlier. And her niece was the reckless woman from whom I'd liberated that damned chalice.

I suspected I was no longer her favorite student.

After Rhys climbed dutifully past me toward the surface, sending more debris sifting down from the overhang, I knelt by the nearest skeleton, at the base of the ladder—and surreptitiously returned the key I'd taken. Then I blatantly eavesdropped.

"Please, Brigitte, sit over here," I heard Rhys say.

The professor asked sharply about "...where you'd gotten to?"

True, I'd stopped by my own place of employment, then by the hospital to check on *Grand-mère*, before coming to relieve Rhys. Telephone service was still out across parts of the city, and it had seemed important to let the Cluny know where I was. When I told the museum director of my discovery, he promised to cast around for outside funding to help the reclamation.

As for *Grand-mère*, she'd refused to see me. The earthquake had shaken none of the ill-temper out of her.

But in the meantime, Rhys had been here all night.

Taillefer said, "You did not tell me *she* is involved."

I moved to another nearby skeleton. It—she—seemed not to have died with anything metal in her gullet. And yet…why did one of the pebbles, beneath the ribcage, catch my attention?

Might it be more than a pebble?

Rhys said something about not thinking my involvement mattered, followed by, "You two dislike each other…."

The professor raised her voice. "And you do not?"

I heard Rhys mention "Alexandria" as I blew gently at the unnaturally square little rock. Twisting around for a brush among the supplies, I cleared the worst dirt with a few careful whisks and was rewarded with the gleam of something not quite metallic. "And what," I whispered, "did *you* swallow, *chéri?*"

Now I could ignore the escalating conversation above me. I took note of the item's size and shape, then—with a measuring stick laid beside it—photographed it. Josette stepped closer as I did. "You found something?"

"Amidst all this barrenness? Yes."

I thought perhaps Josette also wished to eavesdrop. But she crouched beside me. "What is it?"

"I believe," I murmured, trusting myself to reach for it only now, "that it may be a tile or inset." I touched it—

She throws herself in front of the guard as he tries to shoulder his way into their salon, tiles hard in her throat. These, they will not take. But can Isabeau hide the rest?

"Make way, by order of the Committee of Public Safety!" As usual, they have made their raid in the middle of the night.

She throws herself against him. "My friends and I are loyal, citizen! My husband fights in the army. We've a brick from the Bastille on our mantel—only look!"

He backhands her across the face. She sinks to her knees from the shock of it, tears burning despite her desperation. The blow hurts nowhere near as much as the death of her ideals.

If Isabeau has time to hide the letters, there is hope of their dreams surviving, even if the Sisters of Mary do not.

If Isabeau has time.

"We have orders to search this house," warns the guard. *"We have heard reports of your seditious sympathies."*

She does the last thing she can to distract him. Kneeling as she is, she reaches out a trembling hand toward his trousers—the full-length style, of course, not the fancy breeches of the upper class that the sans-culottes *have disdained. She feels his body stir with anticipation beneath her touch. "Just a little more time,* monsieur, *to dress and make ourselves proper...."*

Monsieur—*it is a deadly mistake. Such language has been outlawed in favor of the more egalitarian "Citizen." She has just insulted his patriotism and destroyed her own.*

Again he strikes her, then again, screaming at her for having the sluttish morals of an aristocrat. At least he is distracted, *she thinks, as others storm into her home to tear it apart and, she is quite sure, to plant false evidence. When he leaves her, she crawls to the stairs.*

Please, let Isabeau have hidden them, *she prays. Isabeau races down the stairs in her nightgown and gathers her close, berating the men as beasts....*

I gasped—and yanked my hand back as if from a

snake. I'd been someone different—rather, seen through different eyes.

What the hell was happening to me? And yet…Sisters of Mary? *Soeurs de Marie.* SdM. I now understood SdM.

Except…they sounded like nuns. They did not act like nuns!

"Mademoiselle Dauvergne," insisted Josette, as if she had already said my name more than once. I lifted dazed eyes to her. "Professor Taillefer is asking for you."

Indeed, that was the professor's voice, not asking but insisting that I "get up here *immédiatement!*"

Normally, this would be the quickest way to ensure that I not move until she brought her own decrepit ass down the ladder to me or shut her mouth. However, still dazed by midnight raids and the taste of imagined blood in my mouth, I found it easier to simply comply, for once.

At least Rhys was insisting that the professor calm down.

"We ought not leave the students unattended," I reminded them, taking his outstretched hand to step from the ladder.

My lingering detachment faltered when I found myself face-to-face with the woman I'd once wished could be my grandmother. Small and stooped, the professor wore her long, white hair in a crown around the top of her head. Her faded eyes burned at me.

"How dare you?" she demanded, much like my real *Grand-mère*.

How dare I…plummet into the gaping earth during a natural disaster? How dare I try to save what I'd found there? How dare I lust after her attractive teaching assistant? I smiled coolly, feigning confusion. "Could you be more specific, *madame?*"

She all but spat the words. "You dirty little thief!"

From his lodgings above the locksmith shop, Grimaud watched through a crack in his curtains as the honey-haired demoness stepped off the ladder to speak to the old lady. Luckily, with the avenue blocked off, he had little else to do with his time.

He must better understand how he could have failed so miserably the previous night. Had he thought she posed such a challenge, he might not have attacked while the women were awake. But he'd feared them complicating matters by hiding the key, or locking it away, and he felt certain the key was…key. Even without instructions—his letter could not possibly have reached its destination yet—Grimaud knew he must do *something* to contain the evil. And yet…

He was on God's side. He should have won. How…?

He yearned for instructions. He wanted to protect France. He wanted to fulfill his family's purpose. He ached to serve on the side of the angels.

But for now, considering his previous night's failure, all he could do was watch the two-hundred-year-old devils.

Escaping.

Chapter 4

The worst part of Professor Taillefer's accusations came after she slapped me.

She accused me of stealing that chalice, of betraying her. I noted that she and her niece had come to me with that piece of stolen property, risking my reputation as well as theirs. Rhys tried futilely to referee, finally turning away in disgust.

"But which one of us sold it?" demanded the *professeur*.

I smiled coolly through my fury. "The smarter one?"

The old woman slapped me. I recoiled, more startled than hurt—until Rhys, spinning back at the sound, *grabbed my arm!*

As if I commonly hit old ladies. Or even hit them back.

I watched a mixture of realization, shame and defiance play across Rhys's unshaven face—and some little part of me died, even as he let go. I'd thought he…but I'd been wrong.

He turned on her. "Brigitte, that was uncalled for."

"She was my favorite!" Now she made a play for *pity?*

"Do not pretend you cared for me," I hissed—to both of them, now. "Or that old ladies are helpless. I know better."

"Catrina!" I'd never seen the usually calm Rhys so irritated. Not even when I'd taken—that is, *kept*—the damned chalice.

"Rhys," Professor Taillefer said decidedly, her voice quavering in a calculated way, "I do not want you working with this woman."

He took a deep breath before saying, gently but firmly, "Brigitte, I love you, but I will work where I am needed. The Sorbonne already approved this project, and we're working against time. Personal biases cannot be a factor."

Which is when the old woman simply stalked off, around the security tape and back toward the bus stop.

"Brigitte!" Rhys called after her. He took a step in her direction, but she made good time for her age. His shoulders dropped and he jabbed a hand through his thick, dusty hair.

"Bitch," I muttered. She had, after all, hit me.

He spun back to me, scowling. "Catrina, *sod off!*"

And he stalked away in the direction opposite the bus stop.

Even if Scarlet were correct about Rhys Pritchard in some way wanting me, he must *not want* to want me very, very badly.

* * *

Luckily for my ego, the geophysicist Rhys had mentioned soon arrived with his handheld computers and sensors and math to investigate the location's role in the Paris quake. This scientist from the Paris Institute of Earth Physics was sharp-eyed, sandy-haired and single.

I flirted outrageously. By the time he had finished his initial investigation, Léon Chanson and I had a date for the next night.

"*Incroyable*," murmured Josette to me, before the dust from Léon's ascent up the ladder had even settled.

"The trick," I told her, using tweezers to collect another of the odd little tiles, "is not really caring either way."

That trick helped me focus on my task at hand after the disturbing morning. That, and my fascination for what we found.

Too dreadfully, many of the items that had been dumped with these bodies had rotted beyond saving: heavy layers of clothing and leather-bound books, for example. Dishes and mirrors lay broken, although we collected them for a closer look at the Sorbonne. But other items remained whole—candlesticks, buttons, silverware, a bayonet, a cedar writing box and bits of jewelry. Those, we winched up in boxes and loaded into a nearby van for Charles and Josette to take back to the *université* when their shift ended. And we wondered, often aloud, how they could possibly have been left here. The late eighteenth-century had been a time of desperate poverty. How was it that the workers who dumped the bodies had not stolen all this while it was still good?

When a new shift of students—Paul and Georges—arrived, Charles and Josette drove our latest salvage off to safety. Scarlet came by to check on me and to photograph the excavation. Though the cameras she'd had on her the day before were as mysteriously useless as our cell phones, she'd brought replacements. I found myself drawing her to one side to whisper as if we were best friends in secondary school. When I told her about the phrase from my vision, the Sisters of Mary, she bounced with excitement, recognizing—as I had—the connection to SdM, and she promised to research them further. And to "blog" about it. "You never know who's out there reading your blog," she said.

After she left, Paul and Georges eventually stopped discussing her and moved back to the favorite subject of the day—earthquakes. Yesterday's quake had felt so alien, and yet…people had faced worse disasters throughout history. The 1382 earthquake in southern England had destroyed churches. The 1755 Lisbon earthquake, which had killed over 60,000 people, had lost the Jesuits much of their hold over Portugal.

Then we heard the rumble.

Our heads came up slowly, all three of us, as the shudder of it rolled closer, louder. With a crash, the earth shook!

"Storm coming," called Rhys from the top of the ladder, startling us from our paralysis. "Everybody out."

I would have thrown something at him if I weren't afraid of missing him, hitting the unstable rock ceiling and finishing the job yesterday's quake had begun.

Georges and Paul obediently hooked their half-filled boxes to the cable we were using to winch items up while Rhys continued, "Stay with the van for a while longer, if you will. I've gotten permission to move the bodies."

He'd been busy for someone who'd not slept since yesterday.

I went back to what I'd been doing—following a strange wire that seemed to run across the floor, wondering at its purpose. By the time Georges and Paul had their boxes and themselves out, I'd traced the wire into a crack in the wall, directly opposite the high stack of skulls.

"It's time to go, Catrina," insisted Rhys, from up top.

"I'll take my chances," I called, bending even nearer the wire. Where could it go? It had to be from the same time as the mass grave, if not earlier. Carefully, I tugged.

The wire pulled easily, as if not attached to anything. But how long was it?

Blowing out a particularly aggrieved sigh, Rhys said, "Then at least stand back. I'm sending down shovels and body bags."

So I did, and he did, and I tried not to feel ill when another, louder roll of thunder shook the ground around me. More dust drifted downward from the damaged ceiling. But I did not mean to give up on these ladies and their mystery until the last possible moment.

Hopefully I could climb a ladder very, very quickly, if the need arose.

Since saving the bodies was our highest priority—both for what they could tell us before their state-mandated reburial and to ensure the road repairs above did not further desecrate their remains—I left the mys-

terious wire *and* my annoyance in order to help Rhys
with that. As he dug up the earth around and beneath
each skeleton, I eased a body bag under the area he'd
freed. Each time we had a skeleton, a skull and their surrounding debris and dirt zipped securely into one of the
black, heavy-duty body bags, we labeled it by number.
Then we winched it up to our companions above.

We'd managed three of the five in total silence—
apart from the increasingly frequent rumble of thunder
outside—before Rhys finally spoke.

"I apologize," he said. "For this morning, I mean."

Secretly pleased, I worked thick plastic under the soil
of the feet as he held much of it up with the shovel. "You
have no control over what Brigitte Taillefer says or does."

He made an annoyed noise, and I looked up. The
halogen lights that burned against the underground
gloom gave him something of a halo. But rather than
looking agreeable, his eyes were angry again. "I was not
apologizing for Brigitte. You did not have to goad her."

"Didn't I? You heard what she called me, saw what
she did."

He muttered something under his breath that sounded
like *"Uffach cols,"* and he went back to digging.

"For someone who once was a priest," I teased, re-
suming my work, "you make a poor apology."

His words came out through gritted teeth. "I was apologizing for my language, Catrina, as well you know."

Again I shrugged, this time deliberately baiting him.
I *liked* Angry Rhys. "Your French, it is not so terrible."

He rolled his eyes. I know, because I was sneaking
glances up at him through my lashes, despite that we

continued to work at our gruesome task. "What I am sorry for was not in French."

Sod off is of course a British expression. Though there are French equivalents, they are not always as satisfying.

"All the best vulgarities come from the Anglo-Saxon," I agreed easily. "I have certainly heard worse."

Again with the rude noise. When I raised my eyebrows in question, Rhys tried more Anglo-Saxon. "I am not surprised. You *piss me off*," he explained in English, quite on purpose, before he switched back to French. "I'm not sure why."

"It is a talent," I assured him.

"You need not sound so proud of it."

But the alternative would be shame. *Merci, non.*

Rhys's body seemed to radiate an extra heat that smelled good amidst the decay surrounding us and felt even better against the chill of the coming storm. I believe I have already mentioned finding the bodies of even average men quite sexy? He was not average.

Consider me a connoisseur, if you will.

We sent the last skeleton up to Georges and Paul in near silence. They called the lightning show above *"fantastique"* and encouraged us not to stay too long. Then they left to drive our macabre day's work back to the *université*.

Again thunder crashed around us, the kind of thunder that shakes the world. Dust filtered down from the damaged rock above. The air smelled of electricity.

"After you," called Rhys, over the cacophony.

"Not until I have to," I insisted. And I went back to the wire I'd been examining earlier. Another tug won me no more than another arm's length of wire, with no apparent end to it.

He followed me. "I won't leave you alone down here."

I glared up at him, the judgmental protector of mean old ladies. "Do not dare use your gallantry to manipulate me! We each have a choice. I am making mine on my own. I suggest you make yours in the same manner."

Whether he chose gallantry or chose to stay for his own purposes, he sank into a crouch beside me. "What is that?"

"I have no idea." Another pull brought yet more wire, rough from lying underground for so long. It was not insulated, of course—this was from the 1700s.

"Let me help." And between the two of us, we retrieved more wire than we ever could have imagined—what Rhys guessed was nearly a hundred meters' length—before finally the loose end pulled free.

Well. That was an anticlimax. Except…

"The end is sharp," I murmured, my words punctuated by another crash of thunder. I held up the bit that had caught my gloved finger and, unlike the weathered wire itself, the edge shone in the lantern light. "As if it were freshly cut."

Rhys was already following our wire in the other direction, where it turned out to be spiked solidly down just beneath the stacked skulls of the catacombs, near the base of our portable table. It had been laid to run across the width of the excavation.

"Like a trip wire," I murmured, even more disturbed by this than by the way the thunder shook our cave.

"Or…" ventured Rhys. But he stopped himself.

I crouched beside him and his hard warmth, beside the stake that had secured the wire for almost two hundred years. "What?"

"A common fear in Victorian times was the fear of being buried alive," he explained slowly, as if thinking this out even as he spoke.

I snorted. "These women were beheaded!"

"I know that!" His voice somehow mixed annoyance with more attractive amusement. "Which is why this doesn't make sense."

I waited, now regretting my interruption, and he gave in.

"Because of that fear, it was common to bury people—those who could afford it—with wires. The wires ran to the cemetery above and attached to bells. The idea was that if someone awoke after being buried, and thrashed about, his movements would pull on the wire and ring the bell, alerting the groundskeeper to dig him up. But, as you say, these women clearly had no hopes of regaining consciousness."

One certainly hoped not.

I looked out to where the skeletons had lain until we'd moved them. *Trip wire*, I thought again. "What if someone wished to be alerted to the movements of someone other than the dead?"

I am unsure what Rhys might have answered to that, though. Because at that moment, I saw a flash of movement from the fissure above us.

Something white. Cylindrical. Perhaps a foot long. It fell—

And, as in my vision of the woman dodging the guillotine blade, I tried to throw myself out of the way of something falling too fast to be dodged.

Unlike in Isabeau's vision, I threw myself against Rhys, knocking us both under the utility table—

Just as what I'd recognized as a pipe bomb exploded on impact, and the entire world seemed to collapse upon us.

Chapter 5

This is your fault, Catrina....

Rhys Pritchard's arms closed, hard and protective, around me. Something over the table crushed him against me, heavy, then heavier. I caught a flash of halogen-lit, rattling white before hiding my face into his lean shoulder. Bones. Then rock pushed us down, and back. Dirt surrounded us until we would drown in it. Rhys choked into my hair. I gasped into his shirt, more grateful for him at that moment than for anything, ever, in my life.

Who would have thought not dying alone would mean so much?

Except…thought began to creep back as the worst of the rock-fall became shifts and shudders in the debris around us. Air remained amidst the dirt.

I *wasn't* dead? Not yet.

I heard an odd hitch to Rhys's shaking breath. Was *he* dying? Then I recognized, mingled in his gasps, catches of Latin. "*Dimitte nobis debita nostra, sicut et nos dimittimus debitoribus nostris....*"

Forgive us our trespasses, as we forgive those who trespass against us. The Lord's Prayer.

I opened my eyes to gritty blackness. I moved my face from his shoulder and into his neck, for more breathing room. I whispered a shaky, "It worked."

Floating dirt dusted my tongue.

He gasped, in English, "What worked?"

"The praying. We're alive."

"Don't be daft. That's not how prayer works." More coughs wracked him, and I realized he might be hurt. Because he'd stayed. Worse, because *I'd* stayed.

Because he'd tried to take the brunt of the cave-in.

"Are you all right?" I asked.

When he laughed, his jaw rubbed my head. "I'm well. And you?"

"I am sorry."

After a long pause, Rhys said, "*You* caused the explosion?"

"No!" No wonder I apologize so rarely. I've no talent at it. "I'm sorry for not leaving when you asked. If I had…"

His breath rushed past my ear, with us lying cheek-to-cheek. Our inhales and exhales rocked us together. "The table saved us. How did you know to push me?"

"I saw something that looked like a length of PVC fall from the street, and…I thought it might be a pipe bomb."

"As one does."

"I used to date an anarchist." He'd thought there was shock value in discussing things like that.

Rhys said, "Thank you, Catrina."

"But what if we die down here?"

"No matter the results. But we aren't likely to die tonight."

"Why not?" I asked—actually, I asked, *Pourquoi pas?* Each of us was shaken enough to revert to our mother tongues.

"I can sense air moving on my cheek, from the left. I think we'd best dig in that direction."

"Instead of waiting to be rescued?"

"Georges and Paul did not know we would stay."

Merde. I hadn't thought of that. "And unless we know why the first bomb was dropped…"

"Then we cannot discount the possibility of a second."

So we fumbled outward, into a chaos of what I realized, from the feel and sound of them, were broken bones. Thousands of broken bones. They pressed against us on all sides, crushing us, scraping us. Everywhere Rhys's warm body was not, I felt cold, dead bones. And we had to dig through them by hand?

Thank God we'd worn leather gloves.

Time passed, what felt like hours of clawing and squirming blindly through femurs and skulls and flat pieces, like pelvic bones. At least this particular catacomb wall had been made out of the large bits, although the explosion and collapse had broken many of them to the sharpness of weapons.

The only benefit—beyond our hope of survival, of course—was my inappropriate enjoyment of Rhys's sinewy body writhing on mine as we struggled to clear room for both of us together, bit by bit, in what we hoped was a consistent direction. It made for great distraction. I did not imagine his body's appreciation of that same writhing against me. But, him being a man, that increasing hardness—rounded and warm and alive in a world of sharp, cold, dead things—might mean no more than a blink or a sneeze. More's the pity.

Sometimes we stopped to rest, panting through each other's hair to filter the dust as we caught our breath. I had to bite my tongue to keep from tasting him, then. Why frustrate matters further? Although, to judge by his jeans…

At the risk of being blasphemous—it may have been quite a waste, had Rhys Pritchard remained a priest.

Occasionally we would gasp comments back and forth: "Still here?" or "Let's go." But for the most part, the work was too difficult, too necessary, to waste breath.

I began to fear we would die here, our bodies rotting to leave only our bones, lost and forgotten amidst an entire catacomb full of them. But I would not stop before Rhys did, so I went on. Millimeter by millimeter.

Then I gasped as my hand emerged into open space. "Rhys!"

"It may just be a pocket," he warned, but we renewed our scramble. With a loud clatter of falling bones, we squirmed farther into absolute, black nothingness—

A nothingness where we could breathe.

"Take care," Rhys began, but I was already pushing free, with the kind of desperation that makes drowning victims fight their own rescuers. Not that I hurt *him*, mind you.

But my blind tumble down a slide of bones to land, hard, on damp stone knocked all breath out of me.

"Catrina?" Rhys's voice took on an edge of panic. *"Cat!"*

I tried to inhale, to shout a response, but I couldn't. So I slapped my hand on the floor several times, splashing in something I hoped was run-off.

I began to panic. I *would* breathe again, wouldn't I? We couldn't make it this far, just for me to die of a fall!

Only as more bones hailed down onto me did I catch that first, glorious breath. Rhys landed solidly beside me. I heard each foot firmly hit, and felt the presence of him. "Catrina?"

"Here." I reached, and his hand found mine in the darkness, and we pulled ourselves into each other, clinging…alive.

I arched upward to find his lips—and his found my forehead first, damn it. "Thank God," he whispered, after an annoying, big-brotherly kiss. "Do you have to be quite so fearless?"

"Yes." I shrugged off my backpack purse as he drew back. "Yes, I do."

The purse was barely enough to contain necessities. But one of those necessities…yes! I flicked open my cigarette lighter.

For a moment I just looked at Rhys—his eyes a deeper blue for reflecting the flame, his face scraped, his clothes torn and stained. Assuming that I looked the same, I barely glanced at the passageway around us before closing the lighter again, to save fuel. The tunnel led in only one direction, the landslide of bones and rubble from which we'd emerged blocking the other side. A thread of water snaked down the middle of the passage, pooling against the rubble a meter or so from Rhys's jeaned hip.

"May I please see that?" asked Rhys, so I handed him the lighter. Then, with shaking hand, I found my pack of *Gauloises.*

I had been quitting for some time. Seeing one's grandmother hospitalized with end-stage cancer presents a harsh argument. But nothing makes me need a cigarette more than the realization that I cannot have one. Lately I had managed to go as long as a week at a time without a smoke. But give them up entirely? The two times I'd tried, I'd panicked and smoked a pack—so, not yet.

Rhys flicked open the lighter again, to better study our surroundings. He started when I caught his hand, then smiled when I used it to light my cigarette. Smoke filled my lungs, relaxing and deadly. Yes....

It wasn't sex, but it would do. "Do not waste that," I suggested. He closed the lighter and pressed it into my hand.

Then he said, incongruously, "May I please see that?"

Perhaps he, too, was shaken by what we'd just escaped? I tried to give him back the lighter. He said, "I meant the fag."

So I passed him the cigarette, and he took a long draw of his own. By the faint red glow of his inhale, dramatic against the underground blackness, I could barely make him out. Him, and the skulls behind him.

The catacombs cover many kilometers—miles—and

hold an estimated five to six million bodies. One legend told of a man who'd vanished down here, only to have his remains found twenty years later, identified by his keys. But we would not suffocate on dirt, buried in bones. That was something, anyway.

Rhys passed back the cigarette. It was cool down here. The audible trickle of water past our feet hinted at the promised rainstorm. I settled closer against his side for warmth before handing over the *Gauloise*.

He did not push me away. He looked disarmingly like a bad boy, smoking so easily, with his shaggy hair and his disheveled clothing, with his desperate need of a shave.

"How very sinful of you," I murmured, impressed.

He made a rude noise. "Dirty, perhaps. Certainly unhealthy. But *sinful* might be overstating matters." He handed back the cigarette. "Besides, I haven't had one in years."

I haven't had one in almost a week. But to say that would sound pitifully like justification, or a plea for approval.

When I tried to pass him back the cigarette, he said, "No, thank you."

Feeling a twinge of something suspiciously like guilt, I inhaled deeply, then breathed the smoke out with an audible sound of enjoyment—"Ahhh!"—before I carefully stubbed it out.

I only smoked halves. And it might be wise to ration.

The ground vibrated—probably a clap of muffled thunder. Worse, the trickling water had, at some point, become a gurgle.

"Perhaps we should…" Rhys began.

I was ahead of him, flicking my lighter open and forcing my attention from his world-weary face to the stream widening down the center of the tunnel, pooling against the dead end. The runoff seemed to rise even in the moment I watched it, before I again closed and pocketed the lighter.

This is one of the common warnings the police circulate, to try to keep cataphiles out of the tunnels beneath Paris. One could get lost. One could fall. And, in the case of flash floods, one could drown.

Rhys stood. "Perhaps we ought not wait here for rescue."

I was surprised when his hand closed around my wrist and he tugged upward. It threw me off balance, but I'll admit, that is not the only reason I fell into him.

Into his hard, T-shirted chest. Into his sinewy arms. Rhys was warmth. Strength. Life.

Then I allowed him to help me right myself, and I let go.

Or tried.

I hadn't expected his breath, redolent with wine and fresh smoke, on my cheek. I hadn't expected to have to tug from his grip as well as from my own. Interesting...

"So we need not waste the lighter," he suggested. A moment later, a different glow lit the tunnel around us.

"You have a cell phone? *You could have called for help?*"

"It does not work underground. See?" He showed me the display, and the warning of *No Service* printed across the top. But the blue light of the display lit our surroundings. I could see that the floodwaters from the storm had spread to about a meter across, just that quickly.

The tunnel itself was only about three meters across.

Rhys and I exchanged solemn looks, both aware of what the growing stream meant and neither willing to speak the truth. I shrugged my purse back on and we began walking. Quickly.

Limestone wall loomed close on one side of us, the tightly stacked skeletons on the other, leering in the unnatural glow. Random bones littered the floor ahead of us, to trip the unwary trespasser in the shadows.

Since downstream was blocked, we headed upstream.

Within a few minutes, our steps began to splash in the spreading water. And this was only the start of the storm! I remembered urban legends my one-time cataphile boyfriend had shared about tunnel residents being swept away into the Paris sewer system…or into oblivion. He'd taken particular glee in describing what happens to a body as it is rolled by a rushing current, battered across rock and tightly packed bones, then left to bloat in the eddies that linger after a storm.

He is one reason I came to prefer older men.

Now the water writhed ankle-deep across our feet. Worse, it ran strong, as if deliberately trying to trip us. It caught and twisted the faint illumination of the cellphone display.

Then, with a sudden rush, it rose to a battering knee-deep.

I drew my breath to call to Rhys, whose long stride had drawn ahead. Before I could, his free hand swung back and closed solidly around mine. "Hang on!"

"We need a cross tunnel." I caught up with extra effort.

His words took on a sharp, sarcastic tone. "Do you think?"

"Pray or something."

"I told you, that's not how it—"

One misstep, just one, and I went to my knees, wet to my shoulders now. The flood swept me backward a half meter before I caught myself with a foot on the rock floor, with Rhys's hand still gripping mine. He twisted, fast, to better hold me, even as I reared back out of the suddenly thigh-high water. But the quick movement cost him.

Now Rhys went down and, like that, washed past me, his wet hand pulling loose from mine.

I dove after him. The cold current tossed us downstream with incredible force, but only he fought it. With two kicks, I caught up to him, grabbed him around the waist, tried to regain my footing instead of pulling him deeper, tried not to breathe water.

Stopping us was far more difficult.

I *think* I helped. Everything got confused with flashes of absolute darkness and swallowed water, with submerged moments that muffled all other sound and gasping, surfacing moments of echoing, splashing chaos. But my cold hands grasped a belt loop on his sodden jeans. I held on desperately and somehow, somehow, we regained our feet together.

And Rhys was still holding up the telephone. Wet or not, he'd kept it above the surface enough that it still glowed.

On the downside, we'd lost half the distance we'd made.

"My apologies," he muttered thickly, over the rush, swiping wet hair off his face with his free hand while I still held tight around his waist. "I should have…"

I could have pointed out that I'd fallen first. Instead I tried, "You kept the light, anyway."

For a moment we just stood there together, panting, water pushing against our hips. Then Rhys's arms came around my waist too and, hip-to-hip, we forged against the rising floodwaters.

"Do you rehearse being this abrasive?" he asked. So he'd probably noticed on his own that I'd fallen first.

"Daily," I assured him.

"Practice makes perfect," he grumbled. I laughed, and caught only a glimpse of his grin, but it strengthened me for the struggle ahead. And it was a struggle.

Beneath the muffled boom of the storm, the pounding water rose to waist depth. Splashing heavily into the landslide of rock and bones behind us, its current circled back in tricky eddies and undertows. If Rhys and I hadn't held so close, I doubted we could have kept our feet, much less made progress.

But we *had* to. The alternative was to drown.

"There's one!" called Rhys, suddenly.

I peeked from under his arm. A deeper shadow to our left hinted at the intersecting tunnel we needed. We took forever to get there, every straining step a fight against the current. When we reached it, the backwash where the flood splashed off the tunnel's side churned even more dangerously.

For a moment, I feared we might both go down. The ground dropped from beneath me, leaving me with no foundation except Rhys. Taller, he kept his feet in the momentarily neck-high wash while I held on with one hand, swam with the other, tried not to inhale water, tried…

Then my feet touched submerged floor. We were waist-deep and, better, out of the current. When we reached relatively dry tunnel, we staggered a safe distance from the water before dropping to the ground, panting. We'd made it!

The first thing Rhys said, when he caught his breath, was, "Perhaps we should rest here."

But he didn't rest. While he pulled himself up and explored the tunnel a little further, I squeezed water from my shoulder-length hair and busied myself opening my purse and feeling across its contents—wet, but thankfully not sodden. I laid everything out to dry. Rhys returned with a discarded bottle, and filled it in the rushing water of the flood beyond us, insisting that I drink my fill.

"I've done my share of camping," he insisted, against my protest. "The more we drink tonight, the less we'll need tomorrow. Assuming nobody finds us right away, that is."

"Do you know what could be in that water?"

"Moving water is marginally safer. In any case, we're under one of the most advanced cities in the world. Once we do get out, we'll visit a hospital and get antibiotics. Agreed?" When I said nothing, he added, "Catrina, we can manage without food for days, if necessary. But we need water."

Days…? I drank as much as I could before remembering that I did have food, of a sort. I rattled the tin. "Breath mint?"

Having refilled the bottle, Rhys sank wearily and wetly back beside me. "Perhaps for breakfast."

Then he shut the phone, plunging us into complete darkness.

That's when I fully accepted that we would not escape this labyrinth tonight. Perhaps not the next night. Perhaps….

Whoever had blown up the *Soeurs de Marie* site might yet have killed us. Had that been his intention? Or had he meant only to destroy whatever secrets had been buried so long ago?

"We should let our clothes dry while we sleep," I suggested by way of distraction, pulling my top off and laying it beside me. Chilled, I slid off my boots, my wringing-wet socks. Then I unbuckled my belt and wriggled out of my trousers.

Only then was I gratified to hear the distinctive sound of Rhys's zipper sliding open.

Against the rush of the flood beyond, I listened to the trickle of water as Rhys wrung out his clothes, then the wet slap as he laid them out, piece by piece. Then, because it was cold and he was alive and I felt alone, I slid up against him.

He caught his breath. Like me, he still wore his underpants. Though cold and wet, they did not inhibit his body's slow but promising reaction to the length of me.

Rhys had a long, strong body and a gratifyingly hairy chest. His large, warm hand, on my shoulder, slid down my bare back—a good sign—but then he breathed, "You're…topless."

"Do not be so British. Have *you* ever worn a wet bra?"

"I…no. Catrina—"

He did not need to say more. I heard the hesitance in his voice. My pout was, perhaps, in mine. "I know. You do not *want* to want me. But I am chilled. I am tired. I am—" *Frightened?* But that, I would not admit. "Lost," I substituted. "I could ease your discomfort or not, as you wish, no strings attached. I dislike strings, in general. But all I ask is that you hold me."

"My 'discomfort' is my own concern." He sounded annoyed, but that could be frustration. Or embarrassment. He may not have lain with many naked women before me.

I rolled over, so that my back was to him, his "discomfort" pressed deliciously into my rear, and I drew his arms around me. I tried not to think about how he would feel in my hand, how he would taste in my mouth, if only he *would* let me help—my offer had not been selfless. But his body was his own. Damn it. At least he was wonderfully warm. "Then go to sleep."

After a long moment, Rhys quietly asked, "That's all?"

My laugh echoed. "Were you *hoping* I would seduce you?"

Instead of answering, he closed his arms more tightly around me and growled, "Go to sleep, Catrina."

But I noticed that one of his forearms pressed possessively across my bare breasts, and I felt…hopeful. Safe. Not alone.

It was not sex, but with him, it would certainly do.

Somewhere above, in his doorway off the Avenue Denfert-Rochereau, Grimaud accepted the truth. God *was* on his side.

How, other than divine intervention, could one explain how easily he had made the bomb? Nobody had even noticed the explosion! They must have thought it more thunder. God's concealment.

Finally, Grimaud dared to creep back to the edge of the rubble that had once been the archeological site. Rain spattered hard across him, the torn pavement, and the sprawl of rock and dirt and twisted ladder where once evil had dwelled. He felt elated. Even without guidance, he'd done it! He'd stopped the spread of evil. He'd fulfilled his family mission.

And he'd pleased God.

Not bad for a poor, uneducated locksmith.

Chapter 6

To save the batteries of Rhys's abused phone, we walked in darkness. We went slowly. Since the rough bare walls sometimes jutted out at odd heights, we tracked the walls and occasional side tunnels by echo—or by my impact with one of them. Sometimes we opened the phone to reorient ourselves by its meager light.

Only after a long argument did Rhys agree to let me go first. It had nothing to do with selflessness on my part, and everything to do with the fact that if I hit a sinkhole, Rhys—with a hand tight around my belt the whole way—had strength enough to keep me from falling.

Were our order reversed, the first time Rhys stepped off an edge I would be alone down here. No cell phone. No warm human blanket. No hope of eventually seducing him…and of course I had not given up that hope, which is one reason that I pushed the question of why he'd given up his former calling.

"I left in order to marry. She died. I did not go back."

"Ah," I said over my shoulder, extending my gloved hands ahead of me to minimize collisions with the bone walls. "That explains everything. Except for how you managed an engagement while still a priest. And how she died. And how long you were married before that. And why you did not go back. And why you still act as if you are a priest."

He barked a laugh. "I do not act—" Then he seemed to catch on. "You mean last night? That any man who does not succumb to your ample charms must have taken a vow of celibacy?"

At least he thought my charms were ample. "Only that he must have a very, *very* good reason," I assured him modestly.

"Perhaps I just don't like you. Would that be reason enough?"

"Not always," I said honestly. It must be noted that both our tempers were strained. We'd had a meager breakfast of three breath mints each—and, in my case, a birth control pill. We'd drunk a little water from our bottle, since the flood had subsided into a muddy ditch. After that, we'd dressed in our still-damp clothes, and we'd been walking ever since. I banged my gloved hand against a wall of what felt like closely packed femurs, or perhaps humeri. Until now, I'd not fully grasped what "millions of skeletons" meant. But now…

"I apologize," said Rhys, more softly. "That was—"

"Oh, stop it. Why do you not like me?"

"You did steal from my friends…." Thus continued the same argument I'd had with his boss the previous day, with one extra detail. "Even if you'd had noble motives," he granted, "it does not excuse your accepting two million dollars for its sale."

I almost stumbled. "*How* much?"

"My friend Maggi bought it back for two million dollars. Do not pretend you did not know."

I'd received a payment for sending it on to an anonymous buyer—what a private collector gets free he will not cherish. Most had gone to my grandmother's hospice care. But not *two million dollars!*

I disliked feeling sick, so I said, "Then she got the cup back. All's well that ends well."

"And you don't feel at all—" But he cut himself off, retreated to that distance he'd worn too often in the past. "I'm being judgmental, Catrina. I apologize."

"Well, don't! We're alone—let down your guard for once. Sleep with naked women or push them away. Call me a bitch. Shout. Curse God if you must! God is a big boy. He can take it."

"I've already tried that," said Rhys softly. "It did not—"

But with a sharp scream, I dropped into gaping nothingness.

One moment there was stone beneath my feet. The next moment—I plummeted. I jerked to a stop by the waist as Rhys caught me. He had to roll backward to haul me up, two-handed, using his body for leverage while I helped by scrabbling on the rock. After much gasping and straining on both our parts, I kneed myself over the edge and fell onto a momentarily exhausted, still-damp man.

And stayed because he, too, was a big boy. If he could hold tight to me, breathe big gulps through my hair, who was I to push him away? I thanked him by nuzzling his jaw.

He did not push me away, either.

"I lied," he admitted, hoarse, as we caught our breath together. "Perhaps I do not *wholly* dislike you. Even when…"

"When I am being a bitch," I finished for him.

"I just do not under—"

I interrupted him with an eager kiss, my blood rushing from this latest brush with death. He kissed me back, his lips redolent with breath mints. And I am unsure why, but I began to shiver then. At least, inside.

When was the last time kissing a man had shaken me so?

Even after a second and third kiss, the exquisite trembling got worse. Finally he sat up, me still straddling his wet-jeaned thighs. That seemed a request to stop the kissing.

"We are both of us being affected by the dark," he panted. He lifted me off him, and he stood to continue walking. "It makes this too easy."

But I saw nothing at all easy about this.

Once we'd skirted the shaft and moved on, I dragged the subject back to what he'd omitted about leaving the priesthood. He said that he had loved the church his whole life, loved being an altar boy, felt honored to be allowed to touch the sacred vessels.

"I could feel God in them," he explained. "I only ever wanted to be a priest. But then, once I had my own church—I met her."

She had been Mary Tregaron. She'd been pure, kind and devoted to good works. They'd struggled with their attraction for well over a year before Rhys had asked to be transferred to another parish. Instead, his bishop counseled him to at least consider other possibilities.

"I joined a movement within Catholicism petitioning to allow priests to marry. This is how the church changes, after all—always from within, by the people who love her. But those changes come slowly. The change in me, however…I realized that I could no longer preach a doctrine that I questioned, and no matter how hard I prayed, I could not stop questioning it. So I petitioned Rome and waited for the papers to come through. For three years we waited. But she was in an auto accident."

And he'd already said… "Before your papers came through?"

"A few days before they arrived, yes."

"So the two of you never…?"

"I longed for her. For three years I dreamed in private of our marriage and gave her communion in public. We avoided spending time alone. Lord in Heaven, some nights I felt…" But that part, he did not choose to share. "If we'd not both respected my position as seriously as we did, I don't know what might have happened between us. But we had faith that by waiting, we could eventually be together without sin. It would be worth all the sacrifices."

We walked in silence for some time, both very aware that their reward had never come. So much for true love. Then Rhys added, "I did kiss her, one time. As she was dying, after the accident. I gave her last rites, but first… First, I kissed her. I don't know if she was even aware. Then the papers came, and I left the priesthood—as much as any priest can do, since ordination is considered permanent. For some months, I left the church entirely. But that part didn't keep. Not exactly."

"You're simply pursuing God through secular means now," I finished for him. When we'd been working the site in Alexandria, he'd gone often to the Coptic Museum in Cairo. He'd spoken with interest about the fourth-century Gnostic Gospels from the Nag Hammadi find. "And apocryphal sources."

"I want to understand the early church." He took a deep breath before adding, "I'm looking for the Holy Grail."

Then he waited, as if he expected me to laugh.

I could not laugh at him. So I asked, "Why?"

"I suppose I got it in my head that to find the Grail would be proof of God's forgiveness, or a way to truly know Jesus, or… It's a foolish quest, I know. But it's mine."

"I," I admitted, "have dreamed about the Sisters of Mary."

"You've dreamed about the who?"

So for the second time in two days, I explained about my visions, and how SdM might stand for *Soeurs de Marie*, and how powerfully the thought of them affected me. Secrets have been hidden with their remains. Mysteries. I meant to uncover them.

Or I had, before someone *blew them up*. Before we'd found ourselves lost beneath the city. Before...*had* everything ended?

At least Rhys Pritchard did not laugh at me, either.

By the time we stopped for the "night," I was desperately hungry. We finished all but two of the breath mints and took ibuprofen against our dehydration headaches. We were down to less than half a bottle of water, despite our rationing. My body ached from my falls... and from something far more primal. Worse, I was starting to lose hope.

"There should be litter," I insisted, stripping blindly from my drying clothes. From all of them. "Codes scratched onto the walls by cataphiles. Grafitti."

"Perhaps we missed it," Rhys assured me, over zipper and wet-denim sounds.

"Sections of the catacombs are completely closed off." As I had the night before, I slid with exquisite friction onto his barely dressed body. "We could be trapped."

"Or we may not be." Then, just as I was wondering how much God would hate me if I tried harder to seduce him, Rhys kissed me. Hard. Fingers twisted into my hair, pulling it loose from its makeshift tie. When I sighed my pleasure, he rolled me over so that he was on top and kissed me harder, his hips grinding down onto mine, hot and hard despite his briefs.

Unexpected, but I hated to interrupt the kissing to question his change of heart.

Matching Rhys's dry thrusts with my own, tongue and hips alike, I scored my nails down his bare, arched back and over his tight, cotton-covered ass, still damp from his wet jeans. I drew a foot up and down one of his hard calves, enjoying the sensation of it. It seemed to go on for an ecstatic forever.

When Rhys groaned and moved his kisses from my tingling mouth to my jaw, my throat, I writhed beneath him—and I began to shiver again. Did something about this man frighten me? Ridiculous. I trusted Rhys. And yet…

Perhaps that was why I shivered. I *did* trust him. I try to make it a habit never to wholly trust anyone, but I wanted—

I nearly screamed my frustration when he abruptly stopped in his blind worship of my body, his face still between my breasts, his briefs tented tight over his own hot need. "I did not expect…" He tried to explain and gulped. "I never…"

"You never…?" I prompted, palming his whiskered cheek, stroking my knee up and down his inner thigh. Then I understood—and wondered how I could have imagined otherwise. He'd been a staunch Catholic. His one true love had died after only a kiss. True, he'd been a civilian for well over a year, but…

"You've never been with a woman," I finished.

"And I did not intend to— Please stop that."

My knee stilled as I considered this. *A virgin.*

Now he seemed able to speak. "I feel things with you, impatience, annoyance…lust. And I ask myself, why *not* now? Here? With you?"

Not a pronouncement of undying love, but that hardly bothered me. I was not looking for love. "You wish to do this because we might die," I guessed. It seemed cliché, and yet—

"No," he contradicted me. "I wish to do this *despite* the fact that we might die. I would sell my soul for this. That's how powerfully I want you. But we may yet get out, and I…I no longer intend to have another relationship. I am no good at them. It would not be fair to you. You must understand—"

Ah. He was merely laying down the terms—something the average man waits until the morning after to begin.

"I do not want a relationship, either," I whispered back. "I do not believe in romance and marriage. What I so desperately want from you, my dear Rhys…"

I drew his face to mine, close to his ear—to his ragged jaw—and whispered *exactly* what I wanted. In the most clear and vulgar of Anglo-Saxon terms. So there could be no confusion.

To my relief, he sank back onto me, tasted my ear, covered one of my breasts with his large, warm hand…

In defeat, or liberation? Either way, it was ecstasy.

I would have liked light, to see his chest and the line of his body. But there was much to be said for exploring each other by touch, sound, smell and taste. Rhys's hands, sliding across the curve of my hip or testing the weight of my breasts, felt…awed. And what my hands told me of him…?

I helped ease his briefs off his straining erection, quite happy with how firmly and thickly it filled my palm.

Then Rhys caught my wrist, tight. "I…do not want…"

Merde! Merde, zut, encule un chien!

And no, I will not translate that.

"You changed your mind," I muttered, flopping back from him. Chill air curled across my flushed body—

Then he was back against me, his scratchy cheek on mine, a smile in his whisper. "I do not want to do it *badly*."

Men! "Then I will teach you," I assured him. Sliding back onto him, I kissed down his jaw, his throat, his collarbone, his hairy chest. There was much fun to be had there before I moved on down his hard, hairy abdomen to his harder…

"Cat!" he gasped. "I…cannot…"

"Relax," I whispered, licking his engorged penis. I held back the urge to nip, even softly. "Do not try…"

He tried anyway. Every muscle in him strained to fight it.

"We have all night," I insisted. My breath—across where I'd just been licking—made him shudder. Then, with some effort, I drew him deeply into my mouth, then deeper…

Rhys bucked beneath me, but I was prepared for that and gently sucked around his penis, my tongue tracing the hard line beneath, my hand sliding under…

I was also prepared for his long shudder, his cry and the hot spurts into my throat. Which I swallowed. Breath mints, a birth control pill, ibuprofen and perhaps some protein.

I withdrew to purr, "Good," before he could possibly think otherwise. "Now that we have taken the edge off…"

And I slid back up beside him, wrapping myself around him. I stroked one of his forearms until he gradually relaxed, then I drew his hand to the wetness between my legs. "Your turn."

Catching on to the fact that we were nowhere near done, Rhys rose to the occasion. So to speak. The man learned quickly. I stretched beneath his caresses, then his less tentative incursions, only to climax around his hand—hard, convulsing orgasms, like my own personal earthquake—long before I'd expected to. Rhys captured my cries in his mouth, kissed me deeply—and, his fingers curious, did it to me again.

And again. So much for my role of teacher.

I don't know how long it took him to get hard again. I'd lost track of everything except what Rhys was drawing out of me, giving back to me, by the time *he* drew *my* hand back to his own thick readiness. No wonder his kisses had started to smile.

I whispered, "A moment, please."

"Catrina!" he protested adorably.

Spilling my purse onto the rock beside us, I fumbled for a condom—for more reason, of course, than birth control. I curled back onto him, tearing open the package as I did, warming the latex roll with my breath before I pressed it into his hand to show him what I had. I made him cover my hands while I pinched the rubber tip and slowly, slowly rolled the protection down him.

"Lie back." I swung my leg over his hips to straddle him. I had no intention of letting his first time be the poke-and-prod slapstick I knew from my misspent youth. Instead, I put one of his hands on my hip, the other inside my thigh, to "see" what I was doing. I shifted myself....

And slowly, gloriously, I lowered myself onto him. I was so wet that he slid in easily. Thoroughly. Impressively.

Rhys made a guttural noise of amazement which, leaning down onto him, I kissed right out of his mouth. "Now," I began—

And he rolled over with me, almost too abruptly, slamming my shoulder blades and butt onto the rock with his weight, but I could not mind, considering what came with that. Again, the man showed incredible aptitude and, this time, endurance.

My words, after that, were mere gasps of "yes," and "there," and "please, please, *please*…"

If he'd not been holding me so tightly, his thrusts would have pushed me across the tunnel floor. Deeper. Harder. Forever. With a scream, I climaxed, well before he did. Twice.

Then, with his own cry, Rhys came, too.

Only after he'd stilled, after he seemed to start breathing again, did I show him how to slide out of me before the condom became a problem. Then I let him fall back, let him gather me hard against him, tight in his arms, until we slept.

I woke to the scent of cigarette smoke, and opened my eyes to the faintest bit of light in our tunnel.

I made out the skulls first, their eye-holes blank and jaws gaping, staring down at me from high on the wall before I rolled over—and caught a glimpse of Rhys's dark expression in the faint glow of the *Gauloise* in his hand.

I'd hoped for afterglow. Possibly a smiling, head-ducking embarrassment. Not this.

He looked…fallen. After something like thirty years of purity, he'd fallen. *Because of me*. Then his long-lashed gaze dropped to me—and he smiled. I could not tell if he was sincere.

He also offered me the cigarette. "I did intend to share."

Surprisingly, I did not want a smoke. Instead of taking the *Gauloise* from him, I said something unusual. Blame my half-asleep state. I said, "I am sorry."

For a long moment, he said nothing. Then…

"I'm not. That's what concerns me."

Intrigued, I kneeled and, chest to bare chest, leaned into him.

We were both starving. Literally, now. Hunger gnawed at me, and thirst. But he made it easier not to dwell.

"We," I admitted, "are bad for each other, aren't we?"

"We are," he agreed, his voice husky. Then he kissed me, long and absolute. One kiss became another, then another, before his stomach growled, and we stopped and tried to smile.

Only then, as we caught our breath, did I notice that he did not taste of nicotine. He was not smoking, just… keeping his options open. "Good morning, Catrina."

One vice at a time, I suppose.

We ate the last of my mints and came close to finishing off the water. We cleaned up as best as we could. Then, reorienting ourselves with the faint glow of the cell phone—which beeped a low-battery warning—we headed out into the dark, Rhys's hand on my belt.

We talked about childhoods and our families—mainly his, back in Wales. We spoke of music and films, and why we enjoyed history. We tortured ourselves with favorite restaurants and dishes, his mother's currant bread and my paternal grandmother's cabbage soup, until our dry throats were too sore to say anything else.

Then we could only know each other's presence by our shuffling footsteps, our grumbling stomachs and our touch.

The battery on the cell phone died. We reverted to using the cigarette lighter. The bone walls to either side of us took on an extra eeriness in the sparing flicker of the flame.

And then, despite having skirted several sinkholes successfully, I dropped again.

I was so weak, so hungry, I'd lost my reflexes. One misstep, and down I went. Rhys's grip tightened on my belt.

Then, with a smash of glass, we dropped farther! I thought for a moment he'd caught me, but we lurched farther yet.

Only then, at last, did I find myself dangling from my belt, somewhere in the darkness. Nothing more happened. Specifically, I didn't start to rise again. Above me, I heard Rhys's gasped breath. "Cat."

Was he as weak as I was? With a groping hand, flailing above and behind me, I realized that he'd held on with only one hand himself. The other must be holding him on the ledge where he lay. *Merde!*

I spread my arms, feeling across a wall of rock for something to help myself climb out. My gloved hands found nothing useful, so I used my teeth to tear off my left-hand glove, spat it into the void and tried again. I also tried not to notice that *I couldn't hear my glove land*, far below me.

This was not helping my fear of heights.

My bare fingers found tiny fissures in the shear of limestone where my gloved hands had not. So I bit off my other glove as well, and found another crack with my right hand. It would have to do.

Rhys's arm, my only connection to life, trembled now. He could not hold on much longer. So I swallowed until I could manage to call, "Let go."

"No!" Dry throat or not, he shouted that.

"I…can climb." I hoped. But Rhys still didn't let me go—not willingly. Instead, I fell free.

"Catrina!"

I slammed into the wall and lost one handhold—but only for a moment. Scrabbling on steep rock, I found another crack. My booted feet had just enough purchase to hold me in place.

"Still here," I gasped. "Broke a nail."

Carefully I tried to boost myself up a centimeter or two. Then a few more. But I was so tired I felt sick. Thirsty. Hungry. If I let go, I could fall to a quick, easy death….

Then I thought of the guillotined woman from my first vision. I thought of how desperately she had wanted to live.

I thought of whatever secrets she had died to protect.

Besides, Rhys might feel rather bad about dropping me, if I died. Even if he died mere hours later. So—another centimeter…

A golden glow bloomed above me. My lighter. Rhys's hand caught my wrist before the light went out. In the darkness—the image of him still imprinted on my retinas—his other hand caught me as well. With him pulling, and me able to use my free hand and my feet, I hauled myself onto level rock. At the end, Rhys caught me under the arms and lifted me the rest of the way out. He drew me against him with a groan, holding on as we collapsed.

Eventually we sat up. Rhys took my hand and carefully had me feel an edge of sharp glass—and a touch of cool liquid. It was the last of our water, the bottle broken in my fall. He guided it to my mouth, and I was so thirsty that I swallowed with animal desperation. Only then did I realize he'd abstained.

So I kissed him, so that he could suck at least a little of the moisture from my mouth.

Somehow, we managed to stand. Rhys had to try the lighter twice for us to see our way around this latest drop. We edged around the precipice, on a narrow, crumbling ledge. Then we began walking again. And walking. And walking.

Until Rhys, who'd been moving more slowly since my fall, dropped to his knees—and stayed there.

I leaned against a wall of bones to touch his clammy face. I feared if I kneeled, I wouldn't get back up.

He shook his head. "Go on."

"Not without you." I tugged at him.

"When…we fell…" He shook his head.

So I slid down the bumpy wall to sit beside him. I felt across his butt to find the lighter, then lit it. He looked awful, his blue eyes glazed with pain, his Welsh skin—already on the pale side—now ghostly. He wasn't just tired. He was hurt.

The lighter flickered and went out.

I tried it again, faster each time. I got only a spark, no flame in a horrible strobe. It was out of fuel, and we were condemned to darkness.

"Go on," Rhys repeated.

"Sod off," I returned, in English.

Perhaps he no longer had the strength to argue with me, because his arms came around me then. He leaned his head on my mine, and said no more…except for the faintest of voiceless whispers in his breathing.

After catching a few Latin words, I realized he was praying again. Pleas? Repentence? Me, I felt more like cursing.

His whispering voice fell silent, and he slumped to the floor. I felt for his pulse and found it, barely.

And then I must have started hallucinating, because I heard ghostly, echoing voices. *German* voices. Discussing catacombs.

My German is not as good as my English. But my slow-moving mind managed to place the lecture as that of…a tour guide?

I tried to shout, but that was not going to happen. So, with a final kiss on Rhys's cheek, I began to crawl.

After some meters, strengthened by the nearness of the voices, I staggered to my feet. Then—I saw a faint light!

I went for it like the proverbial moth—and was stopped by the rusted bars of a grilled doorway, welded shut. *Non!*

The tour guide was saying something about "Kingdom of the Dead" as they came around a skull-packed corner, barely a foot from me. Their halogen lantern felt garish on my eyes.

I reached through the bars and grabbed a man's arm. With a screech, he spun—and punched me.

Chapter 7

Ah, well. That is what hospitals are for.

I regained full consciousness in a private room. An IV snaked into my arm, and the bliss of hydration and painkiller flowed through my veins. Scarlet sat there, looking remarkably concerned for someone with such monochromatic red hair.

"Rhys?" I gasped, my throat barely working.

Scarlet was wise enough to say, "He's just a few doors down, he'll be fine," before she began to gush. "You couldn't imagine the reporters who want to talk to you. I wouldn't mind some pictures myself, but hello, friend first, photographer second, right? Still, look at all the flowers!"

Finding the correct buttons on the bedrail, I sat myself up to see the room. *Mon Dieu.* I might as well have

died, to deserve such arrangements…although the
balloons and fruit baskets might have been less apropos
for my demise.

Or not, depending on whom I'd alienated.

"They are…." Just as well that I could not speak
until Scarlet gave me some ice chips.

"I know," she said, grinning. "It's because you're ce-
lebrities, for returning from the dead. A lot of them are
from strangers. But that one over there—" she pointed at
a large teddy bear holding more balloons "is from a certain
Léon Chanson. There's a note asking you to call him to
reschedule last night's date. I hope it's okay that I looked."

I could not find the strength to mind. I'd forgotten the
geophysicist, what with the almost dying…and Rhys.

"The carnations? Those are from the tourist who hit
you. No good can come from ghost tours. And *that*
one—" she pointed to a tasteful basket of heather with
a curling arch of willow over it "—that's from the Cluny.
Your boss brought it himself. He asked me to tell
you…" She pulled out a notebook. "'He has found
sponsors for further study of the artifacts.' They're some
philanthropic Italian family, the Adrianos. Ever hear of
them? I've never heard of them."

I thought I had. Instead of answering, I asked,
"Shower?"

She popped to her feet. "I'll get the nurse. But once
you're cleaned up, I *have* to tell you about the Sisters
of Mary. After you gave me the name, I did some
research. So far I've only found two references to them.
Catrina, the Sisters of Mary weren't nuns at all!"

I imagined an underground resistance, or disguised

nobles, or spies. What I did not expect was for Scarlet to announce, "They were a literary salon!"

"The Sisters of Mary were a book club?" repeated Rhys, when I got to visit his room that evening.

My IV had been removed, but not his. He looked worse than I did, despite being clean and, now, clean-shaven. He no longer looked like a bad boy. His beautiful chest, which I knew by feel better than sight, was tightly wrapped in gauze. According to Scarlet, he'd badly cut his hand—on the broken bottle, I assumed, when I fell—and despite wrapping it, had lost too much blood. Between that and the dehydration, he'd almost died.

"A literary salon," I corrected. "Like the Hôtel de Rambouillet or the bluestockings who met with that romance writer, Madame de Scudéry."

He arched his brows doubtfully.

I leaned back in my chair beside his bed, tucking my feet under the edge of his mattress. After three days not only in his company but in his grip, our separation felt strange. "Fine. But those book-club ladies, they are trouble. Oh, they *seem* all innocent and readery. But look beneath the surface…"

"Then they were executed as upper-class intellectuals?" But surely Rhys knew better. Some citizens *had* been guillotined for the sin of wealth. But who else had seen the proof of their existence destroyed with them?

"Many leaders were intellectuals. Robespierre and Danton were both lawyers. Marat studied medicine before he went into publishing. I thought…do you think the Sisters may have been killed for their religious beliefs?"

Rhys frowned.

"It was dangerous to be openly Catholic during the Revolution," I reminded him. "The church had abused its power in France for centuries, with torture and executions—"

"And hundreds of priests were murdered. Churches converted to secular use. It became illegal to display the cross."

So why was he not convinced? "But…?"

"But something about that Mary medal that we found."

I leaned forward, across my knees. "What?"

"I will need to study it more closely to be sure. But something just didn't…fit."

I nodded, watching his lips. And the fall of clean, black hair over his forehead, shadowing his bright blue eyes, which darted to and away from me as he spoke. Perhaps he was just as aware of what we were *not* saying. That our intimacy might not survive outside the catacombs.

Someone had gotten him a pair of pajama bottoms, damn it. But Scarlet had brought me a nightgown, peignoir and slippers, so I suppose I ought not complain. I'd kissed that chest, rubbed my face in the sweeping whorls of hair, nuzzled under the holy medals he still wore. He'd held me so tightly with those bare arms….

He cleared his throat. "So where do we go from here?"

"My boss at the Cluny has found sponsors for our study of the site—what we salvaged of it, in any case. Nobody knew about the bomb, so they have no leads. And—"

Rhys gently touched my hand. "I meant, where do *we*—"

My foot almost slipped off his bed. "You said you were not looking for another relationship," I suggested casually.

"So did you," he reminded me. I'd been right to say so, then. Who needed the agony of being regularly compared to his dead love—the virgin, Mary? If men saw women as one of two extremes—the Madonna and the whore—I understood where I placed. If I ever made the mistake of wanting more from Rhys Pritchard than his friendship, more than his body…

I feared he could break my heart. Despite the assertions of those who believe I do not have one.

Thinking of people who doubted my heart gave me the perfect escape. "I almost forgot my *grand-mère*. I should go see her and break the news that I survived."

"You…?" Rhys looked understandably confused.

"My *grand-mère* is on another floor of the hospital," I explained, standing. Not surprisingly, we'd been brought to the Hôpital Saint-Vincent de Paul, the one nearest the catacombs. "She will be asleep soon, so I should see her now."

One crisis at a time.

The nurses protested my leaving the floor, but I went anyway. I even brought one of the smaller of my aberrant teddy bears. The toy would not hurt overmuch when she threw it.

Getting off the elevator at the cancer ward, I went to the nurse's desk. "I know visiting hours are over," I admitted, letting her understand from my nightgown that I, too, was a patient. "But I wish to simply check in with my grandmother. I have been…unavailable, for the last few days. If she heard anything of it, she might have…" Not worried. "Wondered."

The night nurse could not seem to place me.

"Room three-fifteen," I prompted. "Catrina Gide?"

"Yes," she said, finally. "We've been trying to reach you."

Trying…? But then I understood.

Suddenly, foolishly, I did not want to hear the rest. I strode toward room 315. The nurse grabbed my arm, but I shrugged her off and pushed open the door.

A middle-aged man lay in the bed, his luggage still out, surrounded by his loving—and now startled—family.

The nurse closed the door firmly between them and me.

Rhys was watching the overhead television in his room when I went back to him. He looked over from a news show with a grin. "You did not tell me you're a hero."

From the TV I heard a young woman. "Before poor Eduard could reach me, the road, it tore in half! But Mademoiselle Dauvergne—the one they found in the catacombs? She took my hand, and even when I fell in, she did not let go! She—"

I reached up and turned it off. "She had such a tight grip on me, I would have had to chew off my own arm to escape."

"Of course you would," agreed Rhys with excess solemnity. "Because you are haughty and indifferent, and…Catrina?"

He said that last as I drew the curtain around us and climbed onto his bed. "I do not want to sleep alone tonight," I explained, finding the button to lower the head of his bed.

"I—" He gave it up. "My IV might complicate matters."

That almost made me smile. Almost. "Just to sleep."

He rolled onto his side, gritting his teeth against lingering pain. "Is your grandmother all right?"

"Better than ever," I lied.

He looked unconvinced—so apparently the belief in my duplicity would survive *Grand-mère*. Still, he erred on the side of acceptance, turning off the lights over the bed and easing himself down. "It is odd. Suddenly trying to sleep alone."

I nodded, my head on his shoulder. "No strings attached," I promised quietly. Though who I was promising? I could not say.

The yell woke us.

It came from down the hall—in the direction of my room. I sat upright, suddenly cold without Rhys's arms, then swung my feet out of his high bed and headed for the door.

"Wait," he protested, trying to free his IV lines so that he could follow me. I went on ahead. Nurses and a security guard were rushing toward my room, calling about police, and I needed to see what had happened—and, if it were merely my absence that startled them, to let them know I was here.

It had not been my absence. When I pushed past the other onlookers, I saw that my hospital room was in pieces. Broken flowers lay in lumps of crumpled stems and scattered petals, yet their vases sat whole on the shelf. Foam stuffing from the pillows spread across the room like a snowdrift. The mattress had been gutted. The curtains that hung from the ceiling, to be drawn around the bed for privacy, fluttered in shreds. The large teddy bear that Léon Chanson had sent hung by its fuzzy neck, a length of bed-curtain tied like a hangman's noose. It had been gutted, its button eyes cut out…and yet three balloons still bobbed merrily from its plush paw.

In fact, none of the balloons had been touched. Why…?

He did it silently, I realized, trying to fit my mind around the destruction. He did not break machines or pop balloons because they would have made noise….

But the worst stained the walls in red: *Stop the evil. Fear God. Death to false prophets.*

"You're all right!" exclaimed the night nurse. "I was so afraid that you'd been taken, harmed, when Moe called out…."

Her expression of relief stilled, as if at a worse thought.

"Is that blood?" I tried to ask. My voice wasn't working.

"Enough," insisted the security guard, herding health workers out of the room. "This is a matter for the police. Go on, mademoiselle. And you, monsieur. Back to your rooms."

"This *is* my room." I managed enough voice for that, unwilling to leave before I understood. To my relief, Rhys appeared at my side, his pajama top hanging open. I noticed that he no longer wore the IV—and that a drop of blood stained the back of his hand. Getting the IV pole through the crowd must have proved too difficult.

One of his hands caught my waist as he looked at the gory grafitti. The other made the sign of the cross.

"Mademoiselle Dauvergne," asked the nurse, too gently. And here it came. "Did *you* do this? The third floor called to let us know. Your grandmother's death, on top of everything else you've been through this week, would upset anybody."

"Do not be ridiculous," Rhys chided. "How could—" Then he frowned down at me. "Your grandmother *died?*"

A guard interrupted their stereophonic demands on me. "Out of the room until the authorities arrive."

I swallowed, ignoring Rhys's arched disbelief and the nurse's cloying pity both to repeat, *"Is that blood?"*

"I believe so," she admitted.

Rhys's hold around me tightened to steer me from the room. He leaned closer to murmur, *"Better than ever?"*

But I had no explanations. Let him believe the worst of me, if he must. People generally did.

Instead, I stared at a small card on the floor—the kind that accompanies floral arrangements. It must have come since Scarlet left, or surely she would have mentioned it.

It read: *The earthquake was deliberate. Reclaim the Black Madonna before it is too late.*

Grimaud stabbed his knife into his kitchen table. He wanted to cry, but not from the self-inflicted cuts, just enough for blood, on his arms. It wasn't fair that she'd not been in her room! But nothing had made sense today, not since he saw on the news that the demoness and her consort had been found alive. *How?*

God approved of what he was doing, didn't He? Or…did He?

The doubt that bloomed in his gut felt awful. What if his grandfather had made up the tales? What if he himself was insane? If his ancestors had really pledged allegiance to such a power, and to people who knew how to wield it…would those people not have contacted him by now? This possibility felt like waking from a glorious dream into a hellish reality. He'd risked his life stalking the demoness—rather, the woman. He'd bombed an archeological site. He could have killed people! And all based on…what?

Old stories and a faded address in the family Bible.

That, and the dream that he might be special. Now he stared at himself in the hall mirror, his face unshaven, his arms bandaged, his eyes wild. He did not like what he saw. He was not special. He was the worst kind of fool. He needed help.

He almost didn't hear the ringing of the telephone, despite the early hour. But years of providing a service had trained him well. He picked it up, managed to form words of greeting.

"Your loyalty impresses us," whispered the voice on the other line. "Your discretion does not. Let us decide what must be done. Then…you only need do it. Yes?"

Grimaud closed his eyes to a joy beyond description.

He had not imagined it.

He was not alone.

Chapter 8

"**Y**ou and Rhys *did it?*" repeated Scarlet, as we strolled through early-morning Paris two days later. Of everything I had told her, *this* was what she lingered on. *"In the catacombs?"*

"Yes," I agreed. "And the earthquake *was deliberate*."

"Why not ask the geophysicist about it *on tonight's date?*" Scarlet laughed at our continued emphases. I did not.

"That is exactly why I called Léon. I was not responsible for the last earthquake. I do not intend to be responsible for future ones. *He* suggested we discuss matters over dinner. And why not?" I asked. But Scarlet's narrowed chocolate eyes did not let me off so easily. "Rhys and I have no relationship."

"Ah. Just sex then." Her eyes flashed. "Does *he* know that?"

"He barely spoke to me yesterday, when he helped me make arrangements for my grandmother." At Scarlet's blank look I added, "She died. He is angry I did not tell him. And if you are my friend, you will not expect abject grief. I hated the woman."

"Still, it was kind of him to help you make arrangements."

"I did not ask him, he just did. The man was a priest. He understands the administrative necessities that complicate dying." To be fair, I added, "And he is a kind person."

One who'd fully realized that I was not. I did not like remembering how my heart had sped when he joined me in the hospital offices—or how it had sunk when I saw his continued disapproval. And now, this morning, I had to see him again.

I was meeting our financial benefactors outside the building that now held the remaining effects of the *Soeurs de Marie*, to introduce the project to them. Hence I wore my best suit, knee-length. Scarlet wore a flirty miniskirt, a T-shirt and combat boots. "I think you're pushing him away," she said.

I shrugged. Students, on their way to early classes, were a good sign. Still, the Université de Paris is not one building, or even one campus. It consists of three separate universities. Luckily, I had studied *histoire* at this 5th *arrondissement* Sorbonne. I knew my way around.

"You like this man, but now you push him away with both hands. Off a cliff! And then you laugh over the edge—hah hah *hah!* And likely spit, too. As he plummets."

"There was neither laughing nor spitting involved."

"Perhaps he will blame it on grief," she mused.

I glared. *Grand-mère* had managed to drive a wedge between Rhys and me, even from beyond the grave, although I had admittedly helped. I just hadn't wanted... rather, I had wanted...

We rounded a squat, sixteenth-century building and my stomach swooped. There stood Rhys beside a broader, tawny-haired man outside the front steps of our destination. Tall. Slim. Dark-haired. But...impeccably dressed in an expensive suit?

When this man turned, I saw my mistake. Instead of Rhys's fair complexion, this tall-slim-dark man had the olive cast of the Mediterranean. My foolish disappointment warred with vague appreciation. Not only was he perhaps as beautiful as Rhys, with his high cheeks and light eyes...this man *knew* it.

His haircut, his Italian suit, even his shoes bespoke the casual splendor of wealth. So did his posture, and the quick smile that touched his lips at our arrival—and then froze there.

"Good morning," greeted his sturdier, tawny-haired companion. "Catrina Dauvergne? I am Caleb Adriano."

"Monsieur." I offered him my hand. He kissed it with a gallant gesture that went with his Latin complexion, and our gazes locked in a moment of honest appraisal. The sex would be good, I decided in that moment, but this one liked to dominate as he pleased. I would annoy him—as I did so many men.

Perhaps he came to the same quick conclusion. Our eyes smiled at each other and he gave the tiniest shrug of regret. "Please, call me Caleb. This is my little brother, Joshua."

His "little" brother was the one who had reminded me of Rhys although, close up, Joshua and Rhys shared little more than general age, body type and dark hair. I offered my hand.

Joshua Adriano, however, simply stared. At Scarlet.

I caught Scarlet's gaze and she widened it, confused.

"*Fratellino*," chided Caleb—so they were Italian, instead of Spanish or Portuguese? Their French was excellent.

Joshua took a step forward, now frowning down at Scarlet. A single word choked from his throat. "*Zoe?*"

Caleb took a closer look—perhaps her vintage clothes had lost him at first? She shook her head, shrugged—then grinned.

After a moment's obvious surprise, Caleb grinned back.

But I was being rude as well—which, in business at least, I try to avoid. "My apologies. This is Scarlet Rubashka. She has been keeping a photographic journal of the salvage from the Denfert-Rochereau site."

"How do you do, Scarlet Rubashka?" Caleb Adriano lingered an extra breath over Scarlet's hand, and she bit her lower lip.

"Scarlet?" repeated Joshua. He looked suspicious, now. She sidled a little closer to Caleb.

"*Fratellino!*" Caleb smacked Joshua lightly on the shoulder, snapping his brother out of whatever spell he'd been under.

Joshua better composed his features. "My apologies, Mademoiselle Rubashka. You remind me of someone I once knew."

"Truly?" Caleb arched a wry brow. "We had not noticed."

In the meantime, Scarlet seemed to have thrown aside her initial suspicion about Joshua. "You know someone who looked like me? How much? I mean, was it just a passing resemblance, or could it have been a familial likeness? I'm adopted, you see, and I've been looking for my birth family for so long—"

"I am sorry," interrupted Joshua, with what now seemed like honest regret. "She…it was only a passing resemblance."

"Oh. Oh, well. It was worth asking, right?"

For Scarlet, perhaps. I could not imagine flashing my most private longings at strangers—but I was not her, thank heavens.

"Think nothing of it," Joshua insisted, but he backed toward the entryway as he said so, as if he felt similarly about such blatant disclosures. "I am the one who should apologize."

She took the hint well enough. "I'd best let Catrina take you in to show off all the fascinating things she found."

"What?" Caleb's protest surprised us both. "Surely you do not mean to leave us so soon, Scarlet Rubashka?"

He smiled at her, almost too charming—but not quite. She smiled back and bit her lip. I could see that their immediate appraisal of each other went far better than had his and mine.

"Well…" She hesitated, sliding her gaze to me.

"If Monsieur Adriano does not mind." They were our financial backing, after all. They had a great deal of say.

"Please, call me Caleb," insisted the older brother again, offering Scarlet his elbow. She took it happily, her bright blue fingernails a strange contrast to the fabric's expensive weave.

"Caleb," I agreed, and took the elbow that Joshua offered me. The suit—and arm—felt lovely under my fingertips. But I think I am the only one who noticed him frown at his brother as we passed into the sixteenth-century building.

The large, second-story workroom's metal shelves, cardboard boxes and worktables made a stark contrast to once-elegant paneling and stained-glass windows. Rhys—the real Rhys—was at work, his left hand lightly bandaged, examining some of the pieces we'd found. Our gazes touched and then veered away from each other's as I led our guests into the room.

I made the introductions, clarifying that Rhys was the project's full-time coordinator, since I would split my time with my duties at the Musée Cluny. Rhys stood, and they shook hands, sizing each other up the way men will. I did not hear Caleb and Joshua asking Rhys to call them by their first names.

But Rhys was taller.

"May I?" asked Scarlet, lifting her camera.

"Please, this should not be about us," protested Joshua.

With a gesture, I encouraged Rhys to take over the tour of said artifacts. He looked good today, if not expensive-Italian-suit good. His long-sleeved shirt and slacks had been ironed and starched and his shoes shined in preparation for our guests. The fact that he'd likely done the ironing, starching and shining himself gave his appearance an unexpected poignancy.

As did my clear memory of taking his virginity…

"Finding remains from the Revolution is not unusual," he explained with easy confidence. Saying mass must have been good practice against stage fright. "During the Reign of Terror, from June 1793 to July 1794, more than twenty thousand people were executed. The government kept copious records. And yet so far my students have found no record of this burial. What differs about the collection that Mademoiselle Dauvergne…stumbled across—"

His eyes warmed momentarily at me with his joke—and, as before, my heart sped. Damn. It was happening again. I could feel myself getting more foolish by the moment.

"—is that it held a virtual time capsule. For some reason, these five women were not only guillotined, they were interred in a forgotten corner of the catacombs, along with what seems to have been all their worldly possessions. France had rejected the excess of nobility most violently, yet this grave wasted books, crockery—candlesticks!" He indicated the items on one of the large metal tables. "It's unheard of."

Scarlet, never shy, said, "But aren't people buried with their belongings all the time? Pictures or jewelry…" Her voice trailed off with an apologetic look at me, which…oh.

She'd remembered before I did that my grandmother had died.

Rhys stepped easily into her silence. "Rarely people who have been executed. Their belongings became property of the state. From what we found at the Denfert-Rochereau site, we hope to better understand both the mystery of these women's executions, and perhaps their lives."

And on he went, pointing out some of the more intriguing items. Of particular interest was the cracked glass jar I remembered, which had copper wire coiled around it. According to Rhys this was a Leyden jar, used to store charges in early experiments with electricity. "These women may have had a scientific bent," he noted, "and perhaps were fans of the popular 'man who tamed lightning,' as they also had one of these…."

And he made us all smile by producing a chipped dish from our find, featuring Benjamin Franklin's image. Franklinmania in France had so annoyed Louis XVI that he'd had the American's image painted in the bottom of a chamber pot.

"Other items are less easily explained," Rhys continued—and I realized what he meant to show our sponsors next. Perhaps my recent visions colored my paranoia about certain pieces, but…

"Show them the jewelry," I suggested. "Of everything that should not have survived unmolested…."

Rhys beckoned a student over. "Josette, please show these gentlemen the jewelry you've catalogued thus far. Josette's specialty is the history of fashion," he explained—to her obvious adoration—before leaving her to open the proper cartons and begin showing the medals and baubles we'd found. Then he came to my side, tall and warm, a silent question in his eyes.

"I don't want to show them the tiles or key," I whispered.

My eyes begged him to go along—and he did, with a sharp nod. "Explain later," he whispered, with surprising authority.

"—have been Catholic?" Joshua Adriano was asking about the Mary medal we'd found, as Rhys and I rejoined them. "Perhaps even martyrs? Surely Rome would want to hear of it, if so."

"That is one of the theories we are pursuing," agreed Rhys. "What with the precedent of the fourteen Carmelite nuns—"

"The Martyrs of Compiègne," Joshua interrupted knowingly. "But…weren't there sixteen executed?"

"There were fourteen nuns and two servants." Rhys did not interrupt, but he out-Catholicked Joshua Adriano all the same. "All martyrs, guillotined on 17 July, 1794."

I felt tempted to suggest that whoever could name all sixteen martyrs first would win, with bonus points for the servants, but I had my professional face on today. "You see how valuable your support is," I intervened smoothly. "Of course, we have only begun our research, but the possibilities are exciting. What else can we show you?"

"Oh, we've seen quite enough," said Caleb, even if he had been hanging back and trading long looks with Scarlet for most of the presentation. "You have our wholehearted support."

"Yes. Thank you so much for your time." Joshua offered a hand to Rhys, and they shook amiably enough—

I keep forgetting that competition among men does not always mean hostility. "This project is clearly in capable hands."

He even said that *before* he then took my hand and kissed it, holding my gaze as he did. Some men are just made for hand-kissing. I could barely stop my slow, responding exhale.

Only when Joshua offered his elbow again did I recover enough to mouth, *Back soon*, over my shoulder, before the Adrianos squired us out of the room.

Rhys did not look convinced.

"You have no idea," said Joshua to me as we walked out together, "how much we appreciate the opportunity to be part of something like this. To uncover a chapter of history that was previously lost. It is…*magnifico*. As," he whispered, "are you."

This is why Italian men are so popular.

I eyed him at a slant, through my lashes. Between his immediate interest in Scarlet, aka Zoe, and his contrast with Rhys—of whom I was admittedly fond—I had not taken time to wholly appreciate this man on his own level.

Like his clothes, it was a high level. Joshua was handsome. He smelled delicious. And yet…I did not wholly trust him.

Since when had I begun to rank trust so high among my potential lovers? I thought. Likely this was Rhys's doing.

"I am too forward," Joshua murmured quickly, his soft voice a tickle in my stomach. "My apologies."

"No need," I assured him. "I merely—"

But Scarlet interrupted us with a gasp. "Catrina!"

I looked toward her, for a moment foolishly con-

cerned that Caleb Adriano had done something unto-
ward. What I saw, however, dragged my attention from
thoughts of all men except for one.

The small, dark-haired, crazy-eyed man who had
invaded my home the night of the first earthquake,
watching us from behind a tree across the courtyard.

He saw us recognize him—and he scurried away,
like a bug.

I took off after him.

No, I do not know what I meant to do if I caught up
to the strange little man. But I wasn't going to just let
him stalk me like this, and not do anything!

He dodged around students and spun around a corner,
but I pounded after him in my best pumps. Joshua and
Caleb Adriano quickly caught up.

"Him?" demanded Joshua, pointing as he slowed
beside me.

"Yes! He—"

But I did not need to explain further, because he and
Caleb were already pulling ahead of me. Apparently, the
fact that this man upset us was more than enough mo-
tivation for testosterone-drenched Italians to give chase.

The dark man glanced over his shoulder, blanched
and ran faster. Me, I slowed to a trot, then a stride, then
stopped entirely, bending at the waist to catch my
breath—and watch the Adriano brothers disappear down
the Paris street after their quarry. Damn, they were fast.

"What will they do if they get him?" panted Scarlet,
catching up to me outside the pâtisserie where I'd stopped.

I shrugged. For once, Scarlet did not have anything
to add.

To our disappointment, when Joshua and Caleb re-appeared, they came alone. Their suits were rumpled, and Joshua was bleeding from his lip, his jaw swelling. He looked furious.

"The little bastard ambushed us," explained Caleb, breathing hard. "He went down an alley, then he leaped out at us. He knocked poor Josh silly. I could have gone after him, but…"

"You had to stay with your brother," agreed Scarlet, while I moved closer to inspect the damage. As he held a handkerchief to his definitely split lip, his dark hair tousled and his suit stained, Joshua Adriano seemed more attractive than ever.

"We are so sorry," said Scarlet, hovering. Considering that I'd not asked our patrons to give chase, I did not bother to second the opinion, but I did wince at the sight of Joshua's injuries up close. "It's just…he broke into Cat's flat, just last week, and who knows what else he might have done, I mean, just the other night someone vandalized her hospital room, and if only we knew who he was…."

Joshua quieted her with a raised hand, a smile in his hazel eyes easing any imperial edge to the gesture— especially with the accompanying wince. "This sounds like too complex a matter to discuss on the sidewalk. Perhaps dinner? Tonight?"

He was staring at me the whole time he asked, and I felt myself slowly exhaling again under his inherent magnetism.

Caleb cleared his throat. "Our flight, *fratellino*…."

Joshua waved him away. But luckily for their flight,

I, too, had other plans. "I already have a dinner date tonight."

"Then…" Joshua considered this as a dark car drew up beside them. Of course, men like these would hire a driver. "Let me give you a ride to the museum, Catrina Dauvergne. I must know more about these threats to you. And I have information that you, too, may find useful."

I hesitated. For one thing, the invitation had not seemed to include Scarlet. For another, I'd just told Rhys that I would be back soon. For yet another, all women have been warned about getting into cars with strange men. But we knew who these men were. How could I resist such an invitation?

"Scarlet and I," suggested Caleb, "we can walk, so that you may speak privately. If the beautiful lady agrees?"

Joshua's gaze flickered. Either he did not like his brother, or he did not like Scarlet, or both, which also intrigued me. Scarlet's eyes were pleading, despite her careful silence. She wanted to walk with Caleb—and, no doubt, to hear whatever Joshua would tell me, secondhand.

"*Prego*, Catarina," Joshua murmured, holding my gaze. "This may affect your project, as well as you."

Non, I could not have resisted the invitation.

I nodded and let him help me graciously into the car.

Chapter 9

The vehicle was not as ostentatious as a stretch limo. But the backseat was roomy enough that I did not feel crowded. A transparent partition gave us privacy from the driver, but Joshua did not put up the opaque divider.

Besides, it was morning and springtime, not a dark, stormy night. The only real concern I had as we drew away from the curb, Scarlet waving, was suspicion. So I turned on my beautiful host. "I thought my director contacted your family to ask for support, not the other way around. How is it possible you know more about this find than I do?"

Joshua spread his hands. One still held the blood-smeared handkerchief. "He contacted us because he understands my family's interests in certain arenas. To be honest, we doubted this was connected to our area of expertise, though it seemed a worthy endeavor, even so. But if your discovery has already provoked violence…?" He shrugged.

"Your family's interests often provoke violence?"

"Were you not in Portugal about three years ago?" Joshua arched a knowing eyebrow. "The dedication of the abbey exhibit in Tomar, near Fatima?"

Now I remembered where I had heard the name. "I got there late, but…there was a great deal of talk about a patron being carried away in an ambulance. Some said he'd collapsed in the heat, but others said he'd been attacked."

"Max Adriano. My grandfather. He'd been shot by a sniper."

Despite my own issues with my grandmother, that seemed to demand more than a simple, *what?* "Was he…?"

The line of Joshua's jaw was hard, harder than I'd ever seen Rhys's. "No, he did not die. It might have been kinder if he had. Surgeons saved his life, but the bullet destroyed his chest. He can barely breathe well enough to speak. He has been in the best long-term care facility money can buy, since then, but there's little more we can do—except continue his mission."

"That being?"

Joshua leaned nearer. "Using our wealth to oversee history. Especially to uncover proof of histories that have been lost or hidden, especially those of strong women. Warrior women, you might say. It was Max's obsession."

My skin tingled at the very idea of it. But I am a

cynic by nature. So I asked, "Why? You are men. What do you care?"

Joshua's smile nearly knocked the breath from me. "For my grandfather? I believe his fascination had to do with a woman he met during the war. He did not speak of her, not in front of me, but we heard rumors. For me? It is about Max. About doing the right thing. And it is about *not letting the bastards win*."

That last bit of manly bravado sounded especially true.

Seeming to notice how close he'd gotten, Joshua sat carefully back. "History is not dead, Catarina. It affects how we perceive everything, daily. There are those in the world who are threatened by this, threatened by the possibility that what has been considered reality for centuries is an illusion, even a cover-up. The collection that Max was in Tomar to dedicate—it had several pieces that he called 'startling.' But we may never know what they were. After his attack, they were spirited off to the Vatican vaults and locked away before other innocents could be hurt."

I shivered. I had never heard anything that felt so dangerously true in all my life.

"This is why you must be especially careful," he continued solemnly. "The man who shot Max—yes, we caught him. He was killed in prison before he could name his employer. And now, this man who broke into your flat, the one who attacked me? We cannot know who he might work for, but some people will go to any extreme to keep the truth from coming out. Perhaps some of that truth was buried with those poor women. Promise me…"

Here it came. He would say something like, *Promise*

me to contact us if you see him again, or *Promise me to tell us what secrets you uncover from the Denfert-Rochereau find.* Then I would know he was somehow using me.

Instead, he took my hand in his. "Promise me that you will not take chances. If you see anything amiss, do not hesitate to call the authorities. Will you do that?"

Nothing that could inform or benefit him. That, more than anything, modified my lingering suspicion of the Adrianos' seeming perfection. That, and the fact that we'd passed the Cluny at least three times by now, since it is only a brief walk from the Sorbonne. This time, we passed Scarlet and Caleb walking together, Scarlet swinging Caleb's hand and clearly chatting away, Caleb looking amused. Joshua knocked on the partition to signal the driver, who found a place to pull over.

Joshua lifted my hand and pressed an embossed card into it. "In case you need help. Not that I think you will. Or…if you ever wish me back in Paris?" This had, after all, been a business meeting. He was not so gauche as to hint that his family's patronage had anything to do with me agreeing to a date…even if he was Italian.

But, because he was Italian, he still kissed my hand, hurt lip or not. And because I am French, I was happy to let him. He got out of the car first, to hand me out, and I'd shaken hands with Caleb and watched them drive away before I came close to absorbing everything he'd said. If even half were true…

Only once their car had vanished into the traffic did Scarlet throw her arms around me. "*Thank you!* Caleb said Joshua probably thought you'd be more comfortable getting into the car with only one of them along, and I'm glad, because I really enjoyed that walk!"

"Did you?" I disentangled myself from her embrace as if it bothered me. Rather like a slobbery puppy, she was not unlikable, just blatantly eager. That made it even harder to say, "You do realize…"

Then I hesitated. What was happening to me, that I might withhold a catty comment simply to spare someone's feelings?

"That he included me this morning mainly to annoy his brother?" Seeing my expression, she laughed. "Hello? Kinda obvious. But that just makes it all the more fun."

I felt lost. Relieved, but lost. "It?"

"Winning him over," she explained. "I am *so* not what he thinks he wants, but I caught a few glimpses under the mask, and I might be exactly what he needs. And did you notice? Tall. Wealthy. Handsome. Caleb Adriano might be my soul mate."

Now I no longer felt relieved.

"Or at least a really good lay," she added with a wink, and shouldered her camera bag. "If we can get them to stay overnight next time they visit Paris. Speaking of which—what was that little tête-à-tête with Rhys about, while Josette was talking?"

Rhys! That I had forgotten about him was not so strange; have I not explained that I prefer not to dwell on unpleasant matters? I had no reason to feel at all guilty around Joshua Adriano, and every reason to feel guilty around Rhys Pritchard. But I had told him I would be right back, and he had avoided mentioning the keys or tiles when I asked, and… *Merde.*

* * *

"This is brilliant, thanks," Rhys was telling Josette as I reentered the echoing workroom. She'd given him some kind of sketch. His smile, even directed at her, made my stomach swoop. The line of Rhys's long body, that thick, black hair and those solemn lips…

How was it Rhys managed not only to measure up to the wealthy Adrianos, but somehow surpass them? Foolishness.

He and Josette looked up, each with particular annoyance. I did not bother to make excuses. Instead I caught Rhys by his warm, strong hand and drew him away. "Come."

"Why should I?" But he followed, even as he asked.

Josette seemed even more annoyed as we vanished into the hallway. I was petty enough to be glad for it. "Where can we talk privately?" I asked.

Rhys looked around and led me to another room, this one a large janitorial closet filled with shelves, brooms, mops and stacked boxes. He pulled a chain to light a bare bulb, then turned to me. I'd meant to ask about Black Madonnas, tiles and keys.

Instead, I boldly wrapped my arms around him and kissed him. Not Joshua Adriano or Léon Whatsisname. *Rhys*. His body felt perfect against me. For the briefest moment, he kissed me back.

Then he stiffened, and pushed me away from him. "Stop that."

"You want it, too," I noted, nuzzling toward his neck.

He stepped firmly back, holding me off. "You lied to me."

"About *Grand-mère?*" His glare confirmed it. "Not exactly."

"You said she was better than ever. *She was dead*."

I studied my new nails to avoid his gaze. "You don't think she has gone to a better place? Blasphemous. And you a priest."

"I am no longer a priest, and this is not about theology. It's about us." Something in the way he said that made my stomach clench, either from fear or anticipation, or both. There was an *us?* "I thought we were friends, perhaps more than that."

Ah. "And what happened to 'no strings attached?'"

"You are the one who keeps saying that, not I."

I barked a rude laugh. "You are the one who said you did not intend to have another relationship!"

"I did, yet here we are. Cat, I don't—" He ran his unbandaged hand through his hair, as if to contain whatever was going on in his head. "I did not believe in premarital sex, either."

"Like not believing in faeries?" The swooping in my stomach worsened. Here lay the problem with virgins and good Catholics. "You do not mean to propose, do you?" I asked, wary.

"God, no," Rhys muttered, his head still bent. Then it came up. His blue eyes widened as, apparently, we both registered the insult of his words at the same time.

"I did not mean it like that," he hurried to add. "Please, that came out wrong. I just meant, marriage is a sacrament—"

I silenced him with a glare, unsure I trusted myself with words. I'd left foolishness and reached insanity. Of course I did not want to marry him. *God, no!* I did not, do not want to marry *anybody*. So why did his words knock the wind out of me?

Then he had me by the shoulders, his head bowing to touch mine, his eyes searching mine through his lashes. "Please," he whispered. "I know I am no good at this, but Catrina, *please…*"

Unsure what he was even asking of me, I waited.

Until he kissed me, soft, uncertain. Then I reared back. "What a hypocrite you are!"

"I'm sorry," he whispered. Again he looked fallen, like that first morning after we'd been together. But I was tired of playing the serpent in this little temptation drama.

"You could have said no at any time," I reminded him.

"I could have," he agreed. "And I didn't."

"If you're feeling guilty or ashamed, then blame yourself. Leave me out of it."

"I don't." Perhaps seeing my uncertainty, he added, "I don't feel guilty. Not about being with you. I keep thinking that I should, but…well, that's mine to suss out. I simply…" He took a deep breath. "I haven't dated before, Catrina. Not as an adult, and certainly not with such casual intimacy. I don't know how. But I know this much. I do not want to hurt you. And I do not want to be hurt. The rest…"

He shrugged. And, forcing a semblance of poise, I sat on a cardboard box. "First," I suggested coolly, "it is customary to actually go on a date before one considers oneself 'dating.'"

His expression was comical, as if he'd truly not thought of that. "But we…in the catacombs…"

"We were thrown together by circumstances," I reminded him.

"Then go out with me." He remembered his manners. "Please, have dinner with me tonight. We can get a better handle on…no?"

I had winced. I hated to mention it, with him looking so tousled and earnest. I wanted to reward the long-awaited invite. But it had to be said. "I already have a date for tonight."

Rhys folded his arms, raised his eyebrows. "You do."

"You cannot be jealous," I warned him, despite the signs. "Here is another dating tip. One night does not an exclusive relationship make. Perhaps for teenagers, or stalkers, or the occasional love-at-first-sight idiot, but not for the average adult. Only if a couple agrees, after some time together, to make the relationship exclusive is it that."

"And the lovemaking means nothing?" Because to him it was that, wasn't it? Not sex. *Making love*. He might make me foolish, but at least I knew better than to believe in forever after one *good lay*, as Scarlet would put it. "So tonight, will you—"

He bit back the rest before he'd hit full obnoxiousness, but not in time to keep me from *sussing out* what he'd meant to ask. Would I be sleeping with tonight's date as well?

I got in his face, now. "One night of intimacy does not give you say over what I do with my body or my life, any more than it gives me say over what you do with yours. You—"

But we were interrupted by a knock on the door. "Monsieur Pritchard?" asked a familiar voice. "Is that you?"

Closing his eyes for a long moment of annoyance, Rhys then turned and opened the closet door. "Yes, Georges?"

The student looked from Rhys to me, and grinned. "We have been looking for you. Josette found something."

Rhys and I exchanged glances. "Something?" Rhys asked.

"A metal lockbox. I think you will want to see it." And Georges headed back down the hall, no doubt to tell the others where he had found us. Poor Josette.

I began to leave, anxious to learn more, but Rhys stopped me with a hand on my shoulder. "Wait. Did you have something else you wanted to talk about? We got rather…"

Distracted. And not in the way we'd begun to enjoy.

"What do you know about Black Madonnas?" If anybody had the inside track on the Virgin Mary it was he.

"Representations of the Holy Mother, with black features."

"Marian iconography was particularly popular in the Middle Ages," Rhys said. I liked the word *Marian.* "Including black versions. Although there have been more modern renditions."

Mostly those were works of African descent, highlighting a belief that the Mother of God was all-inclusive. "I mean the medieval versions. There are several hundred in France, yes?"

"And Germany, Spain, Switzerland, Mexico—they're a common phenomenon. Why do you ask?"

"I want to understand her. Is she even the Virgin Mary?"

I'd chosen my teacher well. "To the medieval Catholics she must have been. But her iconography is more complex than that."

More questions, then. "And why is she black?"

Rhys smiled. "Nobody knows, Catrina. She's a mystery."

"But you must have a theory!"

So he said, *"Negra sum sed formosa."* When he saw my hesitance, he translated, "'I am black, but comely, oh ye daughters of Jerusalem.' It is from the *Song of Songs*. Saint Bernard of Clairvaux did a series of famous sermons about the book, as well as sermons about Mary as bride of God. Chances are the artists of the time merged the two. But—" Before Rhys could say more, Georges appeared in the hallway to wave us on, so we headed into the workroom…to a discovery that wiped all thoughts of the Old Testament out of my thoughts.

Examining the half-rotted, wooden letterbox, Josette had found a metal lockbox—tightly sealed. My breath fell shallow.

"Perhaps we could find a locksmith to open it?" she asked.

"Or…" I skimmed the labels on our boxes. Finding the right one, I retrieved the key that I'd initially taken. "Try this."

Some part of me already knew it must be the right one. The others watched as I put on a pair of cotton gloves, inserted the key into the lock—and began to turn it. Then it stuck. *Merde.*

"Graphite," Rhys suggested. "Georges, in the janitorial closet, in a wooden milk crate, there are supplies…."

"Ah, yes." Georges headed out. "The janitorial closet."

Josette looked close to tears, until Rhys praised her for the discovery. When Georges returned, Rhys took the small can from him, squirted graphite powder into the keyhole, and worked the key around in it. Then he repeated the process.

"There." He stepped back for me. "Now try it."

Grateful for the honor, I did. The key turned. And inside the box…? *Another key.* A larger one. And, far more exciting, a whole collection of legible pages.

Dearest Isabeau, read the top fold of the top page, and my breath fell short. If my visions were correct, Isabeau was the Sister of Mary—perhaps I should just call them Marians, for simplicity?—who had hidden these very letters while her friend tried to distract the guards downstairs.

They were speaking to us from two hundred years ago.

Grimaud had never felt so confused. On the one hand, God had again blessed him. He'd gotten the best of two strong men, larger and wealthier than he; how was that not proof of divine approval? But on the other hand, he did not fully trust his instructions or the guides who had finally given them.

Everything from family stories to old journals insisted on it. The world was right only when they remained in control. But…

You are calling attention to us. You must be more discreet. If she gets hurt, so be it, but we may yet have use…

Shouldn't evil always be destroyed, discretion be damned?

The guides had known where the demoness would be this morning, where she would be tonight. He had to trust them.

But all the same…he decided to bring his knife.

Chapter 10

Too bad the letters were so painfully boring.

> *Dearest Lisse. We are pleased to know that you made it safely to Lyon, and can only hope the city remains in the hands of the Republic. Austrian invasion remains a fear....*

And on it went. *Vive la République. Vive la France.* The glories of democracy, as Monsieur Franklin espoused. It was all about as seditious as the *tricolore* flag—which is to say, not at all. Carefully turning the pages with my cotton-gloved hands atop an acid-free mat, wearing a dust mask to keep my breath's moisture off the letter, I searched in vain for any sign of why these Marians would have been executed. This letter remained unsigned, as if unfinished. The others had been addressed to "Chère Isabeau," "Chère Manon," and "Chère Alinor."

"Something is missing," I told Rhys, after he'd sent the students to have copies made so that we could store the originals in an opaque, dust-resistant box with acid-free tissue interleaving. We did know what we were doing. More or less.

"With the letters?" he asked. "How?"

"For one thing, they are too easy. I do not trust them."

Rhys seemed intrigued, now. "And things *must* be difficult?"

"For people about to be guillotined? I should think so."

"This Friday, then," he suggested.

Eyeing the newly discovered key, unsure whether I wanted to risk another depressing vision, I said, "This Friday, what?"

"Go to dinner with me on Friday. Please."

Now he had my full, sharp attention. Finally. The date I had wanted for so long, and on my terms. "Yes," I said.

But that, too, seemed far too easy to trust.

Even counting the year-long wait, the explosion, the wandering of the catacombs and the near death, it somehow felt too easy.

My date that night, however, felt unusually difficult. Everything should have been perfect. We went to Le Jules Verne, 125 meters above the sparkling city in the Tour Eiffel. The done-all-in-black restaurant is no tourist destination. In fact, it usually had a two-month waiting list, which said impressive things about my escort. More impressive things than did he. Léon Chanson had not had the easiest week himself—being overworked, finding his home had been robbed in the looting and surviving a minor auto accident. And he spoke of it in tedious detail.

Because what was my tale of catacombs survival, against a minor auto accident? In fact, he so dominated the conversation that we'd left the restaurant, in its tiny private elevator, before I could truly pursue the question for which I'd contacted him.

That being the unsigned note in my hospital room.

"Are you certain last week's quake wasn't deliberate?"

Léon Chanson slid an amused gaze down to me. "Poor Catrina. Is that what distracted you during dinner?"

True, a great many things had distracted me. Thoughts of bombs, earthquakes, dead grandmothers, Adrianos, Black Madonnas and lynched teddy bears. And mostly, thoughts of Rhys Pritchard.

Despite all logic, I felt guilty being out with another man. This was foolish. At the moment, my stomach swooped from nothing more than the elevator's descent and my need to be done with this night.

"Earthquakes are part of what distracted me," I assured Léon, reluctantly taking his arm as we left the elevator to descend stone, canopied steps outside the massive south leg of the Tower. I did not add, *as opposed to your incessant complaints*. About the service. About the food.

"But how could an earthquake be deliberate?" he demanded. "Who could cause it?"

Good question.

Paris is particularly beautiful on soft spring nights, with its elegant architecture, wrought ironwork and the flowering trees of the Parc du Champ de Mars. It is indeed a city of romance. And Léon Chanson was the kind of man I would once have adored. Not only did he have an understated charm about him, with his planed cheeks and gentle gray eyes and short, light brown hair. He was older. For a long time, I'd only dated older men. They have real confidence, not youthful bluster. They've had practice with women, in and out of bed. Or should have had. And one need not feel as responsible for an older man, somehow. *As guilty.*

We headed in the direction of the River Seine, where the Pont de Grenelle crosses the Île des Cygnes—the island with the miniature Statue of Liberty. Our date would soon, thankfully, be over. But my time for questions was running short. I could see the ornate trestle of the Bir-Hakeim Métro station rising ahead of us.

"But could it be done?" I asked, tipping my head just so.

As I'd hoped, he crumbled. "There *are* such things as induced earthquakes. But they generally come from underground stress. Dams, mining, drilling for oil—all these can affect an area's seismic stability. But none apply to Paris."

"So you believe last week's quake to be…?"

"A fluke. I can assure you, Catrina." He stopped as we reached the base of the railroad bridge, with its gray stonework and soaring iron girders, to slide a hand onto my shoulder very near my neck. Not in a threatening way, unless I'd felt threatened by the possibility of a kiss.

Just…touching. "You need not worry. To the best to my knowledge, there should be no more earthquakes in Paris."

Since such reassurance warranted a kiss, I did not turn my cheek when he began to incline his head, his gray eyes softening. I lifted my lips toward his, obligated…

But Léon stilled and frowned over my shoulder. What *now?*

I turned, but could not make out who or what, in the dark scattering of pedestrians, might have distracted him.

"Wait here," he commanded sharply and left me, beneath the echoing expanse of the elevated bridge.

My annoyance warred with relief. *Wait here?* Unlikely. Hearing a train approaching overhead, I made a decision. I pushed through the glass doors onto the street level of the otherwise-elevated station and climbed the long, open-air stairway to the elevated platform. I sped my step as the train screeched into the station with a metallic stop just above me. I fed my Carte Orange pass through the turnstile, retrieved it on the other side and gained the platform.

The train was Line 6, as I'd hoped. But an old man stood in my way. An old man I recognized.

"Restore the Black Madonna," he said.

Despite that the train began to broadcast its warning beeps, announcing the closing of the doors, I took a better look at this stranger. He was gray-haired, frail but well dressed, thin enough that his nose and ears and hands seemed large on him. His eyes gleamed, bright and clear. And I had to know more.

So I let the train pull away, let the handful of people who'd disembarked exit down the stairs, and waited, now alone with this man, for more information. Without the sunlight that usually filtered through the roof windows, the station seemed seedy. The usually dramatic, barred archway over the double tracks was almost invisible against the black sky.

Still, I would have no difficulty knocking *Grandpère* off his skinny old legs if he threatened me. "What did you say?"

He made a polite bow and repeated, "You must restore the Black Madonna, Catrina Dauvergne."

Which is when I saw who had stepped onto the platform behind him—and, with a lunge, I slammed the old man against the white-tile wall. But not merely for fun.

A burly man who'd just crossed the platform behind *Grand-père* had raised a gun. A *gun. In Paris!*

Between me and the wall, the old man said, "Oof!"

Something whistled by us, and I spun to see a small burst of yellow appear against the broad chest of a *second,* equally large man, one who'd apparently approached behind me. His hand flew to the bright plastic fringe that plumed from his chest, and he tugged out what I now recognized as a dart.

He then dropped to his knees, blinking blearily, and toppled onto his face there on the Métro platform.

I spun and faced the first attacker, who seemed to be reloading his gun as he closed the distance between us. A *tranquilizer* gun, obviously with a strong dose. Against an old man whom even *I* could have taken? *Or against me?*

I did not plan to be taken anywhere without a fight. So I closed the space between us and grabbed the gun.

He tried to yank it free, and he was of course very

strong. I only managed to hold on by allowing myself to be slung about, along with the gun, like a rat terrier in the grip of a bear. My dress heels scrabbled for footing on the tile platform. And the whole time his thick hands, so clearly suited to brute force, fumbled to finish reloading his gun. When he raised his hand to strike me, I plucked desperately at the fringe of yellow that still protruded from the half-loaded chamber.

As his free hand crashed down, I stabbed it with the dart.

He froze.

"Tag." I smiled icily. "You are it."

Of course, the large man did not respond. He was too busy collapsing backward, his eyes glazing over. I winced as his head impacted the platform.

Quite a powerful tranquilizer, indeed.

I looked at the gun, now in my hand. It seemed to be made of fiberglass, the better for avoiding metal detectors. I quickly threw it into the trash bin, resigning myself to calling the police, and looked at the old man who, for all I knew, merited being hunted like an escaped gorilla.

He did not help matters. "It is true," he marveled, speaking educated English. "You are your mothers' daughter."

This hardly proved his sanity. "Why are you following me?"

"You must restore the Black Madonna!"

I made a rude noise. "There are Black Madonnas in Chartres, in Aix-en-Provence, in Lyon. None of them are mine to restore, and I have no cause to do so. Why are you—"

A gaggle of tourists reached the elevated platform, saw the two bodies, and ran back down. I was just as glad I did not still hold the gun—though less so when the old man hesitated. "That part…it is not for me to say."

"You're stalking me to say that you cannot say?"

"Take this," he insisted, catching my hand. "Look for more of them. They will help you understand."

Before I could stop him, he pressed something into my palm—

The young noblewoman races through cobbled streets, breath lurching, hair trailing into her face. She tries to hold her brocade skirts high, so as not to trip. The air smells of blood. Her head is filled with screams, some of them her own.

She clutches to her chest a small sack, her mother's most valued treasure. But where in the Lady's name can she hide it? Huguenots have been suppressing Catholics for years, here. Tonight, Catholics are massacring Huguenots. Will the time of the Lady never return? Will—

Horses round the corner ahead of her—large, liveried animals, ridden by soldiers with muskets and blood-smeared swords. The noblewoman skids to a stop, almost falling. It is too late. With a clatter of hooves, horses loom over her. A soldier catches her by one arm and hauls her, painfully, across his saddle. Still she fights—kicking him, biting him. But there are too many. They grab her feet, her hands, tearing at her clothes, laughing their excitement at capturing another heretic on this night of God's glory.

One of them gropes her chest, tries to drag her treasure from her. Even as she clings to the bag, he pours the tesserae into his gauntleted hand.

Lady help her. Lady help them all....

"The bishop will want to see these," he breathes, and backhands her away from him and his plunder—

The vision stopped as her hand left the bag. Suddenly I again stood, not in the narrow street of a medieval château but in the modern expanse of the Métro station.

"What was that?" I exclaimed—perhaps screeched—and my fingers clamped on the old man's frail wrist. Not only was I beyond tired of having these horrible experiences thrust into my memory, but this one wasn't even from the days of the Revolution! To judge by the clothes, this had occurred in the late 1500s, likely during France's religious wars.

What was happening to me?

"It is a tile," the old man said—apparently of the stone in my hand, not of the vision. "It is key to everything else. You should understand more as you find others. This is *your* sacred calling, you see, not mine. You and your sisters must restore the Black Madonna, Catrina Dauvergne. You must—"

For a moment, I flattered myself that my chilling gaze was responsible for his abrupt stop.

Then I felt it, too—a crackle in the air, just as the lights of the Métro platform flickered, then went out. With a horrible, deep groan, the world seemed to sway beneath us.

Another earthquake!

Since I had the old man's wrist already, I dragged him with me as I lunged blindly for the exit stairs—a lot harder to find without the light of the comforting blue "Sortie" sign.

But I had recent experience making my way through the dark.

I was only partway down the stairs before the tremble of the earth stopped. So, it seemed, had everything else. *Stopped.*

I groped in the darkness and found the railing of the high, open-air stairway. I barely noticed when the old man pulled free of my loosening grip, so unnerving was this view of Paris, block upon block lit by no more than the starlight.

Whatever had happened had not affected all of Paris. I could see lights farther away. But immediately below me?

No cars moved.

No lamps shone.

No music played.

Even the Tour Eiffel stood dark, a somehow dead shape against the night. I thought of the people trapped in its elevators in the midst of this blackout.

I shivered. *What was going on?*

"Catrina!" Léon ran to me when I reached street level. "What the hell—you just vanished!"

"So did you," I noted.

So, apparently, had the old man.

Léon scowled. "I told you to wait. After what I just spent on dinner, the least you could do—"

That was enough for me. Deciding the police would surely have their hands full tonight I began walking in the direction of the Left Bank.

Léon followed. "Catrina!"

But at some point, he stopped following me. It was fifteen blocks, at least, before I reached neighborhoods

that still had lights, still played music, still offered working taxicabs. The whole while, I distracted myself with
thoughts of the *Soeurs de Marie* letters. You see, I knew
somebody who might be able to help identify whatever
was amiss about them. Aubrey de Lune was a friend,
though not of the Scarlet Rubashka hugging style of
friendship. Older than me by perhaps five years, Aubrey
was one of the more brilliant scholars that I have ever
known. *Especially* in the area of old manuscripts. And
yet…

And yet I had been less anxious to see her over the
last year, because Aubrey was also the fence who had
helped me place the medieval chalice that I had…lib-
erated. I had asked her for that favor. She had helped me
when I asked. But now, whenever I thought of her, I
could not forget the suspicions that had drawn me to ask
for her help in the first place.

Aubrey de Lune was either an art thief or an under-
cover agent in the world of art thieves. And my instincts
favored the former. Were I to ask her assistance with the
Marian letters, was I further muddying my own morals?
And when had I begun to care so deeply about morality?

Never had the four flights of stairs to my flat seemed
so steep, even dangling my dress shoes from one hand
and taking the stairs barefoot. I found the code for my
new burglar alarm before I even unlocked the front door,
so that I could disarm it quickly. But…when I closed the
door behind me, then turned to punch in the code, I had
a moment of confusion. Why was there no lit display?
Why, when I pressed numbers, did they not beep?

Then, from behind me, I heard the rasping voice.

"Give me the key."

I turned slowly, barely believing it. There stood the same dark, crazed man, easily shorter than me—but, to see him this close, hard-muscled all the same. Behind him, scrawled across my wall in something dark and shiny, was a cross and some kind of threat, just like at the hospital.

And this time, he held a knife.

Chapter 11

I could count the man's eyelashes, and the hairs of his overgrown eyebrows. I could see the sheen of perspiration across his leathered cheek, and the tiny scars etching his fingers as he reached greedily toward me. His left arm bled freely. He smelled of blood and oily metal. He was really here.

"The key!" Spit flew out of his mouth, and I winced back.

As if the knife weren't bad enough.

"I do not have the key," I told him, surprised by how calm my voice sounded. It was shock. I had a burglar alarm, locks. This could not be happening again.

"I heard you talking. You said you took the key!"

"I did take the key. Then I left it at work."

His breath became short, gasping pants. "You lie."

"All the time, but not just now."

"I can see it!" With a quick snatch, he lunged at my neck. I recoiled against the door. Instead of strangling me, he grasped at something and jerked. It wrenched me forward an inch.

I felt the burn of a chain before it snapped, a chain that I had worn so long, I barely remembered it was there.

"Give that—" I started to protest.

He silenced me by raising the knife, closer to my face.

And me unarmed…or was I?

Was I?

"What is this?" he demanded, holding up the chain. His fist shook so hard, the hanging pendant danced. *"What is it?"*

"It is a Virgin Mary medal." A normal, cheap Mary medal, more likely tin than silver. According to my *grand-mère*, it had been given to my mother at her first communion.

He stared at the medal, searching it for something he couldn't seem to find. I took advantage of his distraction to ease my hands behind me, to shift one of my high heels into the other hand.

The intruder's gleaming, dark gaze shot back to my face. For a moment I thought he'd noticed my shoes. But he had other concerns. "Blasphemy!" he exclaimed, with more spit. "How dare you wear a holy image. *How dare you?"*

Rather than explaining how I might *dare* to wear one of the few things remaining of my own mother, I attacked.

One heel, the one in my right hand, flashed out at the hand holding the knife. The other went for his face.

They're called stilettos for a reason.

He cried out at being attacked. The hand I struck curled tighter around his knife, but instead of attacking with it, he drew it protectively back. The heel against his face?

It went right through his cheek!

He screamed. I almost screamed myself. I might have dropped the shoe, if I were not so desperate. Instead I wrenched it from his bloody, torn flesh and struck at his eyes.

Explosions. Tranquilizer guns. I'd had enough!

He protected his eyes with a hard hand, before I could land that second blow, and stumbled against the doorjamb. We'd turned so I was now on the apartment side, him by the door.

Good. I swung again, again at the knife.

"Stop it!" he screamed, as one of my three-inch stilettos broke skin against his wrist. "*Stop it!*"

Like that would happen. Blocking the knife with one shoe, I swung hard for his throat with the other. The first heel caught on his blade, hard enough to impale itself, and we were momentarily stuck together.

The second sank into the side of his neck.

He made a horrible, gargling noise. His eyes bulged almost out of his head. And I could not help myself. I let go. I backed away from the sickening proof of what I could do.

Of course, as soon as I did that, I realized my foolishness. Spinning, I dove for the kitchenette, snatched up my largest cooking knife, spun back—

And saw the door standing open, one of my shoes lying on the floor…and no intruder.

I stood there, panting. Had I *imagined* this?

But a glance at my wall saw the cross, drawn in blood. My home was in shambles, cushions upended, drawers spilled. My neck burned, from where the chain had broken against it. As I slowly approached the open doorway, cooking knife still in hand, I could see calling on the heel of my 125-euro shoe.

One of my neighbors appeared in the doorway, just as I reached it, and we both jumped in surprise. He looked, quite concerned, from me to the knife.

I lifted my chin and smoothed back my hair with a shaking hand—the one *not* holding the knife. It was past time. "Please be so kind as to call the police."

Then, not daring to shut the door for fear that I might disrupt some clue, I sank onto my loose-legged coffee table. I wanted to make my own telephone call. It was foolish, childish, weak. I did not need anybody. And yet...

This affected the project, too. When my crazed stalker sought the key again, where would he look? That, at least, gave me a valid reason to telephone Rhys Pritchard. To warn him.

It was not my fault that he arrived at my flat not long after the police. But I was not surprised, either.

I woke surprisingly early the next morning—in my own bed, with a hollow in the pillow beside me but no Rhys. Last night, when neither he nor the police could convince me to leave my flat, Rhys had offered to stay as my bodyguard. *You should be aware that I am something of a pacifist*, he'd warned me. *But I can distract the bad guys.*

He'd intended to sleep in the living room. I hadn't let him. But we'd been so exhausted from our late-night cleaning, once the police finally left, that we'd actually slept together, instead of "sleeping" together. And now he was gone?

Except that I could hear a CD playing out front.

I sat up and went by the WC—the water closet, what Americans might call a bathroom but *sans* a bath—to take care of early morning business. Then I headed into the front room in my sleep-shirt.

Rhys, wearing only his jeans, was finishing washing the blood cross from my wall. We'd used rubber gloves for the first two scrubs, before exhaustion forced us to quit. Now, in the dawnlight, the wall looked as good as new. The dishes that had been tossed from their cabinets we'd stacked in the sink. Now they sat on the drying rack. My flat smelled nicely of furniture wax and lemon cleaner.

All that, and a great view of the long, bare expanse of Rhys's back and the low-slung denim encasing his butt. Tache, sitting primly on the windowsill, seemed intrigued as well. It was the cat, looking over at me, who must have tipped Rhys off to my presence. He turned with a grin, which slowly faded....

Instead, he stared. I felt unbalanced. I should have thought to comb my hair, to put on makeup. I should have—

But somehow, the way he recovered his smile, a flush warming his Welsh-complected cheeks, told me that my appearance was not the problem. Rhys dropped the sponge into the bucket at his feet, wiped his hand on his jeans and came to me. "Good morning," he said. His words sounded thick, perhaps from whatever was curling heat through me. "I called the school to check on their security. You should have the new alarm and locks put in before you leave, so nobody gets the codes except you—and there's still laundry that he went through to drop—"

I silenced him with a kiss, wrapping my silk-covered arms over his bare shoulders. I rose onto my toes, leaned full-body against his furry chest and slid my tongue into his mouth. *Oui…*

Shivers.

He let me—his breath catching, his arms slowly encircling me as if to keep me from sliding right down his body to the floor. He tipped his head, his tongue flirting with mine. When I slid one greedy hand down his long, tight-muscled back and into the waistband of his jeans, he moaned into my mouth.

A curious swivel of my hips informed me of his definite interest. So I hooked my fingers into his belt loops and began to back toward the bedroom.

Rhys followed with a lost sort of look at first, as if I had drugged him. Only once I fell back onto the bed with him, his denim a delicious friction against my bare inner thighs, did Rhys begin to protest. Between kisses.

"It's morning," he gasped, even as he buried his fingers in my hair, held my face still, covered my mouth with his.

"Mmm," I said—my mouth was full. But once I could speak, I reminded him, "You told the school you would be late?"

"We've got…" Now he lost his breath, because I was running my hand down the front of him, through his black chest hair, and felt the warmth of his bruises. Ah, yes. My injured protector.

"You should be on bottom," I decided, and helped roll him over on my bed. Straddling him, I was better able to navigate.

"We've got a great deal to do today," he protested, even as his spread hands climbed my bare thighs, then my hips, up and under my sleep-shirt. Clearly, he wanted me. But clearly…

Merde. I sat back from him, no longer squirming. "If you wish to say no, say no."

The moment stretched between us as Rhys's blue gaze searched my own. Then he admitted, "I do not wish to say no."

So I sank back onto him, and we kissed and explored and admired each other until we could get his jeans off him, get his briefs off him, then get a condom from my bedside drawer onto him. Desperate to sate this pounding need in me, I slid onto the thickness of him—and yes. Yes, that was exactly what I needed. To judge by his expression of ecstasy, dark lashes sinking into eye-closed satisfaction, so it was for him.

Even in full daylight, without imminent death as an excuse.

I'd meant to introduce Rhys Pritchard to quickies. But he seemed to take it as a point of honor to be thorough.

Again, I had no complaints. Afterward I felt so content, so relaxed, that I cuddled against his long, warm body, and he nuzzled my neck and my ear, and we slept together. Both of us.

So why did I again wake up alone?

Again, I pushed myself up in bed, straightened my sleep-shirt and padded out into the front room, wondering what else he'd decided to help fix or clean or—

"Hi," said Scarlet Rubashka, looking up from my copies of the *SdM* letters. "Rhys told me what happened when I came by to talk about last night's tremor. That's awful! No wonder you look shaken. That's sure a beautiful shirt, though. Is it silk?"

The previous night's encounter was not the only reason I felt shaken. "He's gone?"

"He said as long as I was here, could I wait for the locksmith and the alarm company to arrive while he went to check on the Denfert-Rochereau salvage. Want some coffee?"

I told myself it did not bother me. Heaven knows I'd left men's beds often and silently enough myself. And I, too, was worried about the Marian artifacts. But my stomach twisted, all the same. I couldn't help thinking he'd left *because of* the sex rather than *despite* it.

Still, I distracted myself with a shower in the tiny *baignoire sabot*, a kind of seated half-bathtub, off my kitchen. If Rhys could focus on the mysteries of the *Soeurs de Marie* find, then so could I.

My first call, once I toweled off and wrapped myself in a robe, was to my boss to warn him that I would be late. My next telephone call—and by now I could no longer remember why I had hesitated the day before—

was to my ancient-manuscripts-expert friend, Aubergine "Aubrey" de Lune.

I punched my number into her automated answering service. Within minutes my phone rang. "Catrina," she greeted me, instead of saying hello. "What a pleasant surprise."

Because I'd avoided her for months? Unwilling to entertain even that much guilt, I said, "I have a favor to ask."

Only then did I remember that those were the same six words that had started our plan to dispose of the stolen medieval cup, a year earlier. Her "What can I do?" sounded equally familiar.

But this time, there was no stolen property involved. I reminded her of the earthquake; she asked if I was unharmed—and we both sounded, if not insincere, then somehow *cool*. It was one of several reasons we'd clicked so surely, some years back, at a medieval art symposium. We both had the unique ability to be quite passionate about history and somehow dispassionate about people at the same time. Was that so terrible a character flaw?

Since neither of us needed the distraction of small talk, I then told her about the hidden letters. She gave me a fax number, and promised to call if she recognized the anomaly.

Scarlet volunteered to take several pages of my copies to the *bureau de poste*—in Paris, our post offices are more like business centers. I'd barely finished dressing, and Scarlet had just returned, when Aubrey de Lune called me back.

"Too much white space," she announced, without preamble.

"Too much…" But even as I echoed her, I saw exactly what she meant. The wide margins. The broad gaps between lines. The short paragraphs, leaving space before indents and after hanging half lines. "But of course!"

"White space is a modern convenience," Aubrey continued, her voice a clipped mixture of French ancestry, British upbringing and too much time in the States. She had once been a university professor—this much I knew about her, although I'd never bothered to ask which school or when. "Earlier scribes could not afford such luxury. Many illuminated manuscripts do not even include spaces between words, much less paragraphs. During the late 1700s and early 1800s, a middle-class letter writer was unlikely to waste as much paper as do the samples you sent. If you look at some nineteenth-century letters, you can even find examples of cross-hatching, where writers reused a letter by turning it on its side and writing across the previous lines."

I understood. "And if it was harder to read…"

"Then the recipient had the challenge of figuring it out," she agreed. "Like a puzzle. Is that what you needed?"

"For now. Thank you, Aubrey."

"Any time," she said. Despite my best efforts, I winced.

"I mean it. *Thank you*." For too long, I'd been motivated by uncertain, unnecessary guilt. But I was through taking such foolishness out on friends. I need not prove myself to anyone.

"I mean it," said Aubrey dryly. "Any time."

Scarlet bounced with impatience as I disconnected.

"My guess," I told her, "is that something is hidden

in the white space. We must only learn what, and how to reveal it."

"I think I know where to start," suggested Scarlet.

I raised an eyebrow. Even I did not know where to start. But far be it from me either to kick a puppy or to dissuade Scarlet Rubashka from her inspiration, so I waited.

"Ben Franklin," she announced proudly. And correctly.

"I just got the originals locked up," Rhys protested, once we arrived at the Sorbonne. I was not imagining the distance between us, now. When he'd first seen me, he came to my side, but hesitated before leaning down for an obligatory kiss on my cheek. I'd stepped back from him before he could do so.

It had not been encouraging. But he *was* more or less in charge of these remnants. He was also the only person who could get the letters out of the safe for us.

"Why can't you use the copies?" he asked now, wary.

I folded my arms. "Because if there are hidden messages, they are hidden in ways the copies cannot show us."

"Hidden in ways such as what?"

Scarlet and I exchanged a quick glance, fairly certain he would not like hearing this next part.

"Invisible ink," I admitted. Rhys squinted at me, as if he didn't understand, so I repeated myself in English.

"I know what invisible ink is," he snapped, in French. "But isn't the idea a touch dramatic?"

"Scholars agree that Ben Franklin was involved in espionage during the American War of Independence," I explained. "It is not beyond the realm of possibility that women who had admired him enough to emulate his experiments in electricity might emulate other inventions as well. And one common technique from that war was messages written in invisible ink."

"Ferrous sulfate," Scarlet volunteered, from where she'd been poking at the handful of tiles Rhys had been studying when we arrived. "Or lemon juice, or milk—organic things burn at a different rate of speed, you see."

I fought a wince, knowing Rhys wouldn't miss that pertinent detail. He did not. *"Burn?"*

"Heat," I corrected. "The recipient would reveal the hidden message by heating the paper. So we cannot use the copies."

"You're willing to destroy two-hundred-year-old letters on the chance that they've got secret messages hidden in them?"

"Heat rarely destroys paper," I reminded him. "And we already have excellent copies of their surface text."

His continued hesitation bothered me more than usual, so I added, "Do you even want to understand why these women died?"

He let out a hard breath. "You are a bad influence on me, Catrina Dauvergne," he warned, and walked out of the workroom, leaving me to wonder in how many ways he meant that comment.

"Look," said Scarlet. "These tiles fit together like a jigsaw puzzle to make a castle parapet."

I looked. While I would not have named the toothy pattern she'd created, of a metallic brown against deeper blue, I could see the resemblance to crenellations. "Be careful with those."

"I will. I like the way—"

Then Rhys returned with the box. We chose for our first experiment the half-finished letter with no signature, the one I imagined being interrupted by the house search. He lay the second page—half of it blank—on an acid-free mat and sucked in a wary breath when I lowered a travel iron onto the paper.

"I do not wish to ruin it, either," I groused, sliding the wedge-shaped surface across the parchment once, twice…

My annoyance began to fade as dark, purplish brown lines rose from the previously blank paper. *We were right?*

Now far less concerned for the welfare of the original letter, I ironed the rest of it. The invisible writing was, as Aubrey had predicted, cross-hatched from the surface writing. And these words actually gave us something.

The top half, in a neat hand, was interesting enough.

"*Women are now banned from attending assembly,*" Scarlet read out loud. "*Banned even from gathering! If Manon and Alinor did not live here, I should die of loneliness. Wives, mothers and daughters of émigrés are now being imprisoned. Despite that Alinor's Philippe escaped when it was legal, I fear losing her any day. We distrust our neighbors and are distrusted in turn. Dearest Lisse, our time here on Rue Sainte Sarah cannot last much longer. Thank heavens you escaped. If the worst happens—*"

Scarlet paused, because at that point the neat writing smeared away, replaced by a scrawled, more desperate imitation.

"*After midnight. They are here. Manon delays them.*

I have hidden your true letters and key. You know where.
Please survive. One of us must, or the dream of the M's
may die with us. How will the world endure without—"
But there was no more.

The writer must have panicked and shut all away in
the letter box, then. A letter box that had been confis-
cated along with the women's worldly belongings and
left with their headless bodies, lost to time...

Until the unlikeliest of earthquakes shook Paris.

Rhys crossed himself and murmured something sympathetic. I reread the letter, unable to ignore its lingering panic.

I tried heating the other page—and found nothing.

"She hid the 'true letters' somewhere else," Scarlet
noted faintly, then quoted, "'*You know where.*' How does
that help us? Even if this Lisse person did survive—"

"Lyon was hardly a safe place," I muttered.

"—she is long gone. We do not know where to look,
other than Rue Sainte Sarah...."

"Itself treasonous," Rhys reminded us. "Any streets
named after saints or royalty were renamed during the
Revolution."

"I can find what it was changed to." Scarlet bit her
lower lip, frowning at the single letter. The purple-
brown ink had not faded as it cooled. "But even if we
find the building, how...?"

Merde. I did not want to touch the key. In the last
week I'd dealt with earthquake, explosion, cave-in, catacombs, break-in, starvation, vandalism and thugs with
tranquilizer guns. More than enough. But if you added
the visions I'd been beheaded, beaten and dragged onto

a soldier's horse to be mocked, groped and likely worse. *I did not like the visions.*

But the letter writer had been brave enough to face a very real guillotine.

So while Rhys and Scarlet discussed this new information, I opened the baggie which held the key that had accompanied these letters—not the first, smallest key, which had opened the letter box, but the larger one. I shook it onto the table.

The clank of metal on metal made the others look up—but before they could comment, I curled my bare fingers around it.

With every fresh stab of pain, every time he forced the needle through his cheek, Grimaud felt a stab of confusion. How had the demoness managed to wound him like this? He'd thought God was on his side. Now he stared at his ruined face in his bathroom mirror. He'd used butterfly bandages on the hole in his neck. But the hole through his face…

Again, he pushed the sewing needle into his cheek and drew the thread through his flesh after it. His bathroom was a mess of bloody cotton, spilled peroxide and rubbing alcohol. He dared not go to an emergency room. Not if he could no longer be sure that God favored him and his guides.

The pain of that doubt hurt *more* than the needle.

Desperate, Grimaud thought of tests. God was all about tests, wasn't He? Perhaps this was not a betrayal. It was a challenge, to see if Grimaud's faith was strong, despite the demoness's temporary victory. It was easy to have faith when one outran strong young men. It was another matter, to have faith when a demoness rammed a shoe through one's face.

Encouraged, Grimaud tied off the knot, then plastered a large bandage over the entire mess, so that strangers would not see just how badly he'd been hurt. When his phone rang again, he would not show doubt. He would pass on what the woman had said about the key, and await his next instructions.

But somehow…for some reason he felt unsure whether he should mention that the demoness had been wearing a religious medal.

So he deliberately forgot that part entirely.

Chapter 12

Isabeau stuffs papers into a small, carved chest. She is surprised to see her hands shake as she locks it. She has feared this moment for so long that it almost feels anti-climactic.

The panic in Manon's voice, downstairs—that frightens her. "My husband fights in the army. We marched for liberté!"

Isabeau wraps herself in a cloak, then ducks into a large, empty fireplace and locates a brick at face height. Arching her fingers around it, she eases the brick out and stuffs the chest behind it. Retreating, she sheds the now-sooty cloak.

Bunching it into a ball, wiping soot desperately from her hands, she tosses the cloak onto the roof of the

*building beyond. She hopes whoever finds it is grateful
enough to keep silent.*

*Then she retrieves her quill and scribbles her last few
lines with colorless liquid. Downstairs, she hears
Manon's cry. She slides the letter and the cask's key into
a lockbox, the smaller key to which can, if necessary, be
swallowed—*

I opened my eyes to find Scarlet and Rhys staring at
me. "Did I say something?" I asked, but they shook
their heads.

"You looked terrified, though," said Scarlet.

"There *are* more letters." I somehow caught my
breath, calmed myself. The world I'd just inhabited had
ended over two hundred years ago. "If you can find the
address, Scarlet, I think I can find them."

That, sadly, would not happen instantly. And I had other
distractions. One, foolish or not, was my man troubles.
When Scarlet delivered me to the Cluny later that morning,
I had flowers from both Léon Chanson and Joshua Adriano, while the one man I wanted, despite all logic, seemed
abruptly unavailable. Rhys did walk me home that evening, as temporary bodyguard. We had a light dinner,
wine, and discussed the project. But when night came, he
spread his sleeping bag on my living room floor.

The second distraction hit the next morning. I crossed
my front room to leave for work—frustrated and annoyed about my empty bed—and Rhys said, "Shouldn't
you wear something darker?"

I looked down at my peach-colored suit. "Why?"

"Because today is your grandmother's funeral mass."

Of course he would remember. He set it up. "I'm not going."

"Why not?" When I shrugged, Rhys said, "You should go."

"I did not like the woman so…no."

Now he looked angry. "That ought not to matter."

"It does." I stalked to the counter for a cup of coffee, not to be near him. Even if he did smell freshly showered.

"She is dead." He handed me a cup, scowling. "She raised you when your mother could not and your father would not. If you stay away, it may haunt you for the rest of your life."

"Haunt *me*," I clarified. "For the rest of *my* life. Which means even if it were true—which it is not—it is my problem, not yours. Now if you are ready, I need to get to work."

"Drink your coffee." He put his down to head back toward the WC. Or so I thought. Then he returned to the front room with a hanger over his shoulder. Its black contents were half-hidden by a *Galleries Lafayette* wrapping. "You can change at lunch."

"Put that back!"

"No. Now, are you ready to go?"

The bastard! I tried to snatch the dress from him, but he easily lifted the hanger beyond my reach, and I knew better than to risk dragging on the gown itself. Damn him! Had he really been a priest? Because he was acting more like a bully.

In fact, "You are a bastard and a bully."

"You'll be late for work," he warned calmly.

But he was not the only one who could do calm,

merci beaucoup. I was quite capable of choosing my battles. Rhys could carry the dress to the Cluny if he wished—he even got me to take it from him once there by tossing it…should I have let it hit the cobblestone courtyard? But he could not force me to wear it.

I was the one who forced things around here, damn it.

When Rhys arrived at lunch, he wore a dark suit, probably his best. He must have headed back to his own flat to change clothes. Supposedly for me and my nasty *grand-mère,* which, yes, was sweet of him. But against my firm protests, which was not.

I was not wearing the black dress. But I locked my office door behind him, pulled the shades, and shrugged out of my peach-colored jacket. Then I began to unbutton the beige shell beneath it. He wanted a battle of wills? So be it.

For a moment he seemed to think I *would* change clothes. "I should wait—" But he made no real move to leave as I revealed my favorite bra, antique gold lace. "Ah."

"Could you help me with this zipper?" I came to stand in his body's escalating warmth, gazed for a long moment up into his clouding blue eyes, then at his lips. Only when he moved instinctively to lick them did I spin and present my back, drawing my hair off my neck to give him a better view on his way down to the waistband of the peach skirt.

"I…" But Rhys fumbled at the zipper with his long fingers. It purred open, and my skirt sagged downward on my hips. I turned back, enjoying his focus on my cleavage, then on my legs as the skirt fell to reveal my matching panties and garter belt.

I stepped up against him, circled my arms behind his neck, and kissed him. Deep. Seductive. After a moment's hesitation—always with the damned hesitation!—Rhys kissed me back.

A crueler woman would take him this far—perhaps a little farther—and then laugh at him and say no. Foolishly, I wanted him too much. And I was already struggling with too many guilt issues about him as it was. So I slid my knee up to his hip, along his crisp trousers, and was glad I had locked the door.

But as we drew breath he said, "Catrina...we have to go."

"No going," I protested softly, drawing him by the hands to my desk, which I'd cleared for this purpose. I liked this plan. Two birds with one stone. "You should come. Here. With me."

Rhys swallowed hard but shook his head. "No, I should not."

Determined not to let that hurt, I released his hands— see, I was not forcing him—and perched on the edge of the desk. "But have you ever done it surrounded by ancient *objets d'art?*" We decorate our offices with pieces that don't fit the exhibits.

"You know I haven't. Perhaps another time, but not now. You're not distracting me." He ducked his head and grinned then, stepping farther back. "Not sufficiently, at any rate."

His grin somehow infuriated me. I folded my arms, which improves my cleavage nicely. "That is your last word?"

"About sex on your desk just now? It is my last word."

"Then leave." And I coolly picked up my beige shell.

Rhys groaned. "You were going to put on the black—"

"*No!*" And I surprised myself by throwing the sleeveless blouse at his head, instead. "No, I was not going to put on the black. No, I will not be attending my grandmother's mass. No means no, or do they not teach you these things in seminary?"

He drew the silk off his shoulder and stared, processing the last few minutes. "Then all this was just…"

"As you say, a distraction. That is the kind of whorish bitch I am. I would rather screw you than go to mass. Surprise!" I'd wriggled back into my peach skirt, and now snatched the shell from his hands.

"Whorish…who ever said…? Catrina, *what is wrong?*"

"*You* are wrong!" I felt better with clothes on—of course I could zip and unzip my own skirt. "You are wrong to think that you know what is best, that you can force me through sheer stubbornness to do something that I have vowed not to do."

He raised his voice. *"But it is just one mass!"*

"I asked you to leave!" I screamed back, professionalism be damned. So, wordlessly, he left.

Only then, safely alone, did I sink to the floor—and silently sob. It did not matter that I did not know why, damn it. Feelings have their own truth, even without understanding. *This is your fault, Catrina. Did a night in jail teach you nothing, Catrina? How dare you behave that way, say those things, steal that chalice, not attend mass, seduce a priest…*

It was all a jumble—the attacks, the visions, and now

being all alone in the world…but no, that could not be part of it. I had hated *Grand-mère*, so very much….

Only after I'd sobbed the worst of it out was I able to recover my poise, with copious tissues and a reapplication of makeup. I thought perhaps I would walk to the river and have a crêpe in the sunshine, in sight of Notre Dame. Then perhaps I could think clearly. What to do about safety, without Rhys in the apartment. How to learn more about the *Soeurs de Marie*. Whether I should give up on men for a while…or just until the next time Joshua Adriano was in town.

But when I opened my office door, Rhys sat on the floor just across from it, despite his best suit. He had his head in his hand, and his elbow on one raised knee. When he lifted his gaze to mine, his eyes were fathomless…and no longer angry.

He looked as empty as I felt.

I said, "Do not dare try—"

He interrupted. "I apologize for trying to force you. Just…let me walk with you for a while? I think we should talk."

Talk. That meant a breakup, *n'est-ce pas?* If we'd had a relationship to begin with.

"Fine," I said, walking away from him and expecting him to follow. No time like the present. "Talk."

Perhaps he could get it over with while I was still numb.

"I am sorry," Rhys said again, as we strolled toward the Seine without touching. And now he would say, *But you're quite insane and I must get far, far away from you*.

Instead he said, "You're right. I was being highhanded and petty. I was just annoyed—never mind that.

I should have tried harder to understand why you wish to avoid the funeral."

"You asked," I reminded him, suspecting a trick. "And when I tried to explain, you said it didn't matter."

He didn't defend himself. Instead, he winced—and, catching my hand, he drew me to a seat at an outdoor bistro table. He pointed at something for the waiter and held up two fingers, then turned back to me. "I did not mean that it did not matter. Of course your history with your grandmother matters. What I should have said was that affection is not the only reason to attend services. They can bring closure. It's—"

I pushed my chair back and stood. So much for staying numb. "You're still trying to convince me!"

"I'm not—" He stood, too, took my shoulders, bowed his head over me in that way he had of making me feel oddly…venerated. "It's your decision. Don't go. I can attend for you."

I searched his blue gaze, suspicious.

"Please believe me," he murmured, softly.

Warily, I sat. Rhys sank into the chair across from me, his leg touching mine where the *X* of them intersected. He reached across the table and took my hands in his.

"I just want to understand," he said. "To understand *you.*"

I felt a strange flicker of panic. "Why?"

Annoyance darkened his expression. "Because you are more than a beautiful, empty body, that's why." When the waiter put the glasses in front of us, Rhys snapped, "Thank you!"

The waiter narrowed his eyes. When Rhys paid him,

the man turned with an indignant sniff toward the back of the café. Not all French are rude, but waiters can certainly hold their own.

Rhys had his head in his hands again. But when he slanted his gaze back at me, his eyes smiled wearily over the mask of his fingers. "You really do bring out the worst in me."

I folded my arms. "You are welcome."

"I mean to say—" he began, but I interrupted him.

"Could you simply say things once, and correctly the first time? It would speed matters up considerably."

"I'm figuring it out as I go along. What I meant to say is that you have the ability to make me angry. And high-handed. And petty. I am so used to presenting this composed, moral face to the world, I think I began to believe I was immune to…to the rest. Even after leaving the priesthood, I acted like I was some kind of damned saint, and a martyr at that. And then I hook up with you…."

"And I turn you into a man-whore?" I suggested icily, and took a sip of wine.

"I'm unsure whether to be insulted or flattered." But he grinned as he said it.

I almost smiled myself. "Both."

"In any case…" Again he offered me his hand, and I warily gave him mine. "*You* have not turned me into anything. Something in me may respond to you rather… unexpectedly. But I am responsible for my own decisions. Agreed?"

"My decisions are my own, as well." But we both knew that did not mean quite the same thing.

"We still have half an hour before I must leave for the

mass," Rhys assured me, looking at his watch. "So talk to me, Catrina. Please. Tell me about your grandmother."

He did say please. So, with him still holding my hand, I made the effort. "She was a bitch." Now he would know where I got it, anyway. "She resented being burdened with me, and held my mother's death against me, and relished telling me so."

"Your mother died in childbirth?" Rhys asked.

"My mother overdosed at a party," I clarified. According to *Grand-mère*, only once she had identified the body did she think to ask, *And what about the girl?* Which is how the authorities thought to come looking for me, where I'd been left alone for several days. Even at four, I'd been trained not to cry lest I get us in trouble with the concierge. "*Grand-mère* felt that had my mother not been burdened with me, she may not have turned to drugs. Me, I suspect the drugs were a way to escape *Grand-mère*."

Rhys nodded, but otherwise made no comment. He did look a touch too sympathetic for my comfort, however.

"She did not beat me, if that's what you're thinking," I protested. "The old bat made sure I had food, went to church, got an education. And without the education…"

I'd always been drawn to history, to a past distant enough that the gritty realities of the present felt glossed over by time. But only school had helped me into that world, helped me become a part of it. Not to mention, it had made an excellent escape from constant criticism. So had all my boyfriends.

"You once said you lived with your father as a teenager," Rhys said. "In the United States. Why did you contact your grandmother when you came home?"

But here, I shrugged. Perhaps to prove that despite her dire predictions, I had reached adulthood? To show off my scholarships, or each degree as I advanced? Sometimes when I had a particularly impressive lover, I would allow him to ask *Grand-mère* to join us for dinner. But she had never approved.

And now she never would. But that was not my fault.

"Walk me to the station?" asked Rhys, draining the last of his wine. So I held his arm and walked with him to the St-Michel Notre-Dame stop, barely a block away now. When we reached the station and Rhys hesitated, I started down the stairs.

Rhys followed me from the stairs, through the turnstiles, to the long escalator. It is quite a deep station—between that, and the wait for the next southbound train, he had plenty of time to look questioningly at me. As well he should.

"I might leave at any time," I warned him at last, focusing on one of the oversized advertisements gracing the curved, white-tiled wall across the track. "And I am wearing this."

Rhys kissed me on the top of my head, which was far too chaste for my tastes, but the easiest spot for him to reach. He wisely said nothing. And now…now that he'd stopped trying to force my hand?

I found myself holding quite tightly to his.

The next hour was something of a resolute blur—my childhood church, a casket, flowers, *Grand-mère*'s old friends. Scarlet was there, invited no doubt by Rhys. And mass… The ritual lies dormant in one's bones and reawakens when one is surrounded by the scent of candlewax and furniture polish, the priest on the altar…and, in my case, another one beside me. Of sorts.

Heaven help me, I felt comforted by that—and guilty when, like me, he declined taking the Eucharist at Holy Communion. I'd given up communion out of rebellion, but him? If Rhys Pritchard thought himself to be in a state of sin, I suspected I knew why.

But what stood out most for me?

I turned to leave, with my friends—and I saw the statue I'd blocked from my memory, along with so much else of my youth. A three-foot-tall Madonna statue presided over a rack of votive candles. She was no Black Madonna, though centuries of hard use had darkened her with soot and age. And yet the peaceful expression on her carved, painted face as she cherished the child in her arms struck something deep inside of me.

For months, when I was ten, I had lit a candle each week in prayer for my mother's soul…and perhaps I'd begun to blur the two figures. Because whenever I imagined the perfect mother, I pictured the Madonna. Not the Mary that catechism taught—the Mary of the Immaculate Conception or the Assumption, none of which I disbelieved so much as…neglected. Orthodox teachings were not what spoke to me. What spoke to me was the look in her eyes, the curve of her body, the way she held her baby, not because he was the Christ Child but as if to say that all children were precious.

Somehow I had ignored the doctrinal Madonna and worshipped an archetypal Madonna, both at the same time—at least until my *grand-mère* thought to ask how I was paying for the candles, learned I was lighting them without leaving an offering, and turned that tiny hint of sanctuary into another wrong I had committed.

What if I were not the only person to have blurred the two?

"What if they were not strictly Catholic?" I asked Rhys, after we'd escaped the church and were headed into the Métro station. "The Sisters of Mary? What if they *were* into Mary, but for a reason other than church doctrine, like with the Black Madonnas?"

Rhys and Scarlet looked mildly surprised—should I still be focusing on my loss? I'd worn peach to the funeral. I'd not danced on the casket. *Grand-mère* and I were as good as we'd get.

Scarlet spoke first. "Like the Black Madonnas?" So I filled her in on what Rhys said about the bride in the *Song of Songs*, and how medieval devotees may have merged the two figures.

I must have gotten it right, because Rhys simply asked, "You saw Josette's sketch, didn't you?" When I shook my head, he clarified. "Josette sketched the image on the Mary medals we recovered, in detail. The iconography is definitely confused."

"Confused how?"

"The medal pictures a mother and child, the standard Madonna. But she wears a sword, which would be symbolic of the archangel Michael, and she has a large key, representative of St. Peter. There also seems to be some kind of jar by her feet, but a jar would indicate Mary Magdalene. When I get back to the Sorbonne, I will look more closely at the medals themselves."

"I can walk Cat to the Cluny," Scarlet suggested

quickly, as our train arrived with a rush of air and a long squeal of brakes. We all three got on, since the Cluny and the Sorbonne share a stop. "I have to talk to her about something privately, anyway. Girl talk, dontcha know."

I felt somehow relieved that Rhys hesitated, and even more so when he asked, "Shall I come for you after work, then?"

He had not completely written me off, at that.

"Yes." When the train lurched into motion, it threw me hard against him. Rhys's arm closed hard around me, and I looked up at him, and I understood at least some of my fears from earlier. I was fighting the need to count on him…and I was losing.

Without straightening away from him—we had four stops to go before changing lines, then four more to the Cluny La Sorbonne station—I asked quietly, "Why were you annoyed?"

His brows drew together in honest confusion.

"Earlier," I insisted, over the noise of the rush of train off of tunnel. "You said you'd been annoyed even before we argued, but not why. How did I annoy you? This time, I mean."

Rhys squinted down at me, looking embarrassed, especially when he glanced to Scarlet and back. "It shows me in a poor light," he murmured, stalling.

Whistling with no subtlety at all, Scarlet strode to the other side of the car as if to study one of the overhead ads, the flounce of her black ballet skirt bouncing as she went.

With a half laugh, half scoff, Rhys bent closer to whisper his confession, "I was angry about sleeping on the floor."

I stared, truly stunned. "You *wanted* to come to bed?"

A stocky old lady in a nearby seat, who wore black despite that she likely had not attended a funeral today, pretended not to overhear me. But her scowl deepened.

Squinting again—and blushing—Rhys nodded.

He'd *wanted*… "Then why did you not just say so? Or just climb in? If you want to come to bed, get in the damned bed. It is not as if we have not set a precedent."

"Ah. But if I want you to attend an old lady's funeral?"

"Oh, then definitely try to drag me there against my will. I am sure that will work wonders." But in the end, it had.

Rhys shook his head. "You're never boring, Catrina."

"I have had better compliments," I flirted up at him.

"It is not necessarily a compliment." But somehow, the way he had his head bowed over mine as he said it? Somehow, it was.

Everything seemed right as we left the Cluny La Sorbonne station—I had a lovely, sexy man to spend the night with, and a friend who was helping me track down the Sisters of Mary, and…

And why did I feel an unnerving sense of prescience as a police car drove past us, in the direction of the *université?*

Rhys dropped my hand and ran, quickly outdistancing Scarlet and me. But even he was too late to do anything.

The Denfert-Rochereau project had been robbed.

Chapter 13

"**—**put a note on the door!" insisted Charles, whom Rhys had left to supervise. "And I locked up when I left!"

"—standing open when I arrived, so I fetched a guard like you told us to, Monsieur Pritchard," brownnosed Josette. "Things looked disordered, so I took inventory, and the tiles—"

"—monetary value?" the policewoman who had responded to the call asked, wielding her clipboard. "Your report will carry more weight if you can quantify a clear loss."

Clear loss? I started to surge forward, out of the corner of the workroom where Scarlet had drawn me out of the way. These tiles had come from the dead women's *stomachs!* The Marians had been so desperate to hide them, they'd swallowed them. And if they were in prison for any amount of time, they would have…

I'm sure you understand the digestive cycle as well as I. They may have had to swallow them more than once.

Scarlet pulled me back first. "Let him handle it."

This was Rhys's school, he was the coordinator…and clearly he did have enough to deal with. So I hung back, and felt sick for the poor, dead women we'd let down, and I watched him do it.

Rhys said he believed Charles had locked the door, and took his share of responsibility for leaving the project unattended. Charles looked a little less combative, after that. Rhys praised Josette for her quick response— his hand rested on her shoulder for a moment longer than seemed necessary, but before I could slip into jealousy, it occurred to me that he was probably shaken by the possibility of her arriving when the thieves were still here. He explained to the police that historical value was hard to quantify, but that he would appreciate them assuming that the monetary value was high—and at the very least dusting the area for fingerprints—until he was able to contact our backers and get actual numbers for them.

Our backers. The Adrianos. "I can do that," I offered. Rhys met my gaze across the room and nodded gratefully.

Then Professor Brigitte Taillefer arrived, ostensibly to check on his well-being. "I just heard there was a theft!" she exclaimed—and looked directly at me, her old eyes narrowed.

Disgusted—and clearly of no use there, for the moment—I dragged Scarlet out to head for the Cluny. Lately, she and Rhys acted as if the dark little madman might leap out and attack me at any moment, hence my constant escort. I believe I'd handled him just fine on my own, the last two times…but I didn't wholly mind, either.

"I don't suppose this is a good time to ask Rhys if we can borrow the key from the letterbox," she said now, as we descended the broad stairs to the street. "If it's still in the safe."

"No." Then curiosity overrode annoyance. "Why?"

"Because I found out—at the Bibliothèque Nationale—where the Sisters of Mary used to live," she announced in an excited rush. "The home that belonged to Manon Cannet and her husband still exists. In fact, it's a hotel now. And I thought you might want to go there with me tomorrow, *without* Rhys."

Again I had to ask, "Why without Rhys?"

"The people who own the hotel are unlikely to let us walk right in and take the lockbox Isabeau hid there." Scarlet shrugged, as if surprised by it. "But Catrina, the way they got the house—and it is the same family, even now—they were given it after their family turned the women in."

My step slowed as I stared at her. *Mon Dieu.*

"For unpatriotic activities." Scarlet widened her eyes, willing me to understand. "This family handed the women over to the National Committee, and their reward was Manon Cannet's home. Anything hidden there, they got from that betrayal."

I let the full import of that sink in—and nodded. This was not the sort of thing I wished to mention to Rhys, not without serious consideration. Certainly not before the fact, because Brigitte Taillefer may have been right about me, at last.

"We'll have to steal the box," I concluded.

The home where the Sisters of Mary had met to discuss books and perhaps sedition had become the Hotel du Montfort. It was a narrow, three-story house from the seventeenth century, in the St-Germain-des-Pres district, and walking into it felt…

Surreal. I'd already been there in my visions, remember?

The floor of what had become the small lobby was tiled in slate. The dark paneling matched the dark beams across the white, Tudor-style ceiling. A cluster of older artifacts—suits of armor, weapons—gave the place an aged air.

"The house had been in the Cannet family since the reign of Louis the Fourteenth," murmured Scarlet, as we took this in. "The Cannet who had it built was an Officer of the King."

Any French historian would brighten at the mention of the *Carabiniers du Roi*—better known in popular literature as the Musketeers. "I like this Cannet already."

"Over a century later, Henri Cannet—a lawyer—brought his bride, Manon, into the home. Records show that he joined the army as a captain during the early days of the Revolution. On June 30, 1794, he was executed as a royalist spy."

His wife hadn't known, I thought—but before I could say so, the proprietor of the hotel joined us. "The historian and the photographer!" he greeted, since Scarlet had already contacted him to request a meeting. "I am Etienne Montfort. You have done your research. My family always maintained that the traitors who lived here tried to undermine the Republic, but it is gratifying to hear proof of it!"

Normally, I lie quite easily. But now I could not force my mouth around words of agreement to put Monsieur Montfort at ease. They sickened me.

Luckily, Scarlet did fine. "Undermine the Republic! How very wrong of them," she exclaimed, allowing Montfort to lead us up the stairs for a tour of the hotel. Apparently, she'd given him hopes of a photo spread in a Canadian magazine.

We started on the first floor—one story up—with the three larger bedrooms. Each had its own style, though they all featured stone walls and heavy, dark furniture. One room was done in crimson, another in plaid, another in wide, vertical stripes. Montfort only gave us peeks into those last two, as they were being let by tourists currently out exploring Paris. None of them struck a chord of familiarity, even the one with a large fireplace. Reluctantly, I followed him and Scarlet up the next flight of stairs to what had likely been the servants' quarters. Three of those rooms were decorated in flower motifs.

But the last, larger room, with drapes and bedcurtains decorated with tropical birds? Its fireplace indeed looked familiar. Familiar—and worrisomely clean.

"This was not part of the servants' quarters," I noted, trying not to make a beeline for the chimney. This had once been a wife's study, separate from her husband's for privacy. Situated in the corner of the building, its windows overlooked both the street and the roof of the home that abutted it.

"Did you notice," Montfort said, "that every room has its own private water closet? We upgraded them a few years ago…"

I edged closer to the fireplace, large enough that I did not need to crouch to look into it. *Far* too clean. Instead of andirons, it sported an ironwork candelabra with pillar candles.

No, I thought desperately, leaning closer in hopes of seeing higher into its confines. *Do not be…*

"The fireplaces were sealed off over a century ago," Montfort interrupted himself to tell me, forcing me to straighten without getting a good look. "When we put in modern heating, of course. Messy things, fireplaces. Soot everywhere. Shall I show you the dining facilities downstairs…?"

"Please." Scarlet acknowledged my head tilt toward the fireplace with a tiny nod. "Lead the way, monsieur."

The hotelier did. For a moment I thought it would be that easy, but then he called back, "Mademoiselle Dauvergne?"

So we would have to implement Scarlet's and my plan B.

Deliberately leaving the door cracked, I hurried after them. "I am sorry, Monsieur. I cannot stay for the rest of the tour. But—" Somehow I forced my best, most professional air of enthusiasm "—I am impressed by how well you have merged the building's historical elements with modern conveniences."

He shook my hand as we parted. Scarlet followed him through heavy double doors into what I assumed was the dining room....

And I hurried back up the two flights of crimson-carpeted stairs, my heart pounding. *Do not let the door have closed....*

For a moment, I thought it had. But a sturdy push, with a wrench of the handle, and I was in. I closed and locked the door behind me because, please, what kind of idiot would not?

I ignored the garish bird pattern—with some difficulty—and went immediately to the fireplace. Most sealed chimneys are plugged at the throat, just above the opening of the fireplace itself. If this one had been sealed there, what would I do? Difficult enough to insinuate ourselves this once. Getting back in with a sledgehammer, without admitting our true purpose, might prove beyond even *our* connivance.

I had to crouch awkwardly so as not to kick over a pillar candle as I stepped into the fireplace. I could see nothing but darkness above me, so I slowly straightened....

Straightened...

And bumped my head on a plaster seal—still bent.

Merde! I whispered words even stronger than that. In my vision, the stone I removed had been at shoulder height. If only this fireplace were plugged a few inches higher, I might have reached it! Angry, I pounded on the shadowy bricks before me with my closed fist....

And one of them moved.

I flushed, almost as much at my own idiocy as with relief.

I had never stood in this fireplace before in my life. The stone had been shoulder height *to Isabeau*. From the 1700s.

There was a reason the suits of armor downstairs looked short.

But I could muse on historical standards of living later. For now, I slid my fingers around the brick, the way my vision had shown Isabeau doing it, and wiggled it slowly, slowly out of its hole. The sound of stone on crumbled mortar grated, but eventually the brick slid free—for the first time in over two hundred years. *Victoire!*

With my free hand, I reached in, felt the shape of a box—

I shook off an echo of the memories I'd gotten off the key, the sense of violation as men shouted downstairs, the trembling importance of Isabeau's mission. But as I drew the little chest from its hole, it occurred to me to make sure it was the only treasure stashed there. Securing the box under one arm, I reached back into the gaping shadow left by the missing brick, and my fingers found—

· *Manon rises onto her toes on a stone mounting block, straining to see over the heads of the crowd as they watch the morning's cartload of prisoners creak past. Even more important than seeing is being seen. Gui was arrested for helping people like Lisse escape. If not for him…*

Manon's inaction sickens her. In the novels she and her friends have so loved, the heroine would find a way to rescue her faithful ally. A diversion, a prison break, a bribe. But too many loyal citizens scream for blood this morning. None of it feels real. But it is…and so is her helplessness.

All she can do is give Gui one last glimpse of someone who cares, before his head is taken. Hidden in her pocket, her fist curls tight around a sacred tile, seeking strength....

Sure enough, Gui's dull eyes lift and find hers. His broken posture, in the cart of the condemned, straightens almost imperceptibly. Lisse is safe because of you, *Manon wills him to understand.* So many are safe. Because of you, there is hope....

Does he take solace in that? Or does he, like she, understand that by helping the boldest of the Soeurs de Marie *leave the city, he may have condemned himself?*

Manon cannot tell. But his eyes hold hers, hungry and so very human, for the entire time it takes for the cart to—

A crash lurched me back into the twenty-first century, stone landing on the fireplace candelabra. I'd lost myself so deeply in the 1790s that the brick had slipped from my fingers. Thank heavens it did not land on my foot!

But the faint shout, from below, was perhaps worse.

Stuffing the three flat little stones I'd just found into my pocket, I retrieved the brick, shoved it back into place, and ducked out of the fireplace with the lockbox for which I'd come. I strode to the door, cracked it slightly.

"Don't old buildings commonly have strange noises?" I heard Scarlet calling futilely upward.

Monsieur Montfort's voice sounded closer. "Not like that!"

I would not be leaving by the stairs.

I looked around, wondering where I might hide, and quickly realized that I could not. The water closet and wardrobe niches had no doors, only curtains. The bed sat on a wooden platform. My only way out was, well...

out. Here and now. One window overlooked the street, three stories down. But the other—

Perhaps ten feet below lay the flat roof of the adjacent house. Just over three meters. Have I mentioned I dislike heights? This shouldn't seem high enough to cause my stomach to swoop, but the three-story drop just beyond it did.

I had no time for fears, human or not.

Unlocking the casement window and swinging it outward, I tossed the little chest to the flat roof below. Now I *had* to go after it. I could hear heavy footsteps charging up the stairs as I swung a leg out the window, then followed with the rest of me. I pivoted to hang from my hands as I withdrew my other leg, struggling against gravity. Even more difficult? Slapping the window shut before my fingers gave out, slipping out of the window's way as I dropped.

I landed without plunging through the roof into someone's attic or rolling off the edge. A good sign, that. The chest lay on the gravel of the mansard roof, beckoning me. But I heard the squeak of the casement window above me and rolled, as fast as I could, up against the exterior of the Hotel du Montfort.

I lay immediately below the window—and held my breath. *Do not notice me. Do not notice the box. Do not…*

Above me, I heard Scarlet's voice. "Nothing out here," she called—and met my gaze. She winked. Then she added over her shoulder, "Ooh, do you think your hotel could be haunted? That would be an excellent angle to work into your publicity materials. You could be included in Haunted Paris tours…."

But I heard no more, because I was rolling to my feet, scooping up the chest and running for it. Two connected roofs later, an alley gaped ahead of me like a chasm to hell. For a fleeting moment I imagined myself leaping the two meters, as in some film. But as Manon had needed to face the futility of rescuing Gui, I rejected the idea of so dramatic a jump.

Not me. Not in these shoes.

Instead, I peered carefully, far, far over the edge.

As it turned out, this particular chasm to hell had a fire escape, its topmost platform perhaps eight feet below me.

The idea of jumping over two meters onto iron grill-work instead of solid roof unnerved me even more than my previous drop. The metal bars hardly looked solid, especially with six meters of sheer space to the alley beneath. But I had no other choice.

I sat on the very edge of the roof, clutching the chest like a security blanket. I crossed myself.

And I dropped.

Grimaud yelled rudely at the visitor who pounded at his door. The sign outside said he was closed! He did not dare risk customers asking about his injuries...and he felt too heartsick from his previous telephone call to work.

The key is not old enough, his guide had accused.

"But I took it from the room you told me about!"

It is a replica, made from a mold of the original key.

How should he have known that? Why had God not shown him? "The tiles, though? Those are what you wanted?"

The tesserae will suffice. But you failed to get the

key. We are beginning to question your competence, old friend....

Grimaud felt sick. Angry. Guilty for feeling angry. And now—now, some idiot would not stop pounding on his door!

Grimaud flung the door open to reveal a tall, gray-haired old man who pushed into his shop, stronger than he appeared, and looked around.

"So your family has kept this place, all these centuries," the stranger mused. "What remarkably misplaced loyalty."

"The shop is closed! You must go now. You…" But when Grimaud saw the man's wise, quiet stare, he hesitated. There was a sense of power here, a sense of command. "Are…are you he?"

"If you mean your guide? No. I am merely a concerned observer, Pierre, with some strong advice. Question authority."

Pierre shook his head. He did not understand.

"I cannot save your soul for you," continued the stranger. "But heaven knows you need it, so take heed. Only by each man thinking for himself can true evil be wiped out. Can you remember that?"

Pierre Grimaud shook his head, thoroughly confused. Evil was destroyed through obedience to the forces of right, not through anarchy. Everyone knew that!

With a shake of his head and a roll of his eyes, the old man turned and left.

Chapter 14

I landed with a metallic crash, dropping to my knees. The bolts holding the fire escape to the wall screeched as the whole structure shifted beneath me then stilled. Then I had only to creep my way down the narrow metal stairs and to release the ladder that slid to five feet above the alley floor and clamber down it…one-handed. Because I had a death grip on the box that was my prize.

I could not tell if my increased trembling was from belated nerves or anticipation. Likely the latter.

At least, that's what I told myself.

I reached my flat well before Scarlet did. No madmen waited for me, for once. But I did jump when I heard a key in the lock, only to relax as I saw that Scarlet had brought Rhys with her. Rhys had copies of my new keys and my burglar alarm code, which he punched in as if he'd lived here for weeks instead of days.

Lived here. Have I mentioned how well the previous night went? Rhys took my advice and simply came to my bed and to me. No hesitations, just him and his kisses and his lovemaking....

If I had not felt so guilty for not mentioning my plans with Scarlet, it would have been perfect. Even with the guilt, it came remarkably close.

He looked nowhere near as welcoming tonight.

"I thought we should get the key," Scarlet explained. "Did you know the copy Rhys had made was stolen with the tiles?"

I had not known. "You had a copy made?"

"It seemed important to you and…them."

"The Marians," I clarified. His eyebrows went up, but otherwise he accepted my new term for the *Soeurs de Marie*.

"Josette did not know about the copy, which is why she did not realize it had been stolen. Speaking of which…?"

Ouch. Scarlet must have filled him in on our afternoon's adventure. I should have realized she would be unable to stay silent—and why should she? We'd done nothing wrong.

Not terribly wrong, anyway. "If I may have the key…?"

Rhys might disapprove, but he handed me the key all the same—and cotton gloves and a can of graphite powder. At last I could insert the key into the chest's lock, jiggle it, open it…and behold a thick stack of letters, all of them cross-hatched with messages whose faded, purple-brown color indicated they had all once been written in invisible ink.

They were weighed down by another, larger key—did this make three, now? I carefully avoided touching it.

Have you ever had a pen pal? Have you ever experienced the satisfaction of holding a letter in your hand, knowing that despite incredible distance, you had proof of their thoughts, their existence, connecting you?

For a moment, I could barely breathe. A connection—a real, *tangible* connection—now existed between me and a handful of women from over two hundred years in my past.

By the time Scarlet left to fetch dinner, I'd laid all twenty-two letters out on every piece of furniture and flat surface. Tache yowled her displeasure from where I'd shut her in the bedroom, but I could not have her stepping on any of this. For his part, Rhys poured himself a glass of wine—then a second one—and watched from a safe, thoughtful distance, neither encouraging nor stopping me. I ignored him. By the time Scarlet got back with take-away sandwiches from *Pomme de Pain*, I'd at least skimmed every word…and my head was swimming.

"Apparently," I told the others, as Scarlet and I also took a glass of wine, "the *Soeurs de Marie* helped run a kind of underground route out of Paris. They had a friend named Gui who drove the carts full of corpses to mass graves north of the city. You know, where the Montfaucon gallows had been?"

Scarlet looked blank, but Rhys nodded.

I continued, "The area was still a garbage dump, at

the time. People who desperately needed to escape, if they could reach the Sisters of Mary, would be taken to the stables where the cart was kept. Alinor Geoffrin, who seems to have had a talent for engineering, invented a frame for the floor of the cart to protect stowaways from the weight of bodies. It was not visible, as long as Gui spread enough hay over it. The refugee would hide down there all day, as body after body was thrown in on top…."

Scarlet put down her sandwich.

Glad to avoid further details myself, I said, "This is how the woman named Lisse Clairon escaped Paris—disguised as a boy, and hidden under carnage. She became ill, but a family of secret royalists nursed her back to health until she could collect the treasure. You see, for some time after that, Gui continued to smuggle not just people but 'treasures' out to her, from the other Marians. She doesn't name the treasures, other than an occasional novel—she was desperately bored when she wasn't terrified. But they were willing to risk their lives for it. They also smuggled out what Lisse needed to re-construct a pushcart. That was in letter number seven. Other letters discuss how she walked the treasure all the way to the Languedoc, for months, as a manure ped-dler—which kept people away. Eventually she hid it in a root cellar. Then she returned north to live with an aunt in Lyon, which is where she wrote most of these."

"Was Lyon a safe haven, then?" asked Scarlet.

"No. It was a scene of revolts and then dreadful oc-cupation by the Republic. Over a thousand homes were destroyed, and over a thousand people were executed, some by cannon fire. Lisse wrote of it in letter number thirteen, as recounted by her aunt. It seemed…she wrote that it seemed like the end of the world."

"I don't believe in the end of the world," Scarlet said firmly, though her voice sounded uneven. "Rather…I think one world's ending is another's beginning."

"That was true for Lyon," I admitted, no longer speaking from Lisse's letters, but general knowledge. "They eventually flourished under the Napoleonic Empire that followed. I hope…."

But it was foolish to worry myself about what had happened to Lisse after the execution of her friends. When they no longer answered her letters, surely she would have guessed the truth?

We stayed up discussing other letters. *Now* the Marians sounded like women worth studying! We stored the letters in an appropriate, acid-free box in preparation for copying them. Only after Scarlet had left for the night did I turn to Rhys—who had not moved from his seat on the floor, despite that I'd now cleared the chairs—and ask, *"What is wrong?"*

"You stole these," he said softly. "From the hotel."

I'd assumed as much. But I had my justifications. "The hotelier did not know he had them."

"Does it matter?"

"Considering that the Montforts obtained the building *and* the letters by condemning their true owner? I think it does!"

"What about the project? Are you planning to add these letters to the items salvaged from the Denfert-Rochereau site?"

"I had not planned on it." When I saw him set his jaw, I added coolly, "Nor had I planned not to. I have not considered it. These letters were not salvaged from Denfert Rochereau."

"But you would not have found them without the project."

"And the project could not have found them without my visions. Do you think I mean to shut you out of this?"

"You did this afternoon," Rhys accused.

"If I had told you what Scarlet and I meant to do, would you have approved? Might you have forewarned Monsieur Montfort?"

"I would not have approved," he hedged. "And perhaps…."

I folded my arms. "Then do not pretend confusion that we did not tell you. You are not my keeper." But that sounded…harsh. I am unused to worrying about such things, but with him, I suddenly did. So I hitched myself across the floor to sit beside him. "I have no intention of shutting you out of any findings. You or the project. But I cannot, *will not* report every step I take. So should we not find the treasure first?"

My gut clenched at his darkening, searching disapproval.

"Not to *keep* it!" I exclaimed, haunted again by that damned stolen chalice. "But how can I tell if it goes to a museum, or to the Sorbonne, or to the government of France, until we even know what it is? Do you already have plans for the disposal of the Holy Grail, should you ever find it?"

"This is not about the Holy Grail."

"No. This is about something the Marians needed to keep secret so badly, they risked their lives, perhaps *lost* their lives, because of it. Lisse Clairon escaped the city under a cartload of headless corpses to preserve it. It would be a betrayal of her, of all of them, to spread their secrets without at least seeing what they are. And if you cannot understand even that, or why I must protect that, then to hell with you."

And I began to stand, so I would not have to face that by his beliefs, I likely helped him to hell each time we lay together. But not by *my* beliefs. Not by *my* morals. And I did have them, damn it. Or some close approximation—

His hand, closing around mine, stopped me before I found my feet and pulled me back down, onto him, so that I found myself sitting across his lap. His blue eyes searched my face. Then he said, solemnly, "Does Lisse Clairon name this town, where she hid her treasure?"

"Yes," I said coolly. "She gives directions, of a sort."

"And how do you plan to go about finding the treasure?"

I narrowed my eyes. "I'll decide that when I get there."

He considered that, and I fought the urge to curl into him, to kiss the long line of his throat or his stubbly jaw, to reach into his shirt. I almost wanted…

Well, I would never have his approval. But I wanted his partnership, instead of just his sexual capitulation.

"Then I will drive you," he declared. "Tomorrow." And he slid me off his lap with a solid thump.

"Don't think you can dissuade me from doing whatever I have to do," I warned him, both annoyed and impressed.

"Do not think you can overcome my objections so

easily," he warned back. Thus our lines were drawn in the figurative sand.

But the sex that night was incredible.

I never trust anything when it happens too easily.

The car Rhys borrowed to drive us to the Languedoc was a tiny, three-door Citroën Saxo VTR. It had clearly seen better days, but it ran, so I did not complain. We could have taken the train south, and more quickly—the drive would take us about seven hours, as opposed to the train's five—but once we arrived? Wandering the countryside, seeking the remains of a 300-year-old farmhouse would require more flexible transportation.

We listened to the radio, played silly counting games and talked of Scarlet's obsession with solar flares—the reason she was not with us. We spoke of the Langue-doc's connection to the legends of the Holy Grail, and the region's history of rebellion against the Catholic Church. Rhys's sympathy for the heretics surprised me. I napped. He sang with the music.

May I tell you a secret? It should have felt painfully bourgeois. It did not. It felt...*delightfully* bourgeois. Comfortable. And rather frightening. I am not the sort of person who belongs in such a relationship. The more time I spent with this man, the deeper the wound when we faced that eventuality.

But why not enjoy him until then?

By eating *en route* and making only brief rest stops, we found the tiny town of Lys, amidst the rugged hills of the Aude, in the mid-afternoon. Lys offered only a handful of shops and a one-day-weekly open market—

or so explained the clerk we asked at *la Poste,* the business center of the village. When I shared what directions I'd gleaned from Lisse Clairon's 1794 letters—without disclosing my source—he said he thought he knew the place.

"It still stands?" I breathed. See what I mean? *Too easy.*

"It is for sale," he added hopefully, not so great a coincidence. France, like much of modern Europe, has become increasingly urban. "Are you in the market for a country home?"

I opened my mouth to deny it—but Rhys intercepted me. "We would not mind looking. Do you know where we can get a key?"

Wait…I thought I was supposed to be the devious one.

As it turned out, the postal clerk was also the town's *notaire* and the closest thing to a local real estate agent. After making a photocopy of our driver's licenses and Rhys's passport, he sent us off with the keys.

"If we are closed by the time you return, drop them through the mail slot," he suggested, and wagged a warning finger. "Do not forget. I know how to find you now."

Rhys finally responded to my questioning stare only after we were in the Saxo and out of town, driving slowly up a winding roadway and watching for an unpaved side road *just after the rowan tree beside the old well.* "What is wrong?"

"How do you get people to trust you like that?"

He shrugged. "The house is likely empty," he reminded me. "We have no reason to harm it. And what might we steal?"

Then we both remembered what *I* might steal—if any treasure remained to find—and fell silent again. Rhys needed to concentrate on the driving, at any rate, especially after we turned onto the track past the rowan tree, a tumble of rocks indicating what might have once been a well.

The landscape of this region was rocky, tucked in the foothills of the Pyrenees with a promise of the Mediterranean in the openness to the near south. The little car lurched awkwardly from side to side as it climbed, and struggled for traction at two points. But eventually, we rounded a long, hilly curve....

And there it sprawled in an overgrown hollow, a good-sized eighteenth-century farmhouse, as if it had been waiting for us. *For me.*

I tried to shake off the sensation, but I could not.

The house was blocky, built from the golden stone of that region and capped with a high-sloping, red-tiled roof. The dormer windows upstairs, shuttered like those below, rested in that steep roof. Around the house, past a few faded, red-and-gold outbuildings in disrepair, curved enough overgrown fields to have once supported a single farming family, and a tangled grove of what looked like fruit trees. Beyond that rose rocky hills, as if to cradle the place in the stony arms of the earth.

Home, I thought. But what I said was, "She walked. From Paris. Pushing a manure cart. It took her months."

Reminding myself of Lisse Clairon helped. The homecoming I felt, like the visions, was not likely my own.

"Shall we?" asked Rhys, unfolding himself from the car.

I put my fear into words. "This is too easy."

"How?" He headed to the heavy front door framed by stone.

"The directions were clear, the house stands empty."

Rhys looked over his shoulder with an odd sort of half grin. "Does something have to be difficult to be real?"

Oui. It did. But I didn't want him to be the first one into the house, so I hurried to catch up. These locks, at least, were the twentieth-century kind. I had no particular fear of another vision as we pushed the door open together.

And in fact, no vision overtook me. The only images of the past affecting me were the ones that came from standing in a truly old building. Attempts to modernize the place—some unfortunate 1970s wallpaper, for example—had done the farmhouse no favors. But her bones...

The house had strong bones, even yet. Huge beams from trees already a century old when they were felled three centuries earlier. Cracking plaster that had been painted and repainted over the years—I could imagine an anxious husband, working to please his wife. A heavy mantel over the main fireplace—when I drew my fingers beneath it, they came away sooty. I could picture an ancient homemaker, disapproving of such neglect.

I'd headed for the wooden stairway upstairs when Rhys broke the spell. "Didn't you say the hiding place was in the cellar?"

Yes, I had. Finishing our walk-through of the downstairs in its poorly modernized kitchen, we had to concede that the entry to the cellar wasn't inside. That, and who would mount fake-veneer, overhead cabinets on an eighteenth-century kitchen wall? *Who?*

We headed back out into the spring sunshine, particularly mild so far south, and walked the perimeter of the building to the sound of bees and birdsong. And there they sat, double doors laid into the earth, painted a faded red to match the roof and shutters. A padlock fastened them.

"Merde," I murmured. It was unlikely that the clerk had given us a key—but Rhys tried one from the key ring he carried, and it slid right in.

I felt myself grow nervous again. *Too easy…*

The lock clicked open, and with a great heave and a muffled thud, Rhys swung open one of the two cellar doors and then, for light, the other. A cool scent of earth wafted up from below, with the fading memory of onions, potatoes, coal…. The past. Generations of the past.

"I'll go get the flashlight," he said, and strode away.

Me, I looked at the wooden steps that lead into the void—as much a steeply angled ladder as a stairway. More ladders. I thought of Isabeau, facing the guillotine, and Manon, beaten by a guard as she bought extra time, and of Lisse, smuggling herself out of Paris amidst corpses. And I had to find out now.

I stepped onto the first step. Then the next.

The third step was the one that broke beneath me. Yet again, I plummeted into darkness.

Chapter 15

This time, I landed on my feet. See? Too damned easy.

Rhys got back with the flashlight, saw where I was, tossed it to me and went for a rope. Before he'd returned, I'd quickly glanced around the cellar and found…nothing. Once whitewashed walls. Bits of leaf litter in the corners. Stone floor.

Once Rhys joined me, I did what I knew I must.

I unsealed the plastic bag in which I'd stashed the largest key yet, the one I found with Lisse Clairon's letters. I braced myself and rolled it into my hand—

Alinor's clever invention keeps the weight from crushing her, but not from pressing her breath away. Cold numbs her fingers, despite the insulation of straw—and flesh. She imagines the smell of these bodies, this blood, in the summer's heat….

A slide. A thud. A crowd cheers its approval. It has been like this all day. Soon, another weight is flung atop her, pressing her down even harder. She hears the hollow thunk of someone's detached skull hitting one of the rails of the cart.

She vomits again in the close space beneath her, her face already sticky from the sickness and tears and blood of a day in hell. If this is not the end of the world, she cannot imagine what would be. But she must do anything she can to prevent it.

Assuming the legends are true. Assuming, when the stars align, they will have that chance. If not—

The crowd resumes its calling and taunting. Another victim being led to the scaffold...

"Catrina, stop it!" Rhys snatched the key from my hand, shaking me from this latest trance. "What are you doing?"

The mouthful of breath that I gasped into my starved lungs...it tasted like heaven. And dirt. And the memory of onions. I was safe in this gentle cellar, lit by a wash of sunlight through the overhead door and single flash-light on the ground. I lived.

I reached for the key.

Rhys took a step back and held it high, as he had my black dress. "Not until you talk to me!"

"I was sensing memories off the key," I admitted—he should know this. "Scarlet calls it telemetry. As for what I do during the vision, you tell me. Do I talk to myself? Do I...?"

My blinks felt sticky. A dash of my hand gave me at least one hint of what had happened during this vision, and it startled me. *Tears*. But I never cry out loud. "Do I make noise?"

"Nothing that drastic," Rhys assured me, wiping the tears away with a gentle thumb—but still holding the key out of my reach. "You began to weep, so I took it."

"It happened that quickly?" It had felt endless.

He nodded, so I described my vision. "It makes no sense. These visions, flashbacks…usually I see the last thing the person saw while holding the item." But I didn't always, did I? "Or…the most powerful thing they experienced. *Merde!*"

Rhys waited patiently—one hand, and the key, held high.

"I thought I could hold the key and see where Lisse was when she secured the lock. If I cannot…"

The cellar seemed to mock me. *No treasure here…*.

Slowly, Rhys lowered his hand. "Perhaps if you… ask?"

It was worth a try, so I took the key from him. I felt Rhys's arms surround me as I tried to whisper, "The treasure…"

Gui pulls the woman from the blood-encrusted hay. She falls into his arms, a howl of anguish tearing from her tight throat—

"The treasure," Rhys whispered from somewhere behind me.

She creeps out to the mass grave under the cover of night and digs. Amidst the carnage—dirt-encrusted hands reaching out as if in appeal, dirt-packed mouths open in silent screams—she sometimes finds a package. She secrets each one back to—

"The treasure," Rhys repeated, more firmly.

She smears manure over herself, to keep officials at a distance…. She walks until her feet bleed…. Reaching Lys, she bathes herself, then each tightly wrapped treasure in a spring…

Did Rhys ask something? "Not yet," I whispered, "not yet."

Leaving the now-clean parcels, she prays that they remain safe until the time of transition arrives. She backs out of a tiny room into a larger cellar. She pushes the door shut, fastens the lock she'd brought with her, turns the key with a firm click. "We must plaster over—"

I opened my eyes to point—and found myself sitting on the ground, between Rhys's legs as he held me. It took far more strength than I'd expected to lift my hand. "There."

"Here," Rhys echoed, gently propping my strangely exhausted body against the wall to go look at the spot. "You're certain?"

"We need something to break the plaster away."

Again he left, returning with a toolbox, a tire iron and a box of juice, which he handed to me. "If this does not help, I am taking you to the nearest hospital."

Heaven only knew how far that was from this out-of-the-way place. He waited for me to drink it, too, despite my impatience.

What would I have done without Rhys, I mused, taking several swallows. Then I realized with a sudden, sinking feeling that this, *this* was why the day's treasure hunt had gone so smoothly. Rhys had access to a car. Rhys navigated well. How would I have pulled myself from Lisse's awful memories? Would I have even gotten inside? I doubted I would have been able to convince the *poste* clerk of my innocent intentions, as Rhys had.

Because my intentions were not wholly innocent. Were they?

Justified, yes. After all that Isabeau and Manon and Lisse had been through, how could I not reclaim their secret treasure? My actions were even necessary. But innocent...?

"I am fine," I insisted, finishing the juice despite my now sour stomach and extending a hand for Rhys to take, to help me up. I tried not to think of the last few generations who had lived here before the old farmhouse was finally abandoned to the real-estate market. The quiet grandmother—the kind I had always wished I had—who cooked three meals every day. The stooped grandfather who would have hobbled down these stairs for coal in the winter. They would not mind their descendants moving on in the end. Such was progress. And yet their home...

"Here, then?" asked Rhys, patting his hand on the wall where I had indicated, then lifting the tire iron.

I nodded, the sour feeling inside me increasing—and felt somehow shocked when he swung the iron bar. Plaster crumbled from where he'd struck, in blatant destruction, and he did it again, then again. "Wood," he said. "Instead of earth. And—" He clunked on the wood he'd found. "It is hollow."

Too damned easy by far. And yet, to judge by the way my throat closed, this was not easy at all. But the *Soeurs de Marie* were counting on me, sentimentality be damned, so I pointed. "The lock would be over there."

Rhys swung the bar again, two-handed, his shoulders flexing beneath his T-shirt, and more plaster crumbled to his feet. Clouds of white billowed like ghosts into the shadowy cellar.

When he stopped, I realized I'd backed away and stood pressed against the opposite wall, juice box hanging forgotten in my hand. And not because of fear of what we would find. I had been with Lisse—had *been* Lisse—as she smuggled her treasure from Paris. Despite the ranting of that strange man who'd broken into my flat, I knew that the treasure, whether it had monetary value or not, was something positive, something good.

And yet the sight of Rhys tearing down someone else's wall—

"There's something wrapped in what could be leather," he told me, letting the tire iron fall at last. "Something about the shape of a large padlock. My God, Catrina...."

It was one thing for *me* to waltz in here and take what we found. But, hypocritical or not, I had expected more of him. Perhaps I'd even begun to count on him to be my conscience—my own being nothing very impressive. "Wait," I croaked.

He'd crouched to exchange the tire iron for a camera, in the toolbox, and cocked his head at me. "What's wrong?"

"What do you intend to do if we find nothing?" I asked. "After we've destroyed their wall?" After we'd lessened the building's already miniscule chances of ever selling.

He raised his chin. "I mean to buy supplies, spend the night here and fix the wall. And perhaps a few other things, as long as we're here, as payment for the shelter."

When we'd been asking the clerk about nearby shops, Rhys had included hardware stores. He'd planned that all along. The intensity of my relief surprised me. We could resume our little push-and-pull. I had a safety net, after all. And yet...

I braced myself for the greater argument. "And if we do find something? A treasure?"

Rhys stood without the camera, his hands free as if for battle. "I would make you report it to whoever owns the home."

"Make me," I echoed, annoyance stirring. Like he'd tried to make me go to my grandmother's funeral. Then again, I was just as glad I went. I'd liked not being a disappointment for once.

"Or report it myself. Perhaps you had a point about the Hotel du Montfort," Rhys admitted grudgingly, and folded his arms. "Although I still think you could have erred on the side of respecting the current owners. You're right that the Marians never meant Montforts to have those letters. But this—whatever is locked in here. One cannot build a secret room off the cellar without being noticed. The owners agreed to this. The owners risked treason to hide it. And I suspect the women who hid it here *hoped* for its eventual retrieval, in better times."

"But if we tell the owners, they will claim it."

Rhys nodded. "Yes, they probably will."

"And we have no control over what they do with it." I had seen antiquities mishandled too often. I had given up my summers to volunteer on archeological digs, in part to help protect whatever was found there. I had stolen a medieval chalice from the professor I once revered like a true grandmother, because I did not trust her to protect it. And now, after all the *Soeurs de Marie* had gone through, to just let go… "I cannot do that."

Rhys said, "It's mid-afternoon. There may yet be a store still open. We can start plastering over it now."

"You know I won't do that either. We have to see."

"Then I have to tell. Assuming we find anything of value." Rhys spread his arms now, as if to show his helplessness against the obligation. "Accept it, Cat. I know you won't murder me to keep me quiet. Your ethics may be situational, but…please."

At least he trusted me *that* much. But if I did not act to resolve this, I would explode. A woman can only handle so many earthquakes, cave-ins, flashfloods, be-headings, break-ins and escapes in bloody carrion wagons before she loses it.

And then it occurred to me. The solution. It was crazy— but no more crazy than smuggling oneself out of a closed city in a carrion wagon. "Where are the car keys?" I asked.

"In the car," said my trusting lover. And, considering how out of the way this place was, I supposed I could not blame him.

"Wait here," I said, and scrambled up the stairs, hauling myself over the broken rung.

"Catrina?" Rhys called from behind and below me.

But I was already hurrying to the Saxo. If I moved fast enough, perhaps I could outrun my own good sense.

And, in fact, I did.

By the time I drove back up the rutted drive, the afternoon light had stretched long and orange across the fields and the groves and made the stone of the farm-house glow. I was no longer running. I was moving slowly, as if in shock.

Which I suppose I was.

I almost stumbled on the missing rung, as I descended back into the cellar. Rhys called, "Be careful!" and moved to catch me, but I caught myself.

He still lifted me off the last of the stairs. "Look," he invited. And I did.

He had cleared away all the plaster around what was clearly a narrow, wooden door, and he'd cut the leather wrappings off a large iron padlock. It looked nicely oiled now. I knew Rhys well enough to assume that he'd taken copious photographs first.

"I waited for you," he said—and pressed the key back into my hand. I felt so unnerved, I did not even experience a memory flash off it; perhaps because he'd been holding it all this time. He'd taken the key from me after those last visions.

He could have gone through the door at any time.

My eyes burned with my sudden appreciation of just how quietly kind this man could be. "Thank you."

"So…" He ran a dusty white hand through his dust-streaked black hair and watched me, expectant. "Did you find out who owns the house? I assume that is what you went to ask about."

"A bank," I admitted. "The heirs gave it up almost ten years ago, so a bank took over the taxes."

Rhys said, "Banks are owned by people, Catrina. Everything that a bank suffers, its customers suffer, and they—"

I covered his mouth with my hand, to stop further lectures.

He turned his head away from my fingers, unwilling to let me silence him that easily. "What I mean to say is, I still have to tell the owners what we find," he warned me gently.

"A bank took over the taxes," I repeated. "So I am buying the farmhouse from the bank."

Then I went to the lock, inserted the key, and turned it.

"You—" Rhys could not seem to finish a sentence. "I mean—"

But he fell quiet as I removed the big iron lock and pushed on the door. Rhys had cleared the plaster out from around it, but I felt his tall warmth as he moved behind me to push.

With a hesitation, then a scraping noise—and more plaster dust—the door swung open into a small room, the size of a large closet. In what lingered of the sunlight, we could make out leather-wrapped bundles lying on the dirt floor.

In a moment, Rhys was back with the camera, flashlight and measuring tape. We began measuring, noting, capturing the pieces, one at a time. There were five of them in all.

Only once we'd assuaged our conscience as historians did I kneel by a larger package, like a child on Christmas morning, and carefully cut the thong tying it together, to preserve the knot. The leather had hardened, but I managed to fold it back, and folds of protective material beneath, to finally reveal…

A statue of a Black Madonna, carved out of what

appeared to be jet. She was beautiful, with sweeping lines and a strong, gentle expression. She held a child in her arms, as Madonnas generally do. But she wore a sword on one hip and held a key in her hand. A jug or jar of some sort sat by her feet.

Restore the Black Madonna. But not just any Black Madonna.

Rhys and I said nothing as I opened the next package. It held a triptych, a folded carving of three panels, about the size of a large book, popular in the Middle Ages. This one, seemingly carved from ebony, showed the Lady wielding the sword in one scene, pouring liquid from the jug in another, and offering the key in the third—and in each, holding a child.

The workmanship was exquisite, especially for the medieval period, which had not valued realistic representations.

The largest package was rectangular. When I opened that, I saw it held not one item but seven, each laid atop the other. There were two paintings, one circa the early 1700s and one from even earlier, of the Black Madonna. There were two tapestries—true, woven tapestries—of the same subject. And hidden beneath those lay three hand-embroidered panels. In each of them, the Lady held keys or swords or both. In each of them, she stood near the jug, or poured from it. In each of them, she held a child. Or should I say, the Child?

"Open the other two," I whispered to Rhys, who'd been snapping photographs of the whole process. "Please."

"But this is your discovery. You—"

"No." My gaze caressing the last embroidery—the clear work of a woman's hand, and beloved work it must have been—and I shook my head. "These are more than I could have asked for."

So Rhys unwrapped a second statuette, far smaller, and a diptych—which, of course, consisted of two panels. He stared at that one for a long time, on his knees as I was. His stillness finally drew my attention away from the embroideries long enough to see that it showed the Black Madonna offering water—I assumed—from her jar to a small crowd, male and female alike.

"Like the Grail," Rhys explained, with the briefest of glances toward me, before his gaze returned to the diptych.

This was treasure, all right. I could not imagine what it was worth monetarily—a great deal—and hardly cared. Each piece was artistically exquisite. But its historical value? Even more than the two eighteenth-century medals, these proved a lost version of the Black Madonna, in enough mediums to establish significant presence at least among a limited cult of women and certainly across several hundred years. What had she stood for? How large had her cult been? Why had she been lost? This would send tremors through the scholastic community for years to come. Assuming they ever learned of it. *Should they?*

How could I keep it from them?

By the time we'd emerged from the fog of amazement, night had fallen. Even if Rhys drove as far as Toulouse, he might not find a hardware store open. So we had a picnic dinner together—"Our first date," he pointed out, since it was indeed Friday night. We used

what supplies he kept in the borrowed car to start cleaning the farmhouse I suddenly owned, me bemoaning
that I would need a roommate in my Paris flat to afford
two residences, him offering to do repairs in return for
staying here over the summer, to pursue his quest for the
Holy Grail.

When I agreed, and suggested that I might also spend
much of the summer here, Rhys said, "Even better," and
kissed me.

We made love on his sleeping bag, in the cellar. I'd
never felt so happy. *And the earth moved.*

"Did you feel that?" I asked, my hand stilling on his
hard, naked thigh.

"Feel what?" he whispered teasingly, between kisses.
"This? Or perhaps *this*…?" I soon forgot that momen-
tary sensation…until the following morning.

Then, as Rhys was driving away to find supplies to
best pack our Madonnas and to fix my cellar wall, the
Saxo lurched to a gravelly stop. The reverse lights came
on, and he backed up the rutted drive to the farmhouse.
"Catrina!"

I came to the driver's window, thinking he might
want another kiss—but instead, Rhys turned up the radio
newscast so that I could hear. His blue eyes were more
solemn than ever, and I had trouble catching my breath.

A category seven earthquake had hit Chartres, perhaps an hour southeast of Paris, and dozens were feared
dead.

Grimaud listened to the news bulletin and felt…un-
easy. The first earthquake had released the hidden evil.

He'd been there. He'd seen it. The second tremor had meant nothing…had it? But now this. He had done everything the guides asked of him. They were supposed to be omnipotent. How did the evil keep worsening?

Pierre Grimaud stared at the simple, orthodox Mary medal he'd taken from the honey-haired demoness… and he tried desperately to think for himself.

Chapter 16

It took us two days to reach Paris, listening to reports of the disaster the entire drive. Expecting bad traffic into and out of Chartres, Rhys took us the long route through France, looping west near Italy and Switzerland before coming into Paris from the Luxembourg direction. We never left the Madonnas unguarded. Not at rest stops. Not to eat. When we stopped in Lyon to ask the historical society about records of a Lisse Clairon, Rhys stayed with the car. We slept in the Saxo, with the seats leaned back, which disallowed any lovemaking. When we stopped at a small town outside Dijon on Sunday morning, so Rhys could attend mass, I stayed with the car.

Our cell phones would turn on, but the network was saturated, mobiles and landlines alike. So the second stop we made when we reached Paris was Scarlet Ru-bashka's apartment.

Is it wrong that our first stop was the Cluny, to get the Madonnas into a safe? Rhys agreed with it, so I hoped not.

"I'm so glad you're safe!" Scarlet exclaimed, giving us a big double-hug right there in her flat's doorway. "I was afraid you might've been passing Chartres when the quake hit, and that would be awful, but I couldn't reach you, and even if you were safe, I needed you to get in touch with that geophysicist who took you to Le Jules Verne last week so that we can tell him—"

"Wait," I protested, near to laughing myself. "Rhys has to go check on his students." And on Brigitte Taillefer, from whom he'd borrowed the car. But I didn't like mentioning her.

"He'll want to hear, too!" Scarlet insisted with a bounce.

"I'll still want to hear after I know that everyone is accounted for," Rhys insisted. "And after I've seen what sort of manpower the relief efforts need. If I'm not at the apartment tonight," he added to me, "I'll leave a note."

"And if I'm not there, the little madman got me," I teased. When Rhys actually hesitated, I *did* laugh. "I will be fine! If Scarlet does not watch over me, I'll ask one of the Cluny's security guards to walk me home, agreed?"

We both knew I would spend most of my day with our find.

Not wholly convinced, Rhys nevertheless gave in with a nod and then a long, tender kiss. "Until tonight, then," he said, then winced and whispered, "Le Jules Verne?"

"It was anticlimactic," I assured him huskily, loving how concerned he looked and earning another kiss.

"Take care of yourself, Scarlet," he said to our friend.

She didn't wait for him to reach the bottom of the stairs, much less the door, before whistling. "Look at the two of you!"

Until this weekend, that sort of comment would have worried me, like a jinx. Happiness this intense does not usually last, after all. But I was learning to count on Rhys for more than just his conscience, kindness and incredible lovemaking. So instead I smiled and said, "Wait until you hear my news."

Scarlet squealed. "You're getting married!"

Well…that set me back. "No. I don't plan to marry, and Rhys…" Rhys said he didn't plan to, either. Ever. I hoped it was true, because surely he'd choose a different kind of woman. Some of my glow faded. "It's different news."

"Then mine's bigger," she warned. So we spoke at once.

"We found an entire cache of Black Madonnas," I said, while Scarlet announced, "I know what's causing the earthquakes!"

We stared at each other. She was right. Her news was bigger. "The scientists don't yet know, but you do?"

"Well, I have a theory, which is why I need to contact the geophysicist. To run it by him, so he can inform the sort of people who should know. But I can't remember his name."

Instead of giving her his name, I asked, "And what *is* causing the earthquakes?"

Scarlet looked around us, then drew me into her tiny flat and closed the door. She had a lot of plants, folding furniture and many pictures tacked on the wall. I had the impression she moved around a lot. "Solar flares," she announced emphatically.

Sinking onto a metal chair, I waited.

"Solar flares," she insisted. "Don't you remember? That's why I was on Denfert-Rochereau during the first earthquake—I'd gone to the observatory to check out the solar flares."

L'Observatoire de Paris, established in the 1600s, was the oldest working research observatory in the world. "And…?"

"There were also major flares the morning of your date with the geophysicist, when we had that tremor, but I didn't make the connection because, well, you went to dinner, not breakfast. But the electromagnetic effect on earth is strongest in the twenty-four- to thirty-six-hour window after the flares, so it doesn't matter if it's light out. But I noticed when the quake hit Chartres, because that's why I didn't go with you!"

To study the solar flares. I remembered now. "And…?"

Scarlet plopped into another chair. "Solar flares are explosions in the sun's atmosphere. They're superpowerful, like the energy of tens of millions of hydrogen bombs. The big ones mess with the earth—they disrupt communications, cause magnetic disturbances, stuff like that. So far so good?"

I nodded. I'd probably learned this in secondary school.

"Okay. Every eleven years the sun gets extra active— solar flares, sunspots, you name it. That's called the 'solar maximum.' Then it gets quieter, until the 'solar minimum,' and then it increases again. And guess what this year is?"

That wasn't a great challenge. "Year number eleven?"

But she shook her head. "This is year number ten, Catrina! So if there's a connection between the solar flares and the earthquakes, the authorities need to know, because it's just going to get worse over the next year. Especially if that note you got at the hospital was real, and someone's causing them."

"You think someone's causing solar flares?"

Scarlet rolled her eyes. "No, I think someone's *harnessing* the flares to cause the earthquakes! Think about it! The stars and the sun affect the earth all the time. That's the theory behind horoscopes, right? The fact that we're moving from the Age of Pisces into the Age of Aquarius has major, worldwide ramifications, not the least—"

"His name is Léon Chanson," I interrupted, as much to fend off a speech about horoscopes as anything. "But I suspect he's rather busy, just now."

Scarlet sobered. Who could think of what had happened to Chartres without doing so? We hadn't yet heard about the fate of the famous cathedral, another Notre Dame. But the deaths and injuries were already too much. Still…*on purpose?*

"Well," she said. "I suppose there's been a delay between quakes so far. But can you at least leave a message for him? He made a date with you only the day after the Paris earthquake."

She had a point there. Having covered her unlikely

announcement, we moved onto mine, and Scarlet insisted on coming to the Cluny to see for herself. As we walked first to my flat, to check on Tache, and then to the museum, I filled her in on everything. The roadtrip. The farmhouse. The people I'd spoken to about Lisse Clairon, in Lyon. "If we could only find the letters the Marians wrote back to her," I mused.

When I took her to the vault, to show her the Madonnas, she was as awed by them as I had been, as Rhys had been, as the museum director had been. Their wise, gentle eyes. Their curving, feminine forms. Their dark strength. "But…what are you going to do with them now?" she asked, cocking her head at one of the embroideries. "You've decided not to keep them secret?"

Rhys and I had discussed that matter thoroughly on our long drive home. The problem with trying to keep them secret, he'd insisted, was that it would deny our find the protection of the authorities. Were we to rent a storage facility, or hide them in my apartment? And if we did, and something happened to them, what recourse did we have? But if we brought them to the Cluny, they could be safely locked away and, perhaps, displayed. We could establish their provenance, without which their value dropped significantly, and which helped protect them against being fenced, if ever they were stolen. We could have them cataloged by Interpol.

He'd made a good argument—especially since excess secrecy had been one of the things that allowed me to so easily liberate a certain medieval chalice from Brigitte Taillefer and her niece, a year earlier. But the strongest claim had come from the Madonnas themselves, and I made it now.

"Can you imagine denying the world—especially other women—the chance to see these?" I murmured. "I know the *Soeurs de Marie* did, but their time required it. Ours does not."

At least, I certainly hoped it did not.

Dragging ourselves away from the Madonnas, we went to my office so that I could get the telephone number off the card that came with Léon's flowers. This was the second day after the Chartres quake, but it still took me several tries to get through even on my landline. "Hello, Léon," I purred into the phone, when I reached his message. "Thank you for the flowers, they are still quite beautiful. I, too, am sorry for how we left things. Call me as soon as you can, I would very much like to talk to you."

When I hung up, Scarlet was staring. "Wow. If he doesn't call back after that, something's wrong with him."

I did think it more likely to get a response than simply telling him a friend had an astrological theory regarding the earthquakes. But before I could comment, a light knock on my open door caught both our attentions.

A round, bespectacled man with a large moustache nodded at us. He was the man who'd hired me, and whose patience with my spotty schedule of late had been a great help.

"I hope I did not overstep," said Monsieur Gaspard, the museum director. "Joshua Adriano telephoned to ascertain the safety of the museum employees, and those working on your little project at the Sorbonne. He asked specifically about you."

So far, he hadn't overstepped. "I hope he's well," I said, not only to sound polite.

"He is. His father has asked him to help organize a fund-raiser among French patrons of medieval art, for Chartres. Paris seems the logical location for such a benefit, and the Cluny, in recognition of the two cities' medieval significance."

He was right about that as well. Paris and Chartres had a great deal in common, particularly our cathedrals, each named Notre Dame. Each had been completed in the thirteenth century, with similar facades, even similar rose windows. Each had been built on the site of previous churches.

Gaspard continued, "I mentioned that you had come across an amazing discovery."

Ah. This was where he had overstepped.

Still, the opportunity of it outweighed my caution. Word would spread. Why should it not spread first to those who had shown particular support for my work? More important, I remembered what had happened to Joshua's grandfather…Max? I could not ask for guidance from anyone better versed in protecting unconventional antiquities—and their supporters—than an Adriano.

"I appreciate you telling him," I said, as much because it was politic as because it was true. "Better that he hear of the Madonnas from us."

Gaspard glanced at Scarlet, who was doing her best to look unobtrusive, despite her bright pink boots. And matching earrings. Apparently deeming her safe, he turned back to me.

"Catrina," he said—so telling Joshua Adriano had not

been the overstep, either. "Might you consider allowing us to exhibit your Madonnas as the centerpiece of our fund-raiser? As you know, the Virgin of the Pillar is one of the many medieval treasures which may have been damaged by the quake."

Scarlet risked being obtrusive. "The Virgin of the Pillar?"

"A famous Black Madonna," I said softly. I'd known about her, of course—I'd included Chartres among my lengthy list of Black Madonna sites throughout France. But overwhelmed by the threats to Chartres' Notre Dame, and her famous labyrinth, and the loss of human life, it hadn't occurred to me….

"It is one possible theme," said Gaspard, looking anxious.

"Of course I will consider it," I said. He smiled, nodded and moved on to his other duties, and I turned back to Scarlet.

"If Joshua comes to Paris for the fund-raiser, do you think Caleb will come with him?" she asked. "He called me on Friday, did I tell you? There's something about that man…."

Me, I was remembering Joshua's story about his grandfather—and starting to worry. "We need to get Interpol in here, now."

"It's Sunday," she said.

"Then tomorrow. The insurance adjusters, as well. And Scarlet, is there someplace you can load pictures we've taken of the Madonnas, so that they can't be erased? So we can still distribute them if something happens to the originals?"

"I could set up a Web site," she said. "Link it to my blog. We could even let viewers download the pictures, copyright free. But you'd be losing some of the money you might've made granting exclusive rights."

I shook my head. "What matters is that they don't vanish again. The more press they get, and the faster it happens, the less likely that they'll fade right back out of history."

Because as Rhys and I had told his archeology students, history was subjective. These Black Madonnas represented a completely new chapter. And if there really was someone out there who wouldn't want the world to know about them?

We needed to get this new chapter read by as many people as possible, as quickly as possible.

The next two days flew by. I saw very little of Rhys, between his graduate studies, his work on the Denfert-Rochereau project, and his volunteer efforts. He traveled to Chartres itself on Tuesday, with a relief group. When I asked him what he did there, he said, "Whatever they needed."

"I do not like feeling so guilty," I complained after he'd gotten in, dirty and thoroughly exhausted, and helped himself to some wine. But I'd bottomed out my savings and maxed out my credit cards for the down payment on the farmhouse, and I was so busy with both the details of my mortgage and the fast-tracked Black Madonna Charity Exhibit that I felt overwhelmed.

Rhys surprised me by putting down his wine and coming to me. "You already went through one earthquake this month, and a cave-in. And isn't your Madonna event supposed to raise far more money for the victims of the Chartres quake than any one person could give? Let me get cleaned up, and—"

I did not let him get cleaned up. I could not remember anyone ever making me feel better about myself than he just had…and I had one sure way of returning the favor.

It seemed to work, too.

So why, when I woke alone in the middle of the night, did I find Rhys staring out my window and wearing his fallen-angel expression, a glass in his hand, and almost a whole bottle of wine gone? I am embarrassed to admit that I was afraid to ask what was wrong.

Because I was still afraid it was me.

Wednesday morning—the day a representative from Interpol would finally be in to catalog the Madonnas—I also had a phone message from the Lyon historical society. They had tracked down some letters I might find interesting. Only because Scarlet had walked me to work and come in to see if Léon Chanson had returned my call—he had not—did she overhear the message. She volunteered to catch the train down to Lyon for me.

Frustrated not to be pursuing the lead myself, but unwilling to leave the Madonnas in someone else's care during this significant step in their validation, I agreed to let Scarlet go in my place. And just as well. Analise Reisner, an art specialist for Interpol's Cultural Property Division, proved to be a pleasant surprise. After my first impression, that is.

"Pleased to meet you," she said with an American accent and a grin, pumping my hand. She was an athletic woman of above average height, with pale blond hair pulled into a ponytail that did nothing to improve her somewhat harsh, Germanic features. With makeup, she might be striking, but she'd bothered with neither makeup nor, I thought, an iron. Other than our similar age, we could hardly have less in common.

But I was being a professional. "And you," I purred. "I appreciate Interpol responding on such short notice. If we are to unveil these pieces on Saturday night, for the benefit…"

"You'll need to make sure they're protected, sure," she said. "And confirm the provenance, ascertain the pieces were never stolen. Sheesh, after World War Two, there are no guarantees. You'll want to legitimize the whole kit and caboodle. Makes sense. But that's what I'm here for." She patted the heavy satchel over her shoulder, the strap of which did her tweed coat no favors. "Have laptop, will travel."

I took her to the vault, my suede heels tapping a light harmony to her walking boots, and punched in the security code to open the door. When I led her to the tables where we'd laid out the Black Madonnas, she whistled through her teeth, and her hand caught my shoulder. "Holy Mother of God."

"They are beautiful, aren't they?" I asked, suddenly liking her. There was something about this Analise, something unusually…approachable. Like what I felt with Scarlet.

"Beautiful doesn't begin to…wow!" She moved from one piece to the next, not quite touching the smooth cheek of the taller statue, the sweep of skirt on one of the tapestries. "Look at the features! I've always wondered how a culture that could give us the lines of gothic architecture had so much trouble portraying a proportional human figure, but these…"

"How long will this process take?" I asked, drawing a chair nearer for her to work.

She cocked her head and squinted at the work ahead of her, then nodded. "I might be finished by end-of-day, if everything goes well. Assuming I don't keep losing my concentration and just staring at these beauties. First, I'll closely check the pieces to make sure they haven't already been identified—Interpol uses subtle but permanent markings, and you have to know what you're looking for. Then I'll check them against our database of notable artwork, looking for specific details…like this. Any idea what it means?"

She'd noticed the same detail I had on one of the embroideries, a small symbol like two *X*s, framed with a straight line to each side.

"No." I had my suspicions, but it would require more research before I ever breathed a word. "A signature, certainly, but whose…?"

"Even if we don't figure it out today, I can start a search," she assured me. "Don't worry. We'll get a definitive answer one way or another as to whether or not these pieces are cleanly yours. Once these ladies clear the database, I input as much information as possible— full description, known provenance, the reports your experts have provided—and mark them for future identification. After that, you can exhibit them, sell them, anything your heart desires."

I hesitated while she set up her workspace, glad to see that she'd brought the appropriate tools—including cotton gloves—with which to handle the artwork. And it was only because I'd lingered that I saw the Most Wanted notice that came up on her homepage for Interpol, when she turned on the laptop. My stomach dropped. The figure on the top of the list, represented by a police-artist sketch instead of a photograph, looked unnervingly familiar.

No, it was not me. Thank the heavens, it was not me. The name beside it read, "Dr. Ginny Moon," and it listed a whole series of antiquities thefts with which she may have been involved.

It looked like my old friend Aubergine de Lune.

Chapter 17

Well…this was a moral dilemma. It was one thing to suspect that my mysterious friend was an antiquities thief. It was quite another to see her on Interpol's top-ten most wanted list. The gut-punch of seeing that picture, that name—Lune means "moon" in French, of course—held me through the day. It tainted my further visits with Analise "Call me Ana" Reisner and even my phone conversations with the always-charming Joshua Adriano.

Joshua had agreed that the necessity for haste—fundraisers in response to a disaster really should be held while the shock is fresh and the need immediate—might prove useful. Anyone who would hide the existence of these new Madonnas would have little time to plan trouble. And once enough people saw the Madonnas, and enough press covered it, they could no longer be denied, and the most dangerous period—for the Black Madonnas and for me—would have passed. The Cluny was hiring extra guards for the event, and the Adrianos were contributing extra security.

Which would mean what, if Aubrey de Lune arrived?

I told myself that it did not matter. I would not inform on her. She would not steal from me. But I discovered a touch more sympathy for the handful of people who knew about me liberating that chalice the previous year and did not wholly trust *me*.

What I needed was to talk to Rhys. Even without knowing names, he could surely put this into some kind of moral perspective. But by midafternoon, Scarlet telephoned. "Good! You're there," she shouted over the echoing sounds of a train station. "Have you heard from Léon Chanson?"

"No, and I left another message." Either he was too busy to respond—not unlikely—or something may have happened to him.

Or he may not want to speak to me, but…really. Please.

"My train will be in Paris in just over two hours. I'll walk you home, okay? Wait until you hear what I found!"

At least that, and her call from Gare de Lyon when she arrived in Paris, helped distract me from my own discovery about Aubrey de Lune until Scarlet arrived to escort me home.

"I have no idea how they found them so quickly," Scarlet told me as we strolled along the twilight streets of Paris to my flat. She was practically skipping with excitement. "But someone along the way donated their old family correspondence to the historical society, and among them were a whole stack of letters to Lisse Clairon from Isabeau Volland, Alinor Geoffrin and Manon Cannet. Cross-hatched in that purplish brown color that the invisible ink becomes when it's heated. So we know Lisse—or *someone* who knew the secret— read them."

"You brought them with you?" I asked.

"I brought copies," she admitted. "That's why I couldn't catch an earlier train—I was busy copying everything, and making sure it was legible. Wait until you read them! These women were into astrology, just like me. They say things like how they should have known it was too early for 'the world to shift,' that they just have to keep the memory alive until the new age. They mean the Age of Aquarius. Catrina, we're already on the cusp of the Age of Aquarius right now!"

My doubt must have shown on my face, because Scarlet moved ahead of me to walk backward, frowning. "You think that's just something the bohemians thought up in the 1960s, don't you?"

Bohemians like my failure of a mother. "Yes."

"It's not! The idea of ecliptics is ancient." She sighed with exaggerated impatience. "You really should read my blog. It's all there. Ecliptics are periods of somewhere between two and three thousand years, when a particular Zodiac sign affects society. The Age of Gemini, being an air sign and all about communication, hit like seven or eight millennia ago, at about the same time mankind was getting a good handle on languages. The Age of Taurus—the earth moves through these backward from the sun signs—that was all about the earth and matriarchy, and it's when people developed agriculture. The Age of Aries was all about war, very men-in-power. And the Age of Pisces has been about dualism. Right versus wrong, good versus evil, man versus woman—and winners versus losers—without a lot of room for compromise. I think the Marians were the losers, and knew that if they could just hold out for the Age of Aquarius, they'd have a chance to return."

I wasn't sure I bought all of this…but neither was I sure I did not. "So now it's the Age of Aquarius, which means…?"

"Aquarius is all about personal enlightenment, but we aren't there yet. We're in the cusp, an overlapping period. Personal sun-signs last for about thirty days each, and the cusp goes three days in each direction. So for ecliptics, which stay over two thousand years, the cusps…"

"Would cover several centuries," I guessed.

We reached my building, and Scarlet had to face forward again to tackle all the stairs. But she talked over her shoulder. "Here's the other thing that was really interesting—of course you'll be reading it all, but this is the abridged version. Of all the Sisters of Mary, Alinor in particular was into engineering and science. And she discovered a connection between electricity and the 'tesserae,' which I assume…?"

"Are the tiles," I agreed. "One tile is a tessera—"

"I thought so. She calls them 'our sacred tesserae,' and she tells Lisse about her attempts to use the Leyden jar to electrify them, getting different results depending on which way they faced. Catrina, we have just got to try this. You've got the tiles you found at the Hotel du Montfort, right?"

I did, and the extra tile the old man had given me at the Métro station. And it seemed important to her. Neither Scarlet nor I had been great science students, but even we could figure out that instead of a Leyden jar, all we needed to find electrical current was to cut an extension cord in half, strip some of the rubber insulation off the end and plug it in. The exposed part, we used to touch one of the tiles.

Nothing. After we stared at it a moment, Scarlet even reached down and touched the tile, before I could stop her. "It feels nice," she admitted. "Kind of… friendly."

I decided to take her word at it. "Turn it around."

She did, and again I extended the electric wire—

The tile did not move. But Scarlet, standing beyond it, was knocked back into the settee. "Holy cow!" she exclaimed, laughing. So we tried it again, this time putting boxes and cushions behind the tile, instead of her, and they flew back. We tried it with two tiles then. Facing one direction, they did nothing. Tache walked up to them, purring loudly, and I moved her to the safety of the bedroom. But facing the other direction—

Two tiles not only threw the pillows and boxes across the room, but hurled a small table and ashtray, ten feet beyond that, into the wall. Both broke, and they dented the wall.

"We should do all four," Scarlet was saying when the door unlocked. Rhys walked in, looking tired but, tonight, not filthy. He must have had classes today. He punched the security code into the keypad while she called, "Rhys, look at this!"

"Try four in your own flat," I argued, so she took one of the tiles away, leaving only the one again, and rearranged the pillows and boxes. "Or better yet, an empty field somewhere."

"A field with an electrical plug?" She stepped back, but instead of wielding the exposed wire myself, I handed it off to her and reached up for Rhys to draw me to my feet. Then I slid an arm around his long waist, kissed his jaw. "Welcome home."

He was busy frowning at the experiment. "What is this?"

"We found the letters the Marians wrote to Lisse Clairon, in Lyon," Scarlet explained, touching the wire to the tile, front side out. "This is an experiment they did, modernized of course. Look, faced this way, nothing happens."

Rhys was frowning—in concentration? He crouched and reached for it, before Scarlet could turn it around.

"Be careful," I advised. He hadn't seen their powers of destruction yet. "If the energy hits them the other way—"

He looked up, tile in his hand. "Where did you get these?"

"They're Catrina's," Scarlet explained, replacing that tile with another. "You'll want to stand back—"

But I was no longer listening to Scarlet, because I saw the accusation on Rhys's face…and I felt suddenly ill. For a long, horrible moment, I couldn't say anything. Perhaps I'd misread—

But I hadn't.

"You let me report them as stolen," Rhys said, standing, "when you'd taken them yourself?"

He thought these four tiles were the handful we'd initially recovered from the Denfert-Rochereau site. I found my voice, enough to say, "No, they just look similar."

"You just happened to find some of the same general size, shape, coloring and age. What a coincidence!"

Scarlet had finally figured out that something was wrong. She unplugged our mutilated power cord. "She did, Rhys. When she found the letters at the Hotel du Montfort."

I saw the way Rhys's mouth tightened at the word *found*.

"Stole," I said softly. "Right? When I stole the letters from the Hotel du Montfort. Once a thief, always a thief, even with you. That's how you see me."

He shook his head, still scowling. "These look exactly—"

And I slapped him. Not just because he thought I was a thief. Because he'd been living with me, sleeping with me, for over a week, letting me think he'd believed there was something redeemable about me, when in fact all I'd been, all I could have been, was a good lay, after all.

Then I turned and stalked out because otherwise I would either hit him again or start crying, and I was unsure which was worse. The alarm beeped behind me.

"Catrina!" called Rhys. I of course kept going. Beyond him, I heard Scarlet call, "Rhys, I don't know the security code!"

That slowed him down—even in the middle of an

argument, he must have had the presence of mind not to just shout the code back to her. By the time I heard him hurrying down the stairs after me, I was two floors below him. Now he was shouting.

"Catrina! Stop being a bitch and come back here!"

Yes, that was fine incentive. Two more flights of stairs—I was running now—and I reached the street. It would be an overstatement to call it dark, between the streetlights, the traffic and the brightly lit windows of the cafés and shops. But night had fallen. A light drizzle misted everything around me. I headed in the direction that had always brought me the most comfort—the River Seine and what view there might be of Notre Dame. Hopefully my lover would give up.

He did not give up—and he had longer legs. I hadn't quite reached the river when he caught up to me, a hard hand on my shoulder yanking me abruptly back. "Catrina, stop!"

I slapped his hand away. "Do not dare accost me like some—"

"You hit me!" He towered over me, and at last I saw him at full fury—and still judgmental. "Hitting is never appropriate, Catrina, and walking out like that is childish. All I said was—"

"You accused me of stealing the tiles!" The French may have our own reserve, which other cultures do not understand. We may not smile for no reason, or behave as if a stranger is a friend. But we are passionate in more ways than one. And I'd reached my limit. "Not that it would necessarily count as stealing, since I am the one who found the site in the first place!"

"Rationalize it as you may." So he still didn't believe me.

"I did not steal your fucking tiles!" I screamed, spreading my arms for good measure. People on the street began to give us wide berth. "I have actually tried to do the right thing. I even bought the farmhouse, so that I would not be stealing whatever we found beneath it!"

"And paid for it how?" Rhys challenged. "With money you received from selling Maggi Sanger's chalice."

So now he brought up *her,* Brigitte Taillefer's niece— the woman he really loved, who had married another. And I'd been foolish enough to think he'd given up on relationships because of his virgin fiancée, Mary. My eyes burned, and my throat closed with the desperate need not to cry in front of him. I tried to leave again, tried to make for the river. I did not make it half a block before Rhys was pacing me. "It was not your money, Catrina, so it really isn't your farmhouse."

Nice of him to say that *now*. I wheeled on him. "First of all, I do not know what happened to the two million dollars your beloved Maggi spent on the chalice—I only got twenty thousand."

"Only?" laughed Rhys, but it was an ugly, accusing laugh.

"And do you know what I did with that? I used it to keep my bitch of a grandmother in a private nursing home! That was only a year or so after thousands of elderly people died in that heat wave, because of insufficient attention in the state-run homes, don't you remember? Despite that *Grand-mère* made me feel exactly as misdirected and immoral and worthless as you always make me feel, I did not want to see the old bat die that way, so I spent the money first to move her up on the waiting list, and then for the residence itself, and by the time she went into the hospital two months ago, I'd already broken into my retirement savings, that is how expensive it was! Yes, I feel bad about taking money from your friends, now that I know they are the ones it came from! But I did not know until a week ago, and in any case your precious Maggi was dating a billionaire with so much money he was able to buy my tapestry, *my unicorn tapestry,* out from under the Cluny and donate it to the Cloisters in New York as revenge. So *put things into a little perspective!*"

I expected Rhys to judge me further—perhaps say that it had not technically been my tapestry the Cluny lost, just one we'd had first claim to, one I had loved. Perhaps he'd say that, by spending my ill-gotten gains first, I'd forfeited my retirement savings and the debt I'd just acquired for the farmhouse.

Instead he said, "I make you feel worthless?"

"Is that not how you see me? Why else would you immediately think the worst of someone you've made love to, someone…"

But then I saw something even worse in his dark-fringed blue eyes than accusation. I saw—and felt—dawning horror.

"That's *why* you've been willing to sleep with me," I realized out loud, my voice shaking from more than the spring rain. "Because on some level you *do* think the worst of me."

"No," protested Rhys. But he could convince neither of us.

"Yes. Your morality took a blow when you left the priesthood. You've been rebelling ever since—smoking, drinking too much, and now the sex. But your ethics never once allowed you to harm someone else, even so. Just yourself. You've only ever meant to punish yourself."

"That is ridiculous." But now *his* voice was uneven.

"You do still believe in it. You still attend mass. You refuse communion when you're in a state of sin, despite the fact that more Catholics than not ignore that little rule." If I'd not seen his eyes as I said this, it *would* have seemed too ridiculous to imagine. But I watched his eyes, eyes I'd seen naked before, and I was right. "You have been using me to commit spiritual suicide, because I was safe. I was already damned."

That, he protested. "*No,* Catrina. Of course you're not—"

But I'd had enough, and I turned away. "Leave me alone."

He caught my shoulder, and though he was far more gentle this time, I still struck his hand away as hard as I could.

"*Leave me alone!*" I held his gaze. "No means no, remember?"

Then I left, finally on my own…the way I was apparently meant to be. I fought tears with all my strength and ended up feeling lost, instead. Against all good sense, I'd started to let myself love him, come to count on him for far too much. And now that he'd fallen, it felt as devastating as losing not just a lover, but…a saint.

I dodged traffic across the boulevard that fronted the Seine, then took the damp steps that angled the stone banks of the river to one of the walkways below, walk- ways so close to the water that they often flood when the river rises. Down here, I could watch the lights of Notre Dame, faint through the falling mist and wonder how I'd ever been so stupid as to believe.

Finally I sighed, fairly certain I could contain my tears for a while longer, anyway. "You might as well come out."

"You said for me to leave you alone." But Rhys came out from the shadows under the bridge behind me, its stone arch gracefully shadowing the walkway and river both. When I stared, he added, "I did not want to leave you unprotected, so late—"

But he cut off when the small, dark man stepped out from behind him and pressed a pistol barrel against Rhys's neck.

Chapter 18

"Get under the bridge," my stalker insisted. "*Now*."

"No," I said—only partly because Rhys had risked a faint, negative shake to his head. He did not want to be used for leverage any more than did I.

"I won't just shoot the two of you," he warned. "I'll finish the clip across the river if I have to."

A quick glance showed me a cluster of teenagers in matching shirts, perhaps on a field trip—spring break? They ignored the wet, laughing and pushing at each other, taking pictures…

Someone who was sane would never go through with it. But I'd stared into this madman's eyes, smelled his breath on my face. He was not sane—and more than likely he was angry about the horribly scabbed-over wound marring his cheek, and the one on his neck, where I'd nailed him with my high heels the other week. I obediently stepped into the shadows under the wide arch of the bridge and hoped no other innocents would come upon us. A nice gendarme, yes. Soldiers on leave. Not an innocent.

"I've been thinking about this," the gunman mused. "For myself. I've decided that there's good and there's evil, and evil must be destroyed, no matter what my guides say."

"But why do you think I am evil?" I asked.

He laughed, as if at a joke. "Because you're the one who released them. You're the one who brought their heresy back to the world. Besides, you are a woman. Original sin was Eve's fault, you know. Women ruin everything."

If Scarlet needed more proof of her either/or, Age-of-Pisces thinking, she need not look farther than this guy. "Even if I'm evil, this man is not. He—"

"Shut up!" His arm flexed as he pushed the gun barrel harder against Rhys's neck. I saw Rhys wince slightly. "Kneel. I want you to kneel, submissive for once. *Do it!*"

Which was when Rhys made his move. Using his height advantage, he shouldered our attacker aside, grabbed his arm and tried to wrestle the gun away. "Catrina, run!"

I backed away only two steps before I saw the gunman knee Rhys below the belt, then slam the butt of the pistol into his head. If I had run, it would have bought me enough time to clear the stairs, out of immediate range. Instead, unable to leave Rhys, I saw him fall—and I flew at the bastard. I caught his wrist, bit deep into his gun hand, stomped his foot and scratched four deep furrows down his face with my bared claws. I tried to hit him in the crotch, the way he'd gotten Rhys, who was groaning. That part proved more difficult than I'd expected.

Suddenly, I found myself with the gun barrel hard under my chin, and the madman's arm tight around my throat. He felt hot and sweaty against me, and he smelled of oily metal, and he was in control now. *Merde.* I'd hoped I could fight better than that.

Rhys, trying to push himself up into a sitting position, was looking judgmentally at me again. As if he had more of a right to risk his life than I did to risk mine.

"Stay there," warned my stalker. I felt his hand on the pistol tremble as his finger tightened on the trigger. "You cannot get to me before I shoot her."

"But I've got a fair chance of taking you down as you do it," Rhys half grunted. That kind of blow really does take it out of men, doesn't it? I wondered if he was bluffing, or if he'd suddenly become less of a pacifist. "And if you miss, she will most certainly finish the job."

"I won't miss," the gunman assured us. "God is on my side."

"Bullshit," I said. "God is on *his* side. He's a priest."

"Catrina," chided Rhys, who really did need to learn to prioritize. But I was the one with the gun barrel crowding my tonsils from the outside. I felt my attacker hesitate.

Not enough for me to risk trying to throw both of us into the river. *Not yet.* Beyond the bridge, mist turned to rain.

"Certainly you might consider *me* evil," I continued,

wincing as I swallowed. "You wouldn't be alone there. But Father Pritchard has been, at worst, misled." *Get it, Father Pritchard?*

Spit flew. "You're a liar and a blasphemer!"

"She is not a liar. I am an ordained Catholic priest." Rhys did not add that he'd left his calling. "What you are doing here is a grievous sin. This is not only murder, but suicide. You can't get away. You're destroying your life as well as ours."

"I won't kill you unless you force me. And…and at least I'm giving my life for the greater good!"

Neither of us missed that touch of deference to Rhys.

"If you have any faith at all," I said, hunting for some way to buy more time, "you'll let me give confession first."

"I won't wait for long!"

Startled into action by the unsteady threat, Rhys managed to stand. He crouched by the Seine long enough to scoop water into his hand, whispered something over it and came to me. His eyes, wider than usual, were asking me what to do next. Since I doubted a handful of water would make a difference to someone this unstable, I begged him, with *my* eyes, to go on. *Stall*, I mouthed. It seemed safer than playing chicken with a bullet.

There was no great chance gendarmes or soldiers would stroll up in the rain, but perhaps a tourist with better night vision than sense would notice us and go for help.

Rhys said, *"In nomine Patris, et Filli, et Spiritus Sancti."* In the name of the Father, the Son and the Holy Spirit. The Latin was a nice touch. He drew a little cross on my forehead with a thumb dipped in river water…

which I suspected was now holy. Or, him having left the priesthood...holy-ish?

The gun under my chin was starting to hurt. The chances of knocking it away before it went off hadn't improved. Not yet.

"Bless me, Father, for I have sinned. It has been, um..." Damn. I'd gone to confession only as long as *Grand-mère* could force me, and again sometime in my twenties when, lost after a bad breakup, I'd considered returning to the Church. But...

"Years?" prompted Rhys, with a faint twitch of his lips.

"It has been years since my last confession."

For a moment, all we heard was the rain, the splash of traffic over the bridge above us, and the breath of the gunman beside us. Rhys widened his eyes, prompting me, but I couldn't remember. So he asked, "Do you have any sins to confess?"

"One or two. *Ouch!*" The gun had pressed harder.

"Do not mock the sanctity of the confessional!" warned our attacker. So...his madness had boundaries, did it? At least once in his life, he'd been Catholic. And part of him still believed.

Maybe he wasn't wholly alone, in that. I found a sanctuary of sorts in Rhys's steady, concerned gaze. Sins, huh? "I've doubted God," I confessed, trying to remember what counted. "I've missed more Sunday masses and holy days of obligation than I can count. I've also had carnal relations. Quite a bit."

But of all of that, only one part struck me as an actual sin. "I seduced a man who was pure before I got to him—"

"None of us is especially pure," Rhys interrupted sharply, not missing the fact that I was talking about him.

"Yes, but I certainly didn't help."

"I'm sure…." But a slide of his gaze warned me that Rhys must have seen the gunman's belief in our little ruse weakening, because he let his argument drop. "Anything else?"

"I did steal something, an old cup. Even if I thought I was doing it for a good reason at the time, I was probably mistaken. Oh, and some letters hidden in an old hotel. The hotelier didn't know about them, but I suppose that counts as stealing, too."

"She doesn't sound penitent to me," complained the gunman.

"That is not for us to judge," Rhys snapped, with surprising authority. "Did you mean anyone harm, when you committed those thefts? Were you acting out of greed?"

"I…no." His question, and my admission surprised me. "Though I may have relished my triumph a little too—"

"Let's stick with mortal sins, this man is in a hurry. Have you committed acts of deliberate violence?" Again, Rhys slid his disapproving gaze to the scarred man with the gun under my chin. "Other than in self-defense?"

"Other than self-defense? No." Except for slapping him. But I thought I saw where he was going.

Rhys turned to the gunman. "And you?"

He started, and I swallowed back a whimper. "I… no," he protested. "This is her confession. I don't go to church anymore. The Church became too lenient. Too progressive."

With a look of stern disapproval, the kind a father gives to a disappointing son, Rhys turned back to me and made the sign of the cross. "*Dominus noster Jesus Christus te absolvat—*"

"Wait!" protested the gunman. "You can't absolve her yet. You haven't given her a penance."

"You mean to kill her," Rhys reminded him. "She hardly has time to say her rosary."

"But she hasn't made an act of contrition!" He jabbed the gun again and I winced, mostly from the thought of a bullet exploding through my brain. I readied myself to try knocking him and me off the walkway, into the Seine—

Then Rhys's hand closed, solid, around the gun barrel. "We are hardly in any position to judge her." Slowly, he drew the gun barrel away from my bruised jaw and upward. *He* was upward.

"Father Pritchard," I protested.

"Catrina," he responded, with the same low authority. "Go get help. *In nomine Patris, et Filli, et Spiritus Sancti.*" But this time, he wasn't praying for me. He said that over the now-trembling man, a man who might kill us at any moment. "Please, my son. Tell me your name."

"I…" The gunman's breath caught. "I am called Pierre."

Behind his back, Rhys made a shooing gesture with his free hand—before settling it on Pierre's shoulder. "How long has it been since your last confession? How long have you been lost?"

I backed away, stepping into a wall of rain outside the privacy of our confessional. I reached the stone steps, hating to leave Rhys—who was suggesting Pierre wanted to do the right thing—with a madman who thought guns were right.

"No," I heard Pierre protest, as I started up the steps to street level. "I can't betray the guides…but you're not evil…"

"Don't do that," warned Rhys sharply, and I had to stop. I had to look. Pierre was turning the gun. Rhys shouted, *"No!"*

It fired, a spurt of flame lighting the shadows under the bridge like a camera flash—or a bomb. I screamed, and started back down. But Rhys was moving, unhurt. He stripped off his own shirt to apply pressure, cradling the bloody head of a man with half his face gone—a man who was still trying to talk, blowing bubbles of blood as he did. I thought I heard Pierre slur something about, "Bless me, Father, for I have sinned."

Rhys looked over his shoulder at me, half-naked now, his eyes wild. He didn't need to ask me again. I bolted up the wet stone stairs as fast as I could and went for help.

It wasn't as hard to find a police officer after the gunshot. But somehow I managed to convey that they needed to call an ambulance before dragging them back down to the riverside walkway. *What if Pierre wasn't willing to die alone?* Had Rhys thought to take his gun?

Rhys still knelt with the man who'd tried to kill me more than once, for reasons I might never understand, now. Rhys was drawing a tiny cross with his thumb on what was left of Pierre's bloody forehead, having already closed his remaining eye, and he was saying a long, long prayer in Latin. Despite the number of Amens in it, it went on for a while. *"Per sacrosancta*

humanae reparationis mysteria…." It continued.
"*Amen. Benedicat te omnipotens Deus….*"

He knew it all, I realized as if that should have surprised me. The entire rite of extreme unction. By heart, and in Latin. In so many ways, too many ways, he was still a priest.

I'd been sleeping with a priest.

With a last trinity, Rhys looked slowly up to show the police that he was done. For their part, they'd come close enough to keep watch, several had crossed themselves and one had taken the gun out of the corpse's hand, but otherwise they had waited for this.

I hung back, and not because Rhys had blood on him now.

Once the police drew him away from the body, Rhys turned and slammed his hand, hard, against the stone wall, and swore. I think in Welsh. He looked haunted. I had to go to him.

"What…?" But to ask *what was wrong*, standing beside a bloody body, would be heartless even for me. I was already having to deal with the way my relief, that my stalker would no longer threaten me, warred with my concern for Rhys.

He answered anyway, a gritted, "I can't tell you."

"What do you mean you can't…?" But then, with dawning dismay, I figured it out. "He told you something."

Rhys neither confirmed nor denied it—not with words. But his tortured gaze did it for him.

"If he told you something important in his confession, Rhys, tell me. Tell someone! You already left the priesthood. The confession doesn't count…does it?"

"I told you once before—parts of ordination are permanent. That's why I can give last rites, if necessary. I really did hear his confession and grant him absolution."

"But if he told you something important—"

"Then telling anyone would violate the sacramental seal!" He wanted to tell. I could see that much—if he didn't want to, then he wouldn't be as upset. But Rhys didn't always do what he wanted to do, not anymore. He did what was right.

And that was that. We waited together, leaned against each other for support and warmth, while the police cleared the scene. I looked at Rhys's hand, which didn't seem broken, and made sure the medics did the same before they took the body away. We were brought to the Préfecture de Police, where they found us dry shirts and took our statements.

It was near midnight before we were able to head back to my building. The rain had stopped. But only then did I face facts.

"He's dead now," I said, not quite meeting Rhys's eyes. "I don't need you to bodyguard me anymore. I think…I think tomorrow, you should go back to your own flat."

Rhys caught me under my bruised chin with a gentle finger, urging me to meet his gaze anyway, so at last I did. But I willed him not to make me say it. I *had* been a form of spiritual suicide for him, and I deserved to be more than that. And he was far more of a priest than I'd realized, maybe than he had either. I wasn't angry anymore, not really.

I thought I even still loved him.

But I don't sleep with priests.

Perhaps he could read my concerns in my face. Perhaps not. He merely nodded. "I don't have to wait until tomorrow," he said. "Be careful, Catrina. Please. Try to stay out of danger."

"I will if you will," I whispered. He bent….

And he kissed me on the head. Chaste. Kind. Good-natured.

That was goodbye.

When I got upstairs, Scarlet was still there, waiting for me—and her own brand of furious. "How could you leave me worrying like this? What happened? Did you two make up?"

I shook my head and shivered. The issues that separated me from Rhys, now, went far deeper than a simple fight.

"Oh, honey!" She gave me a big hug—and only then, despite my best efforts, did I begin to cry. We ended up sitting on the settee, me sobbing my makeup off into tissues and onto her shoulder, trying to tell Scarlet everything that had happened. For once, she didn't carry the conversation. She listened, and nodded, and made sympathetic noises, and mostly she held me, and rocked me, and was a friend. A really good, really kind friend.

"At least that crazy man won't be bothering you anymore," she said at long last, her arms around me, her head on my shoulder as mine was on hers. "Am I terrible to be glad for that much, anyway?"

"If so, we can be terrible together. But I don't think it's over. Whatever he told Rhys, it was important enough that Rhys hates not being able to share it."

"Poor Rhys," sighed Scarlet.

"No. No more about him. I can't…"

"Well, then speaking of terrible…" Scarlet hedged.

I leaned back from her, sniffed wetly, and stared. "What?"

"I hate to bring this up, with you being brokenhearted and all, but I think it's important. While you were gone, I got on your computer and tracked down Léon Chanson's Paris address. We need to find him tomorrow, Catrina. Really."

"Why?" I started to ask, but followed her worried expression to the coffee table, where lay my four tiles and the coiled remains of our extension cord. I'd almost forgotten about the Marians' science experiments…but finally, I realized what Scarlet must have figured out some time ago.

"It didn't just have to do with solar flares," I said. "That first earthquake."

"They didn't know why it was so powerful right at the Denfert-Rochereau site," Scarlet agreed. "But the tiles were there, weren't they? Some kind of energy was passed through the tiles, even underground like they were, and they made it worse."

"It can't have anything to do with the Chartres earthquake," I protested, wiping futilely at a mascara stain on the shoulder of her peasant blouse until she pushed my hand away. "How many tiles would be necessary to cause that kind of destruction?"

"I don't know." Scarlet pointed at the dent in my wall. "The energy seemed to increase exponentially with just two."

They were crazy theories, true. But Léon was the only geophysicist I knew. And he'd agreed that there was such a thing as an induced earthquake. So perhaps…

"We'll go to his flat first thing in the morning," I decided. "Leave a note demanding he call us. We can camp there, if we must. Or you could…I'm still working on that benefit…."

"Oh sure. Too busy saving the world to save the world." But Scarlet's laugh managed to draw a weak smile out of me, anyway.

The following morning we did just that—went to Léon's address which, it turned out, was an apartment in the 7th *arrondissement*—which means, the rich part of town. Aristocrats still live along the tree-lined boulevards of this district, as does the prime minister.

"How could a scientist afford this kind of real estate?" asked Scarlet, after we'd used the videophone to request entrance to see Monsieur Chanson.

But as it turned out, he no longer did afford it.

"The man vanished," announced his concierge—polite and reserved, but disgusted all the same. "He left his flat open and empty, with no word. When the month is up, we will re-let. Will that be all?"

"Empty?" echoed Scarlet, disappointed, but I took a page from Rhys's book.

"Could we perhaps see the flat?" I asked, lowering my sunglasses so that he could see the swollen eyes my makeup had not quite disguised. "For…personal reasons?"

Assuming, as I'd hoped he would, that my tears had been for Léon, the concierge made a slight bow and stood back to allow us entry. "If you do not mind the cleaning crew. We do have a waiting list, however."

Just as well. The last thing I needed was more real estate. And even if I were a thief, I doubted I could afford anything like these two stories of splendor.

"No wonder he was able to take me to Le Jules Verne," I murmured to Scarlet, as we looked around the loft-style home. One entire wall was of windows overlooking the street. Another was of windows overlooking the private terrace behind the building. There was modern lighting, a "bathroom" suite off every bedroom, and stainless-steel appliances in the kitchen, where a maid had just finished sweeping up from under the stove and the huge steel refrigerator. Those bits of trash might have fallen off the counters at some point.

I am unsure what drew me to the contents of the maid's dustpan. Perhaps mere curiosity, or perhaps I was coming to sense them. But I said, "A moment, please," and took the bits from her.

Scarlet, looking over my shoulder, gasped.

One of the bits that had been lost in the cracks was a tiny tile, like the Marian tiles. And the rest were nuts, bolts and bits of wire…such as are used in building electrical devices.

Chapter 19

After that discovery, only three things of significance happened before the Black Madonna Benefit for Chartres.

The first is that nobody at the Préfecture de Police believed our concerns about Léon Chanson or the solar flares—which had been active for a week, and promised more activity into the next. A well-dressed gentleman named Carl Montrose, who did not tell us his rank but to whom the police deferred, reminded us that as we were not relatives of the missing man, we were not the ones who ought to file a missing person's notice. Since there was no proof of Léon having committed a crime, the police had no reason to divert manpower to seeking him out.

Also, I thought I overheard one of the officers say, "Ah, so that is Catrina Dauvergne."

But I may have imagined it, just as I might be imagining their increased presence on my street. A lot of good they'd do, if someone had some kind of electrical device, ready to launch a more deadly earthquake than the one in Chartres.

For that and several other reasons, I slept poorly.

The second thing of significance was that I came home on Thursday night to find a small bouquet of violets hanging off my doorknob, with a note: *Wishing you well. Be careful. Love, Rhys.*

They might have been poor contrast to the expensive sprays I'd received last week from Léon Chanson and Joshua Adriano. Yet those, I had left at my office. These I brought inside—as Rhys could have done, since I'd changed neither my locks nor my security code, but he had chosen not to intrude.

The third thing of significance was a gift from Scarlet, on Friday. She and I had stayed in for a quiet night with the Marian letters, eating Italian carry-out and discussing the next night's festivities. The Adriano brothers were coming to town for the benefit, finally getting their double date with us. At first Scarlet could talk of little else than seeing Caleb. Then, after I'd reached the end of the letters and was flipping through them again, wishing there were more, she said, "I have a present for you."

I looked up, honestly confused. "Why?"

She laughed. "Close your eyes."

I peeked, of course—I am not a trusting person. Perhaps expecting as much she hid her surprise between her hands until she'd set it on the coffee table in front of me.

"Open your eyes!" It was a gilt bronze jewelry box

from the eighteenth century with a miniature portrait set into it of a dark-haired young woman, done on porcelain. I began to reach for it, but Scarlet caught my hand. "Look at the bottom!"

Below the picture were engraved the initials, L.C. "Lisse Clairon?" I gasped. "How…?"

"It was in the box with the letters, in Lyon. I bought it from the historical society. I made up a story about you being distantly related—I mean, it *could* be true. If she had two children, and they had two children, and they had two children—"

"And you wanted me to get some kind of impression off of it, right?" I hadn't enjoyed my previous visions, but they'd been useful. And this was only a jewelry box. What horrible images could connect themselves to a jewelry box?

Glad for the distraction from other matters—earthquakes, Rhys, dead stalkers—I took a deep breath, then laid my hand over the box. *Nothing*. At first. Too much time. Too many hands.

I remembered what Rhys had suggested at the farmhouse, and whispered softly, "Show me Lisse."

I closed my eyes—

She spills her jewels onto her vanity table. Every piece of true value from her mother. A necklace from her beloved aunt. Impatient, she scoops all of them into a small bag. She will sell every piece, if it gets her enough gold to bribe her way into Paris and get her friends out. She sets aside only two pieces. One is her Madonna necklace; it would fetch little money and garner suspicion of Catholic leanings. The other

*is a bracelet of cheap glass beads, of even less
monetary value.*

*Her fingers linger on it, and her eyes burn. Gui gave
her that, proudly. A poor laborer, strapping and good-
hearted, he would never have dreamt of such impu-
dence before the Revolution. Early promises of equality
had affected him deeply—but faced with the Terror, he'd
valued basic humanity more.*

*"And so they killed you," she whispers, laying the
bracelet on the letter that tells her so. "But not my sisters."*

I blinked back into my own world, horrified by what
I'd seen. "She went back," I told Scarlet. "She didn't
stay in Lyon. She went back to Paris. Didn't she understand the danger?"

"Lisse doesn't sound like the kind of woman who
cared a lot about danger," Scarlet pointed out.

Once she'd left for the evening, and I'd locked my
three locks and set my alarm, I sat by my window and
I lit a *Gauloise.*

It was my first since the catacombs. Not finding it
anywhere near as satisfying as I'd expected, I stubbed
it out and went to bed.

"Caleb!" Scarlet didn't just call his name—she trilled
it and broke into a run, evening gown and all. Both
Joshua and Caleb Adriano turned toward us, startled.
But Caleb recovered in time to catch Scarlet up when
she threw herself into his arms.

He seemed almost as surprised by his own smile as
he was at finding himself with an armful of Scarlet Rubashka, and he spun her easily in a circle while I caught

up more sedately with his brother. Joshua took my hand and kissed it. Then he turned it and, his hazel gaze holding mine, softly kissed my wrist.

Yes, I thought. *Please do distract me*. But it only tickled.

Still, the night was young—a perfect spring evening for our Black Madonna benefit. Floodlights lit the great medieval gate through which patrons in formalwear— those with invitations, at any rate—passed through the protective wall into the festive courtyard, then the museum itself. The Cluny, which is actually the Musée National du Moyen Âge-Thermes et Hôtel de Cluny, generally closes before 6:00 p.m., but it was not unusual for us to host private events in the evening. For this one, however, our public relations coordinator had outdone herself.

Wine flowed. Crystal sparkled. All twenty-three rooms of the former Abbey Hotel, with its vaulted ceilings and arched windows, were open to be explored by the culturally inclined. Although the underground *thermes*, or ancient Roman baths, required a guide, our very best docents had volunteered to lead groups through.

My hand on Joshua's tuxedoed arm, we made our way to the Notre-Dame de Paris Hall, which displayed works off the great Cathedral herself—decorations and sculptures that had been torn off during Revolution. Particularly disturbing were the heads of the Kings of Judah, statues that had been torn down and beheaded just as the Sisters of Mary had been. An aristocrat had smuggled the heads into his home, where they'd remained hidden until the 1970s. Now, dozens of guests wandered amidst the statuary, or sat at the handful of white-draped tables at the back of the room. To one side, a choir performed pieces by Hildegard von Bingen, the famed twelfth century nun who wrote so much beautiful plainchant, much in praise of the Virgin Mary. Their clear Latin voices echoed off the stone walls like a church at high mass.

It sent shivers through me, even as I remembered my duty to mingle. I was not, thank heavens, the hostess. Not being a people person, I had preferred to do my work in setting up the function and in allowing the event to unveil "my" Madonna relics to press and patrons alike. Neither had Joshua lied about not focusing on his family. I was unsure just how much funding they had contributed for the decorations, the refreshments, the musicians or the extra security, but it had been a great deal.

To borrow an English saying, they'd put their money where their mouths were. But they kept quiet about it.

Still, even without being the center of the event, our respective roles demanded a great deal of socializing. I had to look past the history that surrounded us and, for once, focus on the living instead. Some people I knew from their continued support of the Parisian arts—this included nobility and members of the National Assembly, as well as those patrons who were simply ungodly rich. The usually reclusive Elise Villecourt was there in full grand-dame style, her barely gray hair upswept from a strong face, her expensive gown and diamonds timeless—did that woman never age? She was speaking to the director of the Banque de France and the producer of the film that had won the most recent Palme d'Or at Cannes.

And over in a corner stood Ana Reisner, looking

wholly out of place in a navy suit vaguely reminiscent of Catholic school uniforms. When she smiled in recognition at me and waved—so American—some glimpse of true beauty shone through. She could be handsome, I mused, if she did not work so hard at being ugly.

"Hi, Catrina!" she greeted, coming to my side when I extended a hand of welcome. "This is some swanky party you throw. And look at you! You're a knockout."

"She is, isn't she?" murmured Joshua. Tonight he looked even more tall, dark and handsome. This time, I made the effort to meet him halfway as his gaze slid down my body. I was wearing a sleeveless, jade-green Chanel—probably one of the last designer gowns I would ever buy, even on sale, now that I had a mortgage. The draped neckline looked almost modest in front, until you saw how far the drape plunged in back. I'd accessorized with a collar, bracelet and earrings of gold filigree that I'd purchased once in Portugal—filigree being an excellent way to get the most effect from only a little bit of gold. I wore my hair swept up in a loose twist.

When Joshua used our position against the wall to run his hand discreetly down my bare spine, he was able to start at the very base of my skull, drawing his warm fingers all the way to the curve of my derriere. *Yes*, I thought, with a slight shiver. *If I make the effort, he might get me over Rhys yet.* Get my body over Rhys, anyway. Which was a start.

Since there was absolutely nothing positive I could say about how Ana looked, I tried, "How has your week been?"

Her eyes twinkled. "I've made an intriguing discovery about one of your embroideries, but I want to double-check a few more facts before I get your hopes up. Maybe we can meet about it Monday. Can you believe this music?"

We proceeded to praise the performance, compare the group's CDs of the visionary nun's work and generally enjoy ourselves. Strangely, talking to Ana did not feel like an obligation.

Or, as Scarlet put it when I beckoned her over for introductions, "She *does* feel good, doesn't she? Like we're already friends. Good to meet you, Ana!" She grinned, patented Scarlet. "Or to reunite with you in this lifetime, anyway."

Ana laughed—but Scarlet drew me away from her and Joshua.

"I saw the woman in black," she whispered dramatically.

I blinked at her. Unlike Ana, Scarlet did not look out of place; she'd chosen an art nouveau gown which, on her delicately boned body, gave the impression that she'd stepped out of the 1920s. Even the silver key around her neck looked intentional.

But then she said things like that. "Woman in black…?"

"Haven't I told you about her? Every now and then I see a woman in black watching me. At least, I think it's the same woman. I'll have to show you some of the pictures I've caught of her—I'm very sneaky, but so's she. Most of them aren't especially good, but it's fascinating, all the same."

"Ah," I said.

"Caleb and I tried to intercept her, but she was gone

before we could." She shrugged. "Anyway, we're going to cut out early—this is beautiful and all, but it's time we had a real date instead of a family obligation date, you know?"

The way she held my gaze and raised her eyebrows, quite high, I could not possibly have missed her meaning. But I did not know why she was reporting to me, unless…

"I could have Joshua see me home safe," I assured her.

Scarlet lowered her voice further. "Um, yes. About that. Before we go, Caleb wanted a word with you. In private."

I made my apologies to Ana—who assured me that all she needed to enjoy the night was another glass of wine and no roving men to spoil the music—and to Joshua, who asked me to return as soon as possible and kissed me, to give me extra incentive.

There are some men who kiss so well, you don't have to be in love or even attracted to enjoy it. Joshua had that kind of lingering, practiced kiss. His lips were soft. His mouth tasted amazing. "Please do not leave me alone for too long," he breathed, drawing his hand down my bare arm until our fingertips caught, then parted. "I will be lost without you, Catarina."

Which was just so…Italian. But there's a reason Italians are such popular lovers. Husbands, rarely. Lovers, absolutely.

"Caleb was afraid if he came back through the crowd, we might never reach escape velocity," explained Scarlet, as she drew me across the room—

And that's when I saw Rhys.

Tall. Slim. Glowering. He must have seen the kiss.

I met his gaze with a coolness I did not feel as I swept past. Even when we'd been living together, sleeping together…

It was a mistake, to remember that. I bit the inside of my cheek, to maintain my poise, and tried to notice that he wore his usual, uninspired black suit. Instead, I noticed how good he still looked despite it. I remembered him standing beside me for my *grand-mère's* funeral. And I felt sad, and guilty.

But even when we'd been together, neither of us had spoken of monogamy. And besides, Rhys had Brigitte Taillefer standing beside him, glaring with her own malevolence.

Caleb waited for us in the lit front courtyard, beside the ancient well. "Catrina," he greeted, looking uncomfortable—but Scarlet jabbed him in the side, so he forged on. "I apologize if I overstep, but…you and my brother seem closer, tonight."

"So do you and Scarlet," I pointed out.

"Exactly. I am fond of Scarlet, as she is of you. It gives me concern, but…perhaps my *fratellino* has already told you…?"

"He's married," interrupted Scarlet. "Joshua."

That, I had not expected. In fact, I shook my head, as if to make it not be true. I had higher standards than this.

Scarlet is the one who looked truly sympathetic. Caleb simply appeared uncomfortable as he produced a slim wallet and opened it to a family snapshot— Joshua Adriano, gazing down at a black-haired baby in his arms, while a frail woman with my coloring and large doe eyes gazed helplessly into the camera.

"Her name is Pauline," Caleb explained. "Their son is Benny. She hasn't been well. This is not the first time…."

Scarlet took over. "We're so sorry, Cat. As soon as Caleb mentioned it, I said we had to tell you. Just in case…."

Just in case I planned on bedding Joshua, to get over Rhys? After only a few weeks, my friend knew me better than I'd expected. "Thank you for letting me know," I told them, trying to look at the picture—at Joshua's waif of a wife—again. "Not that it matters, since our relationship is strictly professional, but I appreciate your concerns."

Caleb nodded, and Scarlet looked relieved. But after we said our goodbyes, and they stole away, I felt ill. I did not need earthquakes to shake up my world. Joshua was married.

I felt very, very tired as I turned back to the building—and saw Rhys waiting for me by the door. I wished I could walk past him, pretend he was not there, but he deserved better. Perhaps so did I. So I went to him.

It was too soon. My body was still too familiar with him, and the temptation to put my arms around him—out of recent habit if nothing else—frustrated me. I could not stand another lecture.

I did not expect him to say, "You're beautiful tonight."

It hurt. I knew I did, but to hear him say it only reminded me of what I'd lost. "If that's all…"

"We need to talk." His hand moved, as if to reach for me, but he lowered it again. "I know you're busy, and do not mean to keep you, but Catrina, we really must discuss this."

"This?" I prompted.

"*Us*. I need—" He swallowed, and corrected himself. "I would like to see you again. I would like to repair some of the damage I seem to have done. Please say— please consider letting me take you to dinner soon. There's so much…"

His struggle to avoid demanding anything intrigued me. "We have done equal damage, and the situation has not changed."

"I think it has," he insisted. Then, bolder, he tried, "Don't go home with Adriano after the party."

I raised my eyebrows in challenge. Not that I meant to sleep with Joshua, but he couldn't know that.

"I may have no right to tell you what to do, but I can admit what I want. I can hope we might want some of the same things. Please, Catrina, before you do something that drives us further apart. Give us a chance."

There he went, saying *us* again. Part of me longed to try. Part of me pegged it as the ultimate foolishness— walking right back into the madness.

Rhys stepped closer and brushed his fingers softly over my cheek, his head bent over me like a prayer. "Catrina…"

And what madness.

How I could have noticed anything other than him at that moment, I'm still unsure. At least the courtyard was well lit. I gasped, my gaze focusing on a woman just beyond him, just inside the door. It helped that she lifted a hand, to catch my attention, before she slipped into the shadows beyond.

"Yes," I said. "Fine. Dinner tomorrow night. No sex with Joshua. I've got to go now."

Rhys blinked, understandably doubtful. "What?"

But I didn't have time to reassure him.

I had to go find the antiquities thief who'd just shown up at our Black Madonna benefit.

I followed Aubrey by catching sight of a flip of velvet skirt around a corner, the heel of a black boot descending stone stairs. She waited for me in the underground galleries, in a small, rough-walled niche that hid us from other patrons who might wander by.

She was a petite woman, older than me by anywhere from a few years to an unlikely decade. Her brown hair fell into her eyes in a bohemian manner. Her gown of purple-black velvet, form-fitting except where it flared out in the skirt and under the elbows, with black boots and a large silver necklace, gave her a decidedly youthful, Goth flavor—which she pulled off neatly. When I leaned in to kiss her cheek in cool greeting, I sensed it—the same connection that had eased us into friendship, even back when I'd been at my least friendly. The same connection I felt with Scarlet and, I thought, with Ana.

For some reason, that nebulous bond reminded me of the Sisters of Mary, whose friendship was such that they'd died together—or most of them had. I'd learned no more about Lisse's return to Paris. I wasn't sure I wanted to.

The bond hardly made sense. Aubrey and I were close enough that I would not report her, and she would not steal from me—of that, I felt certain. But dying together seemed overly dramatic.

"They are stunning," Aubrey greeted—presumably of the Black Madonnas. "I had to see for myself. Congratulations."

"Thank you." I hesitated, then asked, "Did you also see the Interpol agent in the great hall upstairs?"

"The frumpy one?" Aubrey smiled. "I expect there's more than her. But I've noticed a few too many familiar faces, here. I shouldn't stay. It's just…" She hesitated, looking concerned, and then admitted, "Something's not right here, Cat. I don't know what, exactly. But the guard outside the retaining wall, where the tunnel used to open into the Roman baths, and the guard just down the hall, where the water was once heated? They aren't to be trusted. I thought you should know."

I wished I could ask how she knew that, and why they weren't to be trusted, but I sensed she was taking a chance just telling me this much. "Okay," I said slowly—and made up my mind. Perhaps this shouldn't be my concern. But it was my museum, damn it. And my Black Madonnas. "Could you perhaps do me another favor, before you head out?"

Aubrey was happy to distract the guard for me. Hanging back, I didn't get a chance to hear what she said after flouncing up to him, but damn, she knew how to work it. The way she shifted her weight made the bell of her lower skirts sway. The way she leaned conspiratorially closer gave him a great view of her cleavage. At first he shook his head, but after Aubrey pressed closer to him, with a coy dip of her head and another shift of more intimate weight, he allowed her to lead him away, around the corner, into deeper shadows.

I pushed quickly through the heavy wooden door before he could return to his post, and passed into the dark tunnels of what had once been Roman plumbing, back when Paris had gone by the name of Lutèce and the bathhouses had been an area of huge social importance. I reached to switch on the light—but nothing happened. I stepped carefully forward, and my foot slipped on something like loose gravel. But that was impossible….

Luckily, I'd last used my tiny, embroidered wrist purse before I'd slowed down on my smoking habit. Inside it were my museum ID, several folded Euro notes, my lipstick…and a cigarette lighter. I flicked the lighter and held the flame high enough to see that the light bulb for the overhead lamp was missing. Then I lowered my hand and, as the pool of flickering golden light reached the floor, I sucked in a breath of slow, horrified recognition.

Dozens of little ceramic tiles, of a familiar shape and feel, had been deliberately arranged across the pitted rock floor, almost directly beneath our exhibit.

And my Black Madonnas.

Chapter 20

I hadn't realized until that moment just how frightened I was of another earthquake. As my mind made the connections between tiles and Scarlet's and my experiments with electricity, and then to the handful found at the Denfert-Rochereau site, I understood what this new discovery might mean…and swayed. The last time had been bad enough, clinging to that tiny iron fence around a sycamore while the world shifted around me and the road in front of me *tore in half*. Fear of what would happen if the energy increased exponentially for each new tile…

"Mon Dieu," I whispered. I began to bend, to pick up the tiles. Remembering how Scarlet had been knocked across the room by only two, I straightened more quickly. It's not as if I had pockets, or enough room in my tiny purse for more than a dozen.

I needed help. So I pushed quickly back into the hallway.

The guard hadn't returned. As I hurried up the stairs and rejoined the main benefit, everything felt distant, surreal. People swept past in their high fashion, flutes of champagne in their hands, the haunting medieval chorus floating across them. Should I be shouting out warnings? Should I try to find our head of security? How much time did we have?

Before even I knew what I intended, I'd found and pulled the fire alarm.

Klaxons began to sound. Lights began to flash from overhead, while a taped voice instructed people, in multiple languages, to calmly leave the building.

Hard hands caught my bare shoulders from behind.

"Catrina, why in God's name—?" Rhys broke off when he saw my face. *He understood I had a reason.* "What's wrong?"

Quickly, over the wailing of the alarm and the shouting of evacuees, pushed close by the crowd, I told him. "We've got to stop the electrical charge," I admitted, desperate. "The tiles will be dangerous until we find the trigger. But I don't—"

"What tiles, Catarina?" demanded another deep voice, and we spun to face Joshua Adriano. To trust, or not to trust?

"Tell him," said Rhys shortly, and strode away. For a moment I thought he was somehow…giving me to Joshua? Then I saw that he'd gone to assist Brigitte Taillefer out the door and, presumably, to a cab. Leaving an old lady alone on a dark street would be almost as bad to him as impending Armageddon.

I also feared that the same sense of honor would bring him right back to me. *And back into danger.*

It took longer to explain matters to Joshua, since he hadn't yet heard of the tiles or their strange properties. He caught on fast. His dark-complected face went white.

"Damn it," he whispered, then repeated it more forcefully. "*Damn it!* You go find the trigger, Catrina. I'll get the tiles."

"What? No, you have to get out."

"The security was our job. *My* job. Now go!" And Joshua pushed past several guards—who were doing their final walk-through before shutting the building down—and down the stairs toward the Roman baths. They would have let few people back in, but he had a certain authority over them. Then Rhys was back—his authority less official, but no less palpable. He took my arm, looking after Adriano.

"He's a good man," he said, as if mildly surprised.

He's married, I almost said. But if anybody knew that morality could be complicated by shades of gray, I suppose it was me. Instead I told Rhys, "I don't know where to start!"

"Out of the noise." Rhys pulled me toward the door. "So you think this trigger is some kind of a pulse bomb?"

Trust a man, even a pacifist, to know the names of all the weapons. As soon as he said it, I knew he was right. We were looking for some kind of high-powered electromagnetic pulse bomb. "That's why your cell phone stopped working," he realized.

"Twice," I reminded him. I'd lost the second one after my date with Léon.

"The same thing happened in Chartres." Rhys scrubbed a hand through his hair, which he'd not managed to tame anyway. "People couldn't call for help."

"It won't be here," I interrupted him. By then we'd crossed the courtyard, lit bright as day. He'd been right. Out from under the worst the Klaxons, I could think better. "I mean, not at the Cluny. When I fell into the Denfert-Rochereau site, there weren't any signs of machinery, and there was no other way out. Wherever it is, he must send the electrical charge from somewhere else."

"Somewhere nearby," Rhys agreed. "For less interference."

"Perhaps underground, to give the energy a straight shot?" Joshua hadn't returned. Vaguely I saw Ana shouting something to our chief of security, and it occurred to me that, had someone else pulled the alarm, this would be the perfect distraction for a thief. *But not Aubrey*, I thought. *And not me.*

What an insane world, that the theft of my Black Madonnas would be the better outcome? But real, living people had to take precedence. Then something clicked. "The Madonnas!"

"Do not dream of going back in after them," Rhys warned. Because kindness and honor didn't make him a pushover.

"There was a Black Madonna at Chartres, too," I reminded him, to clarify. "And there were Madonna medals, with the weird iconography, with the Marian remains."

"You're not suggesting that images of the Virgin Mary carry some kind of destructive power, are you?"

I couldn't tell which annoyed him more—superstitions about even a bastardized form of the Holy Mother, or that her powers might be negative.

"No—the tiles, I can understand. Tiles are made of fired ceramic paste, so heaven only knows what was mixed into them. The Madonnas are all different mediums. But what if there's a connection in the head of whoever's causing the earthquakes? And if they're all about Madonnas…"

The need to do something, anything, pounded like my pulse in my throat. Rhys, picking up on my thoughts as if he knew me or something, added, "Notre Dame was untouched."

"What?" At first I thought he meant our Notre Dame, *the* Notre Dame, mere blocks away on the Île de la Cité. Then I realized he referred to the cathedral by the same name, at Chartres. After days of concern, the historical community had breathed a sigh of relief to learn that the town's famed cathedral, with her statuary and labyrinth, had escaped damage.

Nobody except for the intensely religious, who felt it was God's doing, and new-agers like Scarlet, who believed the major cathedrals had been built on some kind of power points, had thought to ask why.

Now I met Rhys's gaze, both of us putting the last pieces of the puzzle into place at the same time. "Notre Dame," I said.

And we broke into a run. When we emerged by the Seine, the great lady stood as she always had, her spires and towers soaring into the sky, spotlights gracing her aged flanks with dignified illumination. We didn't stop, racing across the bridge under which we'd been held at gunpoint, over the river, and onto the island. Perhaps Notre Dame de Chartres *had* survived by the grace of God. Or perhaps…

Perhaps whoever had launched an electromagnetic pulse through the earthquake-causing tiles—there must have been tiles—had been there.

I'd left my shoes behind by the time we reached the wide square, or *parvis*, that fronted the famous cathedral. Only scattered handfuls of tourists wandered through it, and no street performers remained—the hour was late, and the church was most certainly closed. Rhys had been in the lead until then, his long legs outstripping me, almost dragging me behind him. Now, though, as he hesitated before the majesty of Notre Dame, I moved ahead and began to tow him. "Underground," I reminded him.

Me, I tried not to notice the round *point zero* stone set into the pavement. The name, which innocently refers to the fact that all main road distances in France are calculated to this point, took on an ugly double entendre. Instead, I made for the inconspicuous underground entrance, plain as a small Métro stop. Only a square stone pillar beside it, carved with the legend *Crypte du Parvis*, drew the visitor's eye. It was as we went down the limestone stairs that the more specific name, *Crypte Archéologique*, warned of our descent into history.

I had no idea how to get through the locked glass doors. But as it turned out, the one on the end was unlocked.

"Wait a moment," whispered Rhys, and hurried back up the stairs. I did not want to wait. I had to stop whatever would happen, so I only counted to ten—and by then, he was hurrying back down. "I sent some tourists to fetch the police," he explained. "If only for the break-in."

"They did not believe me when I went to them," I muttered, pushing quietly into the empty, echoing, underground museum.

Rhys whispered, "Nor me."

Many of the cathedral's visitors remain unaware of the treasure that lies beneath its spires and towers, the foundations under the foundations, one might say. Archeological crypts displayed remnants of buildings that had been here first, and second, and third. It is not for the claustrophobic. This is true even when the place is well lit, with bright cases full of ancient cups and jars, displays with maps and interactive buttons, and dioramas of what Paris may once have looked like. The concrete-beamed ceiling seems low over the walkway that surrounds and overlooks the exposed Gallo-Roman ruins and Merovingian foundations. Tonight...

Tonight, Rhys and I crept along by little more than the emergency lighting and the glow from the blue *sortie* signs at the exit. In fact, being together with him, underground, felt ironically familiar.

After the mass graves, catacombs and cellars, couldn't this quest take us somewhere in the open air?

From the pit, we heard a faint beeping noise...like that of a clock or car alarm being set. A glow of artificial light bloomed from beyond the pitted, uneven arch of a former doorway.

Bunching up the skirt of my Chanel gown, I slid over the brass railing, swallowed back my fear of heights and scrambled down onto one of the higher bits of shadowy, ancient wall.

"Catrina!" hissed Rhys in protest, but I was already clambering down. I was glad I'd taken off my high heels. The long skirt, however, was more of a problem than I'd expected.

I heard Rhys's breathing as he followed me down.

I crept along a dark, uneven path between low stone walls, once a hallway where some woman of the Parisii tribe may have carried food or fur coverings, gone to check on her children or drawn her man with her to have sex. The arched doorway was from early medieval times, though—perhaps used by Merovingian kings and queens before the collapse of their dynasty. As I peeked carefully around the edge of it, into the rough niche beyond, my imagination had me expecting someone from almost any era of history, from the Celtic Gauls to…to the Sisters of Mary, perhaps hiding priests or royalty during the Terror of the Revolution.

Such fantastic thoughts made my glimpse of Léon Chanson all the more of a disappointment. I'd been hoping he had been kidnapped, rather than guilty. But no. He crouched in the shadows thrown by a bright halogen lantern, beside a machine that resembled a modified microwave oven with one side opened up, pointed in the general direction of the Cluny. He was programming something onto a keypad.

He was our villain.

Merde. Joshua Adriano married. Léon Chanson causing earthquakes. My taste in men had never been good…with one important exception. Rhys pressed himself against my bare back as he, too, took a quick peek around the arched doorway. His cheek on my hair, he breathed the suggestion, "The police should be here at any time."

But there was no sound of them arriving yet, and no guarantee that they would. And considering the increasing hum of electricity coming out of the machine, and the way Léon stopped punching in numbers and leaned back…

No time.

I wished I had my high heels, so that I could hit him with one. Instead, I stalked in, clenched my fists together, and swung them across Léon's head. Sadly, I did *not* knock him unconscious. I just knocked him over.

And hurt my knuckles.

He lay there and stared up at me, as if…as if he wanted us to stop him? Or as if he knew it was too late. The hum of the pulse bomb became a moan, then a whine…

"How do you stop it?" I demanded, but Léon said nothing. I picked up his halogen lamp, thinking that if I swung it hard enough—

But the whine abruptly cut off when Rhys, with a steadier presence than me, unplugged it. I touched it— it didn't seem overly warm. So I picked it up—it was microwave-oven size—and turned around and hurled it out the doorway.

It bounced several times across the rock path, something the Celtic Gauls or Merovingians would never have expected to see rolling by, and lay there in several now-harmless parts. I began to turn back, wishing I were strong enough to toss Léon Chanson in just the same way.

But with a suddenness that surprised us, he leaped up, body-checked Rhys into me, and fled out of the niche.

I took off after him, tripped on my skirts, and with a loud rip, went down hard. Rhys was there immediately, drawing me up, asking if I was okay, as if that was what mattered.

"Go!" At least I only had to yell it once. Rhys bolted after Léon, and I wasted another minute using the rip in my gown to tear the bulk of the skirt off in an uneven strip. My elbow was bleeding. My knee and hip hurt, along with my hands. And I was not about to let Léon Chanson escape to do this to anyplace else—not if I could help it. I climbed out of the crypts, pounded barefooted up the stairs, reached the square, and saw—nothing. For a moment. Then—

"This way!" called Rhys, vanishing behind one of the large wooden doors into the Cathedral itself.

I went after him, and could hear him on the stairs to the north tower. Again, I followed. "How—" I shouted, between gasps, "—did he get in?"

"I," called Rhys, down to me, "don't know!"

And from even higher, a voice came, "It's too late! Leave me alone, Catrina—it's too damned late!"

As if that would make me give up and go home.

The stairs up to the cathedral towers are increasingly narrow, the higher you get. Even after some years living in a fourth floor flat, I found myself losing wind. Never had I wanted so badly to stop at the little tourist shop halfway up, but instead I jumped the chain to the next flight of stairs and kept climbing.

And climbing.

Slowing down the whole way.

Finally, bent nearly double and gasping for breath like a goldfish, I reached the top of the tower and emerged out onto the walkway, high, high above Paris.

The wind nearly knocked me right back in.

I'd been up here before, fear of heights or not—I usually just pressed as far away from the edge as possible, instead of leaning over to admire the sloped roofs and yet more of the gargoyles than those that perched, stained and glowering, above me and along the rail. But never had I been up here at night. The towers of Notre Dame rise almost 70 meters above Paris—well over 200 feet—and the view was remarkable. The River Seine snaked away, broken into segments by tiny bridges, off past the Eiffel Tower. The white dome of Sacré Coeur glowed, floodlit, over in Montmartre, but Paris herself seemed to go on and on, until her lights faded into distance.

And Léon meant to destroy *this?*

Recovering my senses, after that blast of heights, I turned and saw Léon and Rhys standing only feet apart. Rhys had his hands on Léon's shoulders. But it wasn't a gesture of friendship, I realized, as I saw the stone railing that separated them. Rhys was trying to steady Léon, to hang on.

To keep him from leaping off the bell tower.

Had I just wished that I could end up somewhere in the open air? As the cold wind finished off my once-neat twist, raking my hair across my face and flapping what was left of my gown's skirt, I changed my mind. But somehow, I made myself sidle out onto the too-narrow walkway between the towers, closer to our quarry. Age-stained gargoyles loomed everywhere, like stone demons and dragons—and one, oddly, like a little stone elephant.

"—still fix it," Rhys was shouting, over the wind. "Dying now won't help anybody!"

"You don't understand!" Was Léon crying? "You do not understand how big this is!"

"You're not the only person to have ever held this kind of power," Rhys insisted. "It doesn't mean you have to—"

"Yes! Yes, it does mean I have to use it. If I don't…"

Leon looked over Rhys's shoulder—and even in the stark shadows, thrown by the ground-level floodlights, I could see that yes, he was crying. I did not have as much sympathy for his guilt, now that he'd been caught, as Rhys apparently had.

"The first time surprised me," he told both of us now. "Even after I inspected the site, I didn't understand. I knew about the solar flares, and about the lines, but not about the tiles. That is why the second attempt, when we were together—that wasn't me, Catrina. Would I have been fool enough to put myself, put us, in the path of an earthquake? But there were no tiles. That one succeeded only as a pulse bomb. Then we knew."

"What do you mean, we?" I asked, my teeth chattering.

"Come back onto this side," pleaded Rhys. "You can tell us all about it, out of the wind."

"The power was in the tiles," Léon continued, almost as if talking to himself. "The forces they harness!"

"I know," I said. "They amplify energy."

He shook his head. "Their basic ingredient amplifies energy. But they aren't all identical, each one has a slight difference. If they were laid out in particular patterns…"

"Léon," commanded Rhys, his overlong hair flying wild, his hands still gripping the pulse-bomber's shoulders. Léon was clutching the lapels of Rhys's suitcoat, almost as if he didn't notice his own will to live. "Tell us about it inside. *Come on*."

A zigzag of lights began to sweep past us, different from the floodlights, and I risked a stomach-churning glance over the edge of the walkway. The police had arrived. Some of them seemed to have rifles. That scared me, too.

"Rhys," I warned. "Be careful."

Léon looked from me to Rhys, then back. "It's too late," he said again. "For me."

And then, with a great thrust, he launched himself backward off the tower—

Dragging Rhys with him.

Chapter 21

Well—Léon tried.

With a cry, Rhys freed one hand, looping his arm around a leering gargoyle to hold on. Léon was only able to drag him halfway over the stone railing. Then they hung, weight against gravity. Rhys's one-handed grip under Léon's shoulder dragged him farther across the railing with every gusty second. Léon clung to Rhys's coat with one hand, to the railing with another, his feet dangling hundreds of feet over the great stone square that fronted the cathedral.

Me, I flung myself forward and wrapped my arms around Rhys, which draped me partway over the railing myself. I leaned back with all my weight, all my strength.

"Let go!" I screamed to either man. To both of them.

Léon let go of the stained, ornate stone railing and

grasped hold of the arm Rhys had already extended, but not to live. He did not want to live, he wanted to die. And for some reason—panic? spite?—he had decided not to do so alone.

His weight pulled Rhys farther across the rail, farther over the dizzying drop.

Léon was beyond reason—but my lover was not. "Let go," I insisted in Rhys's ear, uncaring if I was begging him, caring about nothing except his life. "Please, Rhys. Please don't die for him. He isn't worth it. Please…."

"Everyone—" Rhys grunted with the effort of holding on, "—is worth it."

"Not everyone," I argued. And I thought, *maybe not even me*.

My back muscles screamed protest at the constant pulling of his weight. My stockinged feet numbed against the cold stone, but Rhys felt warm and alive beneath me.

"For the love of God," Rhys shouted down to Léon. "Make a damned effort!"

And then—

I didn't place the gunshot, at first. It was so far away, more of a pop than a bang. What I understood was that Rhys cried out and suddenly fell backward, with me, onto the narrow stone walkway, no longer encumbered by the weight of Léon. I pushed myself up—and recognized a spray of blood across his face.

"Rhys!" I screamed, afraid he'd been hit.

But when he levered himself up, turned his back to me and began to sob into his knee, I knew he was…well, not okay. But safe. So I took a moment to look over the railing one last time, down down down until I saw Léon's body, sprawled some distance in front of the doorway called the Portal of the Virgin, the police advancing on him.

They had actually risked shooting him? Why?

At the moment, I had other concerns. I turned back to Rhys, and put my arms around him, and held on, as tightly as I could. I knew I would never cry over the death of someone evil. As I've said before, I'm not that nice a person.

But I rather liked it, that he could.

Rhys had recovered himself well before the police showed up on the walkway, and he remained remarkably calm as they brought us to the Préfecture de Police, right next door, for questions. We made our own accusations—

Well, that part may only have been me. But if they had listened to me when I went to them on Thursday, couldn't they have saved us all a great deal of danger?

"We did listen to you," protested Carl Montrose. Yes, him again. He had introduced himself as "with the government," and the police deferred to him, so who were we to question his authority over this investigation? "You and Monsieur Pritchard both. But no further threats were made upon you, and we were unable to locate Léon Chanson. So…"

He shrugged.

Me and Rhys both?

"We will continue to pursue the matter, make sure Chanson was working alone," Montrose continued. "It would help, mademoiselle, if we could study some of the tiles you have mentioned?"

Tiles.

"Joshua!" I exclaimed, and was selfishly glad to see Rhys scowl. Not that I'd meant it that way. "Joshua Adriano went back into the Cluny to get the tiles I found down in the Roman baths. I need to make sure—"

But Montrose's grim expression stopped me.

"Signor Adriano met with an accident."

My stomach dropped. Luckily, he continued by saying, "When the guards reopened the museum, once it was verified that the fire warning was a false alarm? Signor Adriano was found recovering from a blow to the head—"

Oh, no! If I hadn't told him our secret… "Is he all right?"

"But of course. He was taken to a local hospital, and the doctors pronounced him in no danger. However, his family is flying him back to Naples tonight. His story confirms yours," continued Montrose. "He told my officers that he ventured to the Roman baths to collect the tiles, but was struck from behind. When he recovered his wits, he could find no tiles. Either they had been taken, or…."

Or they were never there.

I narrowed my eyes. *"They were there."*

"As you say."

Now I was the one who owed Joshua Adriano flowers.

I could tell, somehow, that Rhys was waiting for me to offer my own tiles to Montrose. But I did not mention them. And do you know why?

Because I didn't completely trust the man, nor his request that we not discuss the pulse bomb or the tiles with anybody else, "for reasons of security." I still didn't completely trust the police, especially since a police officer had taken a sniper shot at Léon, risking Rhys's life had the bullet gone a few inches off target.

Yes, it could have been to save Rhys.

But it could have been to silence Léon.

I am, in the end, a cynic.

The police kept us there until near dawn the next morning, Sunday. After we left the heavily guarded, massive gates of the Préfecture de Police behind us, we hesitated on the quiet *parvis* outside the cathedral Notre Dame de Paris, both looking up. The floodlights had been turned off. No sign of the previous night's death and near-disaster remained.

"I feel like those gargoyles," Rhys said suddenly.

Instead of saying anything, I slid my fingers between his. His hand closed on mine and, encouraged, he continued. "Some people think they represent the evils that the church has expelled. Others think they protect the church, even if they cannot be part of her. But either way, they're always trapped outside, never allowed into God's grace."

Belatedly, I understood the significance of the fact that he'd already spoken to the police before tonight. "You told Carl Montrose what my stalker said, didn't you? During his confession. You violated the sacramental seal."

Still staring upward, pure loss on every feature, Rhys violated it for me, as well. "He wasn't acting alone. It could have been a delusion, but I believe someone was using him. Perhaps Chanson…I don't know. He said they would use you, then destroy you. He spoke of a man-made Armageddon, Catrina. I could not withhold that kind of information. And I could not risk you."

"Because everyone is worth saving," I finished softly. He'd said the same about Léon.

Now Rhys looked down at me. "You are not everyone." He swallowed, as if embarrassed, and looked back up at the majestic facade. "His other rantings…perhaps I could have sat on them, prayed about them. But not his threats against you."

His hand tightened around mine.

"So what does that mean?" I asked. "People are always saying that priests can't violate the sanctity of the confessional, but you did." For me, yet. "So what happens now?"

Rhys's words came out of a tight throat. "Automatic excommunication," he said.

And he began walking across the empty square. Stunned, I stepped quickly to keep up with his lengthy stride, not about to let go. I could not… He had…

Holy Mother of God.

I'd been raised Catholic, for all the good it had done me. I knew what excommunication meant. It was the worst punishment the church could give out. It exiled Rhys from the church. He could not receive rites—not communion, not marriage, not even the last rites he'd given a crazed killer. He could not be buried in a Catholic cemetery.

He could not have done something this huge for me. It was too much. He had to…to take it back.

"You could ask for absolution, right?" I asked hopefully, after a moment.

"I would have to be truly repentant. I am not that."

"Then…" I didn't want to say it. My eyes, my stomach, burned at the immensity of this. But it had to be faced. "Then I really did—"

"*No!*" To my surprise, Rhys grabbed my shoulders, hard. For a moment, I thought he would shake me. He looked like he wanted to. "None of this is your fault. Get over yourself."

I blinked, surprised into silence. At what point had we started using an equal mix of English and French?

"*I* did it. This is *me*. It is my problem, my faith, my lack of faith, my heresy. It is for me to resolve. All you have done, all you have ever done, is to—" He laughed, as if it were a joke. "To find me attractive, to console me, to let me in. Do you understand what that has meant to me?"

I shook my head.

He clasped my face between his hands. "I was attracted to you from the first, Catrina. I kept telling myself that I shouldn't be, for all the proper reasons—and at times because I was distracted by other matters…."

"Like Maggi Sanger," I said, naming Brigitte Taillefer's beloved niece with more than a touch of bitterness in my voice.

"Maggi Stuart," Rhys corrected me. "She's married with a baby now. But you're hardly in a position to throw stones."

I grinned. "You're angry because Joshua Adriano kissed me."

"I'm angry because you kissed him back."

"Good." I stretched up on my toes, wrapped my arms over Rhys's shoulders, and kissed him far, far more enthusiastically than I had ever kissed the Italian. It soothed a fear, deep inside me, that Rhys kissed me back with equal ardor.

Then he scowled down at me. "If you keep interrupting, it will take me forever to explain why I—"

I kissed him again. As we caught our breaths, I started to say, "Then take—"

But my throat closed up on *forever*. Too much. Too soon. As desperately as I loved him, we'd been moving so very quickly, and I did not want to make any mistakes—not any more than I had.

So I said, "Take as long as you like."

"I should like to. But not without a relationship. I won't watch you kiss other men. I can't be uncertain where I will be sleeping every night."

I sank back onto my heels, left one arm around him, and began to walk again, cuddled against his side. "Yes."

Rhys sounded suspicious. "What do you mean, yes?"

"Yes, let us have monogamy. Yes, I want you to come home with me, and I want you to live there, for as long as we can make it work, which I hope will be a very long time. And yes—" I smiled up at him. "I want to hear more about what attracted you to me."

Now Rhys laughed. "Because you are fearless. And unrepentant. And alive. And you help me to live, as well."

And I love you because you are good. Which had to mean there was something good in me, to appreciate it. But I began to hope we would have plenty of time to say such things, as our relationship progressed.

Only once we'd crossed the bridge and were going

to leave the Île de la Cité and Notre Dame—Our Lady—behind us, did Rhys look back once more.

"You will still go to mass," I prompted. "Won't you?"

His eyebrows rose. "You want me to?"

"It is part of who you are. Even if you don't take communion. Excommunication or not, if the church thinks—"

"Thank you," Rhys interrupted, with a smile. But it sounded like it meant much more. And we walked together, back to our flat. And to our bed. And to more hope than I had ever known.

After that, only three more things of significance happened that week.

One was that Rhys, of all people, came up with a method by which I might learn whether Lisse Clairon had reached her friends before their execution.

He'd thought of it during evening mass.

"You won't like it," he warned. And he was right.

But I had to know.

We went to the Sorbonne on Monday morning and I touched every item left of Denfert-Rochereau salvage since the break-in, whispering, "Lisse. What happened to Lisse?"

Nothing. Not from Alinor's Leyden jar. Not from the strange Mary medals. I began to fear that, now that the Black Madonnas had been found and the earthquake averted, I had lost the ability. But then I touched the bayonet—

And I was back.

"Ten minutes," hisses the guard as he shoves her

roughly through the door. *"Any longer, and you may yet die with them."*

Her friends, wearing only their filthy shifts in this cramped cell, stare in a mixture of horror and amazement. Then they throw themselves at her—Alinor, Isabeau, Manon. They hug her so tightly she can barely breathe. She weeps. She, who hardly ever falls prey to that feminine weakness.

Not too late. She is not too late.

It is Isabeau whose joy first turns to fury. *"You* idiot! What are you doing here? How—?"

A small voice from the corner asks, "Have you come to rescue us?"

It is one of their two maids, the younger one, Berthe. Their innocent maids have been arrested with them.

The four women, who began only as a literary salon but sensed more in each other, and became true sisters, exchange weighted looks. It is Manon who gently says, "No, little one. Not even Lisse can help us escape from—"

Which is when Lisse slides the bayonet out from where she'd had it tied to her leg, under her skirts. "But we can take some of them out with us."

"No." To everyone's surprise, it is the bookish Alinor who speaks so firmly. "So much of the Marians' wisdom has been lost—the little that we've recovered is not enough to save the world. But to murder innocents would stain us all."

"Murder?" Lisse laughs harshly. "They mean to kill us!"

Isabeau shakes her head. "And who shall we kill for

*it? The guards, who are only earning a living and prov-
ing their own patriotism? A handful of the crowd, who
cling to the delusion that our blood will cleanse the
world? The poor, overworked executioner? He is in his
own hell. He dreams of blood."*

*Lisse does not ask how Isabeau knows this. Isabeau
often…knows.*

*"They are right," agrees Manon, who has learned of
her husband's death. She has more right to anger than
anybody. "If I thought we could survive, then I would
kill anybody I must. But we cannot escape. It would not
be self-defense, Lisse. It would be revenge. And that is
not the way of the Lady."*

*From the corner, Berthe continues to sob. Alinor
leans closer and whispers to Lisse, "She is with child."*

*And Lisse decides. "Change clothes with me, little
one."*

*Their work is quickly done. Soon, Lisse is wearing
Berthe's filthy shift, only a little too short, and Berthe
is wearing her gown, her shoes, her cloak. "These are
the papers you need to leave the city. Do you understand?"*

*Berthe, who has protested several times, looks terri-
fied. "But…but what do you wish me to do, once I
escape? How can I repay you? Citizen Clairon, you
cannot mean—"*

*They hear the guard's footsteps approaching their
cell. Their time is almost up. No chance to give Berthe
directions to the farmhouse outside Lys. No chance to
explain the true history of the Black Madonnas—or
what little they know of it. So Lisse gives her a quick hug*

and whispers, "Live a happy life. Raise your daughter to do so. And never, never accept that women cannot be equals to men. Can you do that?"

The key turns in the lock, and the guard pushes the door open. "Whist! If you're going, you must—" He stares, then laughs out loud. "The maid?"

"Do you question the goal of equality?" asks Lisse.

Alinor says, "Liberté, egalité, et sororité."

The guard, so hardened against the upper classes, seems more considerate of Berthe than he'd been of Lisse. He will get this "visitor" safely out of the prison. The rest is up to her.

Once they are gone, Lisse flips up her shift to remind them that she still wears her bayonet, high on her thigh. "If anybody tries to abuse us, before the execution…"

"Then kill them by all means," agrees Alinor, and they laugh. What else are they to do? The shock of their imminent death is gone. Half of them have lost lovers already. The world has turned uglier than any of them wish to see. And the Black Madonnas…

Well. They cannot be the only women with half-lost memories of the Black Madonna. When the time is right, so it shall be.

Instead, they stay up all night, speaking of their loved ones, laughing with each other. Isabeau cannot believe Lisse was attracted to a peasant like Gui, no matter how honorable—but she accepts it is so. Alinor shares ideas she will never invent, but she is quite certain someone shall. Manon insists that they trust in the new age that is coming, only two centuries away. And when they hear the guards coming in the morning, to cut their hair and

*take them to their deaths, they pass around their most
precious objects. The medals. The tiles. Even their remaining maid, impressed by their rescue of Berthe,
takes one.*

Lisse swallows the key—

I blinked back to the present, startled to realize that
it had been *Lisse* whose death I had first witnessed,
back in the mass grave. Then I realized that Rhys stood
behind me in the workroom, with its dark-paneled walls
and stained glass windows. His arms were tight around
me, his chin on my shoulder.

Just in case, I thought, and loved him.

"She found them," I said, in answer to the question
in his blue eyes. "She switched places with the maid.
Then she was guillotined."

"I am sorry," he said.

I shook my head, saddened but not…not so very disappointed, at that. "I already knew they were dead."

Someone cleared her throat from the doorway. I
thought it might be Josette as I turned to look. Rhys stiffened.

Merde, it was my old professor, Brigitte Taillefer. His
boss. The one who still hated me for a thief.

"A moment, Rhys," she said sharply, glaring poi-
son at me.

"But of course, Brigitte." But then—then Rhys
leaned down and kissed me once more, on the lips. In
front of God, the old bat and everybody and in broad
daylight—colored through the stained glass of the
sixteenth-century windows.

He winked at me before heading out, and I had no

doubt he would have as much to say to Madame Taillefer as she did to him.

The second thing of significance that week was Rhys's and my encounter with the gray-haired man. We had just had dinner out, and Rhys was inviting me to go dancing. I had already learned that he was a sinfully good dancer. Part of it, he assured me, was having grown up with older sisters. But I suspected some of it came from having channeled into it the energy he'd not put into sex for all those years. He was grinning, spinning me out from him and reeling me happily back in on the sidewalk, when I stiffened and stopped.

Face-to-face with the gray-haired stranger.

Rhys started to step between us, feeling me tense, but I put out a hand to stop him—and the three of us stared at one another.

I broke eye contact first, to look past the old man and make sure men with tranquilizer guns were not following him.

When I looked back, he was smiling. "You did very well, Catrina Dauvergne. Perhaps there is something to this business of letting other people manage their own affairs."

"How condescending of you," I said coolly.

He laughed. "She is a firecracker, this one," he said to Rhys, still condescending. "Treasure that."

"I plan to," said Rhys, whom I had of course told about my other meetings with the strange old man. "Who are you, and what do you want with Catrina?"

"Ah. Welsh." The man nodded with old-fashioned stiffness. "I am striving to remember that what I want,

I cannot always get. I have spent too much of my life in-
terfering, and am still trying to find the right balance. But
for now, it is enough for me to congratulate the lady, and
to remind her that her sisters' quest is far from over."

Then he bowed to us, and turned away.

"Wait," I insisted, less polite. "Can you at least give
us a name?"

The man's twinkling eyes moved from me to Rhys
and back. "Call me Myrddin," he suggested, then
crossed the street.

"Myrddin," I repeated, frowning.

"It is Welsh," clarified Rhys. "For Merlin. The wizard."

"So he is crazy. I am tired of crazy people."

"But at least," suggested Rhys, "this one is not trying
to kill either of us."

As for the third thing of significance?

I got back to my office, at the Cluny, still somewhat
in shock from my appointment with the *notaire*. I could
not possibly have expected…

It made no sense….

Ana Reisner was the one who knocked at the sill of
my open door. "Look who I met on the way in."

Scarlet just walked right in, and so was the first to
see my expression. "Oh, no!" she exclaimed, in the middle of announcing that she had juicy details about her
date with Caleb Adriano. She came immediately to my
side, taking my arm. "Something else bad has happened! Oh, Catrina!"

Ana made a sound of sympathy and moved closer.

But I said, "Nothing bad."

It wasn't until Ana had sent Scarlet to fetch a bottle

of water for me, and sat down beside me with her hand on mine, that I was able to wrap my mind around it.

I waited until Scarlet was back—she sat on the side of my desk—and I wet my throat. Then I admitted, "*Grand-mère* left me money."

"Your grandmother died?" Ana squeezed my hand. "I'm so sorry."

"I knew she loved you!" exclaimed Scarlet, with a fist punch into the air. "Yes! Aren't you glad now that you went to her funeral?"

Ana blinked, but kindly did not ask, *You almost skipped your grandmother's funeral?*

"It's not necessarily a sign that she loved me," I told Scarlet. "I am the only child of her only child. By French law, she could not prevent me from inheriting. But…I hadn't realized she had any money left. I thought she would have spent it all."

"Which she would have done if she really hated you, right?" demanded Scarlet, swinging her feet.

I nodded. It is certainly what I would have done, in her position.

Again, Scarlet punched the air. "I knew she didn't hate you! Yes! How much did she leave you?"

Ana grinned at me, and I liked her all the more for recognizing that Scarlet was not rude so much as…Scarlet.

"Enough to pay for the farmhouse," I told them. "Enough to make an anonymous donation to the Hôtel du Montfort." Since Ana was technically a police officer, I chose not to tell her that the money was to recompense them for the letters I'd taken from their fireplace, letters they'd never known they had. Neither did I plan on ever telling the hotelier, hence the anonymity. I might be trying a little harder to do the right thing…but there were limits. "And perhaps to buy Brigitte Taillefer's old Citroën Saxo, if Rhys would like. He feels guilty for all the mileage he's put on it, and he says she can no longer drive it."

Speaking of whom… "Rhys spoke to Professor Taillefer's niece—her great-niece. His friend Maggi Stuart," I continued. Interestingly, I could now say the name without grinding my teeth. That, as much as anything, was proof of my growing trust in Rhys's feelings for me. "She is a comparative mythologist, and he called her in New York to ask her about Black Madonnas. She has never seen figures like these—with the key, the sword, the jar. But she said to keep in mind that some believe the Virgin Mary figure, in statuary at least, is loosely based on figures of Isis with her god-son Horus. And Isis was often depicted with black skin."

Scarlet slid off the desk. "You think the Black Madonnas represent Isis?"

"No." I was still trying to wrap my mind around just what the beautiful figures did symbolize. Perhaps it was something each of us had to decide on her own. "But it seems no more likely that they truly depict the Virgin Mary, wouldn't you say? I have never heard of the Holy Virgin touching a sword."

Scarlet covered her mouth, as if to stop herself from making a crude joke, and I was just as glad. Though it would have been funny.

The women had in fact come to my office so that we could go to lunch together, get to know each other better. But first, I had to take them to the vault so that we could see my Black Madonnas again. Triptych, statues, tapestries…

And the embroidery. Especially the one with the signature.

I could not blame them. I tended to visit the Madonnas when I arrived for work in the morning and before I left at night. There was something so peaceful about them. So strong. So…mysterious.

"Maggi *Stuart*, huh?" asked Ana, under her breath, as we drank in the sight of them. "I think I begin to understand."

I could tell, just by looking at her, that she had confirmed my suspicions about the double-X marking on one of the embroideries. It was the only one of which I had made arrangements to divest myself. The rest, I would allow the Cluny and the Adrianos—the least I could do to patch my professional relations with Joshua—to exhibit in several cities. But once they'd made their circuit, they would remain at the Cluny.

"It's worth millions, for historic reasons alone," Ana continued. "Probably more than any other piece here. Are you sure you want to just give it away?"

"I…owe them," I admitted. To myself as much as to her. "And if the Stuarts have a child, then this will keep it in their family. Something feels right about that."

Scarlet could not help but overhear us. "What?" she demanded, coming to our side. "What about the Stuarts. You mean Rhys's friend, the one you were jealous of?"

Yes. The one whose chalice I'd stolen.

"See this signature?" I pointed to the spot on the embroidery, with its [X]X symbol. "Sometimes she simply embroidered her initials, MR, for Marie Reine, or Queen Mary. But this symbol allowed her to hide the M."

Scarlet stared. "Bloody Mary was a Marian? I mean—"

"Not Mary Tudor of England," I interrupted. "Mary Stuart of France."

"Mary Queen of Scots," clarified Ana, for Scarlet's sake. "She was born Queen of Scotland. She was briefly Queen of France by marriage."

"But she was raised here," I added, and watched Scarlet's expressive face as she connected the dots.

"The women who were into these Black Madonnas included a *queen?*"

Both Ana and I nodded. That was exactly what it meant.

Scarlet shook her head. "I wonder who else famous was a Marian. We have *got* to find out more about these ladies."

Ana and I agreed. We absolutely did.

But first the three of us—I and my friends—went out to lunch together.

* * * * *

The past calls…and the present is dangerous.
Learn more of the Marians' secrets as
THE MADONNA KEY *continues with*
Ana Reisner's story, Haunted Echoes
by Cindy Dees.
Available October 2007 at all good bookshops.